# THE
# KEEPER

# THE KEEPER

BY ELLEN JENSEN ABBOTT

**SKYSCAPE**

**SKYSCAPE**

TEXT COPYRIGHT © 2013 BY Ellen Jensen Abbott

AMAZON PUBLISHING
ATTN: AMAZON CHILDREN'S PUBLISHING
P.O. BOX 400818
LAS VEGAS, NV 89140
www.amazon.com/amazonchildrenspublishing

LIBRARY OF CONGRESS CATALOGING-IN-PUBLICATION DATE IS
AVAILABLE UPON REQUEST.

ISBN-13: 9781477847022 (HARDCOVER)
ISBN-10: 1477847022 (HARDCOVER)
ISBN-13: 9781477897027 (EBOOK)
ISBN-10: 147789702X (EBOOK)

BOOK DESIGN BY ALEX FERRARI
EDITOR: ROBIN BENJAMIN
MAPS BY MEGAN MCNINCH

PRINTED IN THE UNITED STATES OF AMERICA (R)
FIRST EDITION

10  9  8  7  6  5  4  3  2  1

*For Will and Janie, the best stories I've ever helped to write*

# ACKNOWLEDGMENTS

Thank you to my editor, Robin Benjamin, who teaches me more about writing with each stroke of her pen.

Thank you to my agent, Ginger Knowlton, for her advice, support, and grace.

Thank you to the circle of women who support me in writing and otherwise: Montgomery Abbott, Elizabeth Cook, Leigh Gustine, Margaret Haviland, Dicky Jensen, Deanna Mayer, and Beverly Patt (my Journey Sister).

Thank you to all of my students, but especially my writing seminar students, who teach me even as I teach them.

Thank you to my colleagues at the Westtown School who never fail to ask, "How's the book going?"

Thank you to the members of the KidLit Authors' Club, who make book "events" easier and a million times more fun.

Thank you especially to Ferg, who makes this writing life possible.

# COMMUNITIES IN THE NORTHERN KINGDOM

## WATERSMEET

### KEEPERS

**Glynholly:** faun

**Rueshlan:** shape-shifter (human/centaur), Abisina's father, killed in the battle with the **White Worm**

**Vigar:** human, founder and first Keeper

### HUMANS

**Abisina:** daughter of Rueshlan and **Sina**, born in Vranille

**Elodie:** one of Abisina's closest friends

**Findlay:** Abisina's love, brother of **Meelah**, son of **Hesper**

**Frayda:** Rueshlan's companion

**Hain:** refugee from the south, husband of **Bryla**, leader at the wall

**Neiall:** leader of Old Watersmeet

### CENTAURS

**Braim:** leader of the Golden Age

**Erith:** supporter of Old Watersmeet

**Ravinne:** leader at the wall

**Salat:** leader at the wall

**Torlad:** a palomino who fights for Watersmeet

## DWARVES

**Alden:** Council member, father of **Breide** and **Aldreck**, leader at the wall

**Gilden:** old dwarf taken by fairies

**Haret:** Abisina's best friend, grandson of **Hoysta**, from south of the Obrun Mountains

**Lennan:** healer in Watersmeet

**Waite:** Alden's brother, leader at the wall

## FAUNS

**Anwyn:** supporter of Abisina

**Callas:** supporter of Old Watersmeet

**Farron:** leader at the wall

**Kerren:** leader at the wall

## FAIRY MOTHERLAND

**Lohring:** the Fairy Mother

**Neriah:** elder daughter of the Fairy Mother

**Reava:** younger daughter of the Fairy Mother

# COMMUNITIES IN
# THE SOUTHERN KINGDOM

## DWARVES OF STONEDUN
**Prane:** supporter of Newlyn, a gate-builder, leader at the wall

**Ulbert:** ancient hero, discovered the Obrium Lode and founded the Obrun City

## CENTAURS OF GIANT'S CAIRN
**Icksyon:** herd leader

**Irom:** sentry

## FAUNS
**Darvus:** Erna's mate

**Erna:** supporter of Abisina, from south of the Obrun Mountains

## HUMANS OF VRANIA
**Imara:** cousin of Vigar, brought south by Vran

**Jorno:** former outcast, former supporter of Abisina

**Theckis:** leader of Vranham, from Vranille

**Vran:** founder of Vrania

## HUMANS OF NEWLYN
**Corlin:** leader of Newlyn

**Eder:** member of Newlyn's army, father of **Thaula**

**Landry:** scout sent north to support Abisina, leader at the wall.

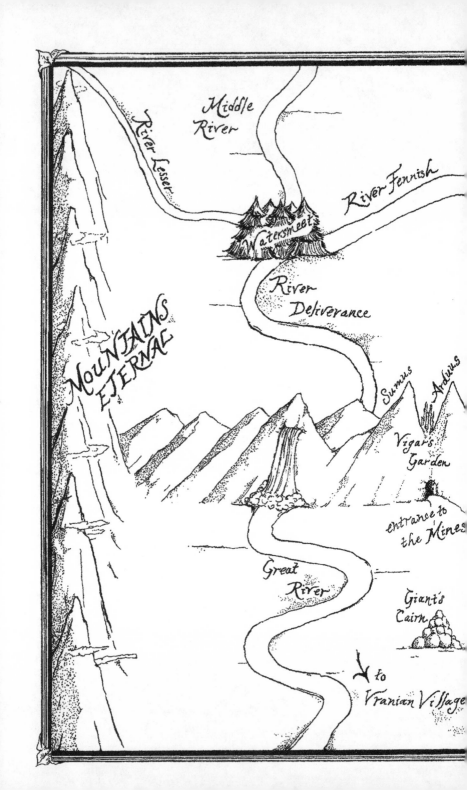

FENS

The NORTHERN KINGDOM

Fairy Motherland

OBRUN MOUNTAINS

Green Man's Cleft

dwarf ruin

PIEDMONT

N

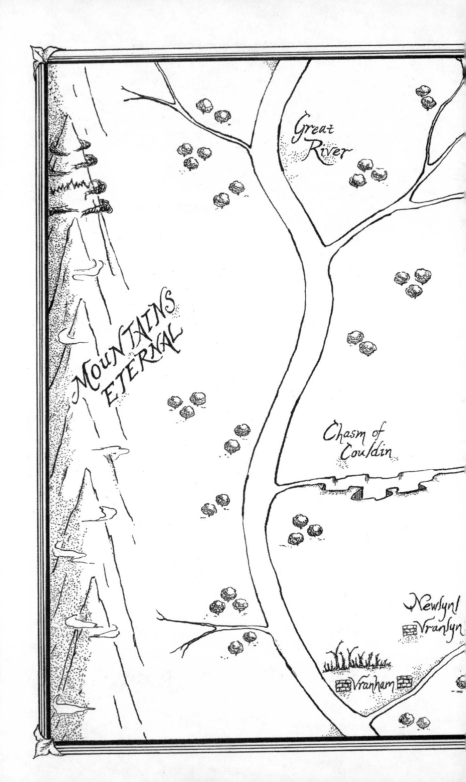

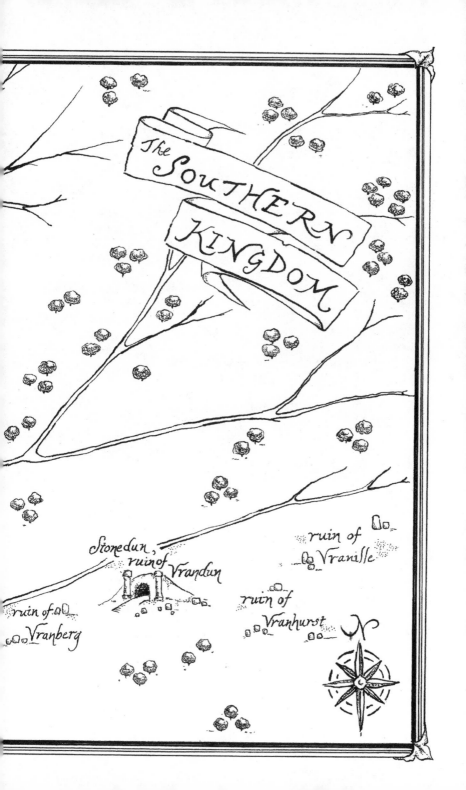

# Prologue

*For weeks the mountain groaned and rumbled. Rocks shook loose far above the line of clouds shrouding the peak and rolled toward the valley, dislodging other stones and then boulders until an avalanche sheeted down the lower slopes. Dust rose, staining the clouds a darker hue. With each tremor, the jagged rift on the rock face widened and closed, widened and closed like a mouth searching for food.*

*This rift had opened three years earlier when the White Worm had reappeared in the land of Seldara, and, through the fissure—as if called by the Worm—had trooped legions of evil creatures: überwolves, tall silver-haired beasts that were able to think and use weapons like the humans they preyed on; minotaurs, huge bull-headed men, and the hags that controlled them as slaves; trolls with tough hides, powerful limbs, and an instinct to destroy; leviathan-birds with lashing serpent tails, steely wings, and deadly talons. The rift brought forth enough evil to carry on the destruction of the Worm, even after the hero Rueshlan had slain it.*

*And now the mountain was ready to release its final horror. As its rumbling intensified, trees lost their hold on the earth and crashed to the ground. Gritty ash rained on the barren slopes. Clouds of debris enveloped the entire mountain.*

*Then with a roar that echoed across the land, the mountain exploded, shaking the folk from the marshy Fens to the southern sea: dwarves in their underground city; folk in the Sylvyad trees of Watersmeet; fairies in their forest stronghold; fauns in their woodland home far to the east; centaurs in their rock cave; and humans in the villages of Newlyn and Vranham.*

*Abisina was waiting in Newlyn for the winter blizzards to pause long enough that she could journey north to her home in Watersmeet. When she heard the roar of the mountain, she touched the necklace at her throat.*

*But none of the folk who lived in Seldara could see the darkness that emerged from the mountain's rubble. Did it move on hooves or feet, claws or paws? Did it breathe with lungs or gills? Did it kill by sting or fang or crushing weight?*

*Did Abisina, with her ancient necklace, sense that the true evil had come to Seldara at last?*

# CHAPTER I

A CRESCENT MOON ILLUMINATED THE HULKING PILE OF rocks. Abisina shivered as she faced the entrance. The air was frigid, and snow crunched beneath her feet, but her trembling was not from cold. She remembered too well the last time she had entered Giant's Cairn: a terrified girl clutched in the arms of a menacing centaur who brought her as a prize to his herd leader.

Abisina shivered again. Icksyon, with his mad eyes, fleshy lips, and dirty-white flanks. Worst of all, he wore a necklace of human toes. One of her own dangled among the others bitten off the bodies of his victims.

*Stop it,* she told herself. *You are not that girl anymore.* She had been fourteen winters and on her own. She didn't know her father, had never been to Watersmeet, had never had a friend. Now she was eighteen winters. She knew what it was to love and be loved. She knew how to fight back. *You are Rueshlan's daughter. Never forget that.*

She transformed from her human shape into a midnight-black centaur. As she shook her hair from her face, the moonlight reflected off her green eyes and the necklace that hung against her chest. The pendant was made of many silver strands woven together into one.

*You have this, too,* she reminded herself. *The Keeper's necklace.*

A shout of drunken laughter echoed down the tunnel leading to Icksyon's den. Abisina squared her shoulders and went in.

The herd's reek hit her before she saw them. Watersmeet's centaurs smelled of clean sweat, river water, and fresh breezes. These centaurs stank of drunkenness, filth, and blood. Abisina faltered. Icksyon's herd killed indiscriminately. Could she convince them to join her alliance? Did she want them to?

Again she questioned her decision to come here. She had to return to Watersmeet! She'd known that since she had been sent the necklace. Glynholly, the Keeper of Watersmeet, had worn it last, and the faun would never have parted with it unless she was desperate. Or dead.

*We need the centaurs. It's up to me to make them see that.*

Abisina pushed herself farther down the tunnel until she turned the corner to the lair. Sixty centaurs wedged into a space uncomfortable for half that many. Icksyon stood a head taller than any other centaur in the herd, but as Abisina forced herself to study him, she saw that he was— diminished. His skin hung loose, as if he had contracted inside of it; his bloodshot eyes roved as though he couldn't quite control them. He looked broken.

The other centaurs showed signs of illness and starvation. Their coats were burred and scarred, dirt was ground into their flanks, and their tails were snarled or hacked short. Their bare human torsos were equally foul, and many had fresh bruises and cuts across their backs and chests. The men wore beards as tangled as their tails, and the hair of both the men and women hung in mats. They jostled for position around a central fire, kicking and elbowing for room. A few centaurs lay collapsed against the rock walls. One female, fighting to hold her place, kicked a fallen centaur in the flanks again and again. He didn't flinch. Passed out from drink or killed? Abisina couldn't tell.

*Their fear of the birds keeps them holed up here.* On her journey north, Abisina had seen the evidence: trees stripped of branches; rotting carcasses of centaurs, minotaurs, and even trolls; piles of droppings that killed vegetation. All the work of the terrifying leviathan-birds.

The struggling herd didn't notice her standing in the doorway, but Abisina remained on guard. Even weakened, Icksyon was a terrible enemy.

Then a centaur spotted Abisina. "Hey! Only tribute of fresh meat buys you entrance! Isn't that right, Lord Icksyon?"

Abisina didn't move, staring at Icksyon.

His eyes widened in surprise.

As she had expected, he recognized her. Her black hair and brown skin made her stand out among the blond and white-skinned humans of the south. In his recent attack on

Newlyn, Icksyon had seen her in both her human and centaur forms. He would certainly remember that.

Icksyon touched a toe on his necklace and said, "This one doesn't come with meat, my friends. She's the one I told you about: the shape-shifter. She looks like us now, but she is human, too. With such beautiful brown toes."

"I have a message for you and your herd, Icksyon. An offer." Abisina's voice did not shake.

"An offer!" one centaur shouted. "We can't eat offers! We want meat!"

"Or mead!" shouted another. Others chorused in agreement.

She spoke into the din. "I know what keeps you here. You need meat but won't face the birds to get it. You've seen what happened to the mountain. How will you survive the new threats it has sent?"

A few shifted nervously. Icksyon smiled. "And you can save us?" he asked. "You and your pitiful friends?"

"No," Abisina said. "Alone, none of us can fight the birds—and whatever else has come from the rift. We have to fight together."

A pause—and then Icksyon started to laugh. Most of the herd laughed, too. But some frowned.

"The humans are using you, shape-shifter," Icksyon said as the laughter died. "They expect you to deliver up the centaurs because you look like one of us. To them, you *are* one of us. And once they've gotten what they want, they'll kill you and hang your tail with ours on their walls.

"And we already have allies," Icksyon continued. "As you know, the hags and their minotaurs were with us for the attack on Newlyn. Who's to say that the rift won't provide us with more such friends?"

"The birds are not your 'friends.' At Newlyn, they killed more of you than us," Abisina countered. "Do you believe it was something friendly that ripped off the mountain-top?" As she scanned the centaurs, a few met her eyes. She saw alarm and fear, though none would speak out against Icksyon. "Look how you're living!" Abisina pressed. "Imprisoned here, surrounded by the rotting bodies of your own herd."

"I will not work with humans!" Icksyon declared. "This land was ours until Vran and his followers showed up. We had no leviathan-birds! No White Worm!" Spit flew from Icksyon's lips. "The humans brought these evils on us. They hack off our tails! So we take our own prizes." He touched his necklace.

"Watersmeet's humans were part of the army that defeated the Worm," said Abisina. "Some of you fought in that battle. You saw what the folk of Watersmeet did. In the north, human, centaur, faun, and dwarf have lived together— and thrived—for more than three hundred years!"

Icksyon's mouth bent into a cruel grin. "They're not thriving now," he whispered.

Abisina touched her own necklace hidden beneath her tunic. "Wh—what do you know?"

Icksyon's smile broadened, exposing broken teeth. "Not so

sure of yourself, are you, shape-shifter? What's happened to your little paradise, eh?"

A few cheered at Icksyon's words, while others watched Abisina closely.

"Alone, we all die," Abisina repeated. "Together, we can survive."

"We?" Icksyon said. "This *we* is you and your friends from Newlyn? Humans?"

"No! Fauns, dwarves, and fairies, too. We have to think of ourselves as one folk—the folk of Seldara!"

The name slipped out—the name she had given this land, taken from the glowing white trees that had sprung from the ashes of her father's funeral pyre: the Seldars.

"Seldara? You've named your new land?" Icksyon asked. "I see you don't lose your human arrogance when you change shape. Enough of this!"

A centaur near Abisina tried to grab her. She reeled back but had no room to turn. He gripped her neck, cutting off her air. She transformed to her human shape to confuse him. He held on, so she transformed again. He lost hold of her, then reached out with his other hand and grabbed her tunic, ripping it and exposing the Keeper's necklace. Light from the pendant shone forth.

"I must have that!" Icksyon shouted. "Kill her!"

The centaurs came at her.

Abisina transformed again to her human form, spinning toward the tunnel to freedom, but a hand yanked her back by the hair. Many hands reached for her, choking her, pinning her arms, scrabbling for the necklace. She transformed from one shape to another, kicking and punching and scratching, but she couldn't reach her bow or her knife.

"Stop!" A cry came from above, followed by Icksyon's scream. "Leave her!"

The centaurs edged away. Icksyon's smug expression was gone. On his back stood a tall figure with black skin, black hair, and fierce dark eyes. *Neriah.* The fairy held an arrow to Icksyon's head.

"We're leaving now," Neriah announced tersely. To Abisina, she said, "Go."

In one motion, Abisina turned and transformed. A few paces down the tunnel she felt the fairy's hand on her shoulder. "I'm here!" Neriah said, but Abisina could hardly sense the fairy's weight on her back.

Behind them, the centaurs fought one another to get through the tunnel's narrow mouth. Abisina and Neriah were racing across the plain surrounding the Cairn before any of Icksyon's herd made it out.

Abisina bolted for the trees half a league away. Hoofbeats and shouts followed her. Her hooves flew faster, churning the snow.

"I'll do what I can to hold them off!" Neriah shouted.

Abisina glanced over her shoulder. In the moonlight, she could just make out Neriah standing on her back—as steady as if she stood on rock. The fairy lifted her bow. Abisina faced the trees again. At the scream of pain from behind them, she knew that Neriah's arrow had hit its mark; but Neriah couldn't take down the whole herd, and Abisina was tiring. She had spent the last season as Newlyn's healer; her strength and stamina were no match for a herd of centaurs that hunted daily. Two arrows sailed past her head, one grazing her cheek. The pounding hooves were getting closer.

Another cry came from behind.

As she neared the dark line of trees, Abisina could see no opening large enough for a centaur. *I'll have to transform.* Using her last reserves, she picked up her pace.

"What are you doing?" The fairy sounded panicked.

"Get ready to jump!" Abisina called as the trees loomed before them. "Now!"

Neriah leapt off her back, almost flying. Abisina transformed and threw herself between the trees. She grabbed a branch and used her momentum to swing herself up. She felt the skin on her palms tear but kept silent as she landed on a pine branch and fought to control her panting breath.

The two centaurs closest to Abisina skidded to a stop as they reached the trees.

"Wait! Where did they go?" one shouted.

"In there!" the other answered.

"I think I got one!" a third said, galloping up. "I shot as they hit the trees."

"Then where are they?"

"I told you! In there!"

"There's no way into those trees!"

The rest of the pursuing herd gathered around them.

"I tell you, I got one!"

"Then where's the body?"

Silence.

"Do you . . . do you really think they could get rid of the birds?" someone asked.

"You want to let them go?" another said.

"Well, if they'd take care of the birds—"

"Are *you* going to tell that to Lord Icksyon?" a female responded. "Oh, Lord Icksyon," she mimicked in falsetto. "I know you wanted that necklace, but I thought it'd be better to let them go!"

"He'd kill me."

"Exactly," the female said. "Irom, you stay here in case that fairy is hanging around in the trees. Herris, you take your lot that way. I'll take mine this way. Icksyon'll kill us all if we don't find that shape-shifter."

# CHAPTER II

"ABISINA." NERIAH SPOKE INTO HER EAR, THOUGH ABISINA knew that the fairy might not be near her. The fairies had uncanny abilities: leaping into treetops, seeing in low light, and speaking as if standing next to you even from a distance. But Neriah's words reminded Abisina that they also had weaknesses: "I'm hurt."

"Where are you?" Abisina whispered as loudly as she dared. Too loud. The sentry Irom, trotting back and forth to keep warm, stopped. Neriah didn't answer.

Abisina peered around her but couldn't see the fairy.

"Up." The voice so quiet, it could have been a breath.

Abisina climbed. She was high in the tree when she found Neriah lying on a slender branch, her arms and one leg hooked around it. Her other leg dangled down. Abisina pulled herself onto the branch and pressed her mouth to the fairy's ear. "Where are you hit?"

"Back," Neriah whispered.

Abisina ran her hand down the fairy's back and felt an arrow embedded above Neriah's waist, its shaft broken off.

"I can't get it out here. I have to bring you down. Can you hold on to my neck?"

As Neriah shifted from the branch to Abisina's back, she groaned, and the sentry, who had resumed his trotting, stopped again. "Bite this." Abisina lifted the hem of her tunic to Neriah's mouth. "I'll try to be gentle." She felt Neriah take the tunic in her teeth.

Abisina made slow progress. Fairies were so light they could stand on twigs smaller than Abisina's little finger, but Neriah was taller than she was, and it was difficult to maneuver her between branches. By the time Abisina was ready to jump from the lowest branch to the forest floor, the wind had picked up, covering some of the moans that Neriah couldn't suppress. To lessen the impact, Abisina hung for a moment from the final limb. Neriah was at the end of her strength, sobbing softly as she clung to Abisina. At their landing, the fairy went limp. Abisina caught her before she fell.

Abisina worked quickly now. *First staunch the bleeding.* The moonlight didn't penetrate to the forest floor, but she could find the vial of shave-weed extract in her healing pouch by touch.

*Please don't wake!* she pleaded silently with Neriah as she grasped the arrow's jagged shaft protruding from the fairy's back. The sentry was no more than two lengths away, but Abisina didn't want to move Neriah farther into the trees until the arrow was out.

*One, two, three,* she counted in her head, and then she pulled.

Abisina's hand, wet with blood, slipped off the shaft. *Come on!* she screamed inside. She tried again, and again her hand slipped.

*Hoofbeats!*

Abisina snatched up the vial of shave-weed. Keeping a hand pressed to the fairy's wound, she lifted Neriah over her shoulder and groped through the dense forest. More centaurs joined Irom, and an argument broke out. Abisina stopped and laid Neriah on the snow, knowing the centaurs' quarrel would cover any sound she might make. Wrapping her hand in her under-shirt, she grasped the shaft of the arrow and pulled. Neriah cried out, but this time the arrow came free. Abisina let the wound bleed freely to clear out any slivers of arrow, poured shave-weed into the gash, and packed the wound with snow. Tearing her under-shirt into strips, she bandaged the wound and covered Neriah in the fairy's coat and in her own cloak. The snow pack would chill her, but the wraps should compensate.

*Vigar help her,* Abisina prayed when she had finished her work and sat huddled close to the fairy. Abisina ignored her own cuts and bruises; her ears strained in the direction of the centaurs.

So many things could go wrong! Had she removed the whole arrow? How much dirt had gotten into the wound? Was the snow she used clean? Once daylight came, Abisina would clean the wound further and try to sew it up, but that was hours away. *It's cold,* she told herself. *Good for stopping infection.*

But it was not good for Abisina. She had given her cloak to Neriah, and her feet were bare, as they always were when she was changing shapes. They had become so tough, boots were hardly necessary, though they still felt the cold. At least her legs were covered. *Thanks to Thaula.* Her little friend in Newlyn had made Abisina longer tunics and knit her loose, footless socks that could withstand her transformations. Even with Thaula's wonderful creations, her fingers soon stopped responding to her commands, and her mind was getting sluggish.

She shook herself. *You'll be no good to Neriah if you freeze to death.*

She loosened the fairy's wrappings and crawled in with her, amazed at the warmth the fairy's light coat provided. As Abisina's body thawed, she shivered violently, but eventually, the warmth burrowed into her clothes and skin, and she could relax again.

Before she drifted off to sleep, it struck her how strange it was to huddle close with a fairy. Fairies were so aloof, so *independent,* with their stoic faces and cold eyes. Many in Watersmeet had warned her never to trust a fairy.

Then again, Neriah had always seemed different from the other fairies. Instead of blue eyes, hers were brown, and her hair was wavy rather than curled. Her speech lost the formality of the fairies when she was excited or agitated.

But her actions were what really set Neriah apart. Last

spring Abisina had visited the Fairy Mother to propose that Watersmeet and the Motherland work together to fight the creatures from the rift. The Mother agreed, but only if Watersmeet helped the fairies build a wall to close off Seldara's southern territory. Abisina's friends in the southern village of Newlyn were trying to transform their community, using Watersmeet as a model. How could she cut them off? Her refusal enraged the Fairy Mother, and Neriah had been the one to help Abisina escape the Motherland—even though Neriah was the Mother's daughter and heir.

Then, last autumn, Neriah had come to Abisina in Newlyn. The fairy carried with her a box made of Obrium, the mysterious dwarf metal, which had once held the necklace that Abisina now wore. Though Neriah couldn't open the box, the latch slipped off at Abisina's touch. To Neriah, this was a sign of Abisina's "special destiny."

Abisina bristled at the idea. She had been born an outcast, marked for death—how could *she* have a special destiny? But Neriah was adamant. She pointed to all the ways that Abisina's life had been unique: the Elders in her Vranian village had allowed her to live, though all children with dark coloring like hers were put to death; she was the daughter of Rueshlan, the hero who had led Watersmeet for more than three hundred years, and she shared his ability to shape-shift; the Keeper's necklace, once worn by the founder of Watersmeet, Vigar, responded to Abisina, glowing when she wore it and coming to her aid if the need was great. Her ability to open the box was just the latest evidence that Abisina had some sort of special power.

And if Abisina hadn't opened the box, she would never have found the letter inside: a letter from Vran, the founder of the Vranian villages, to Vigar. While Vran had tried to drive out the centaurs, fauns, and dwarves living in the southern lands so that his human followers could build their villages, Vigar had founded Watersmeet in the north and welcomed all. Two such different people; two such different visions. And yet, in the letter, Vran called Vigar his sister. Once, the two had loved each other. This letter confirmed Abisina's belief that north and south should unite to create one land—Seldara. As Vran and Vigar had once been united, the land they had lived in should be united again. When the leviathan-birds attacked and the creatures from the rift grew more numerous, unity became a matter of survival.

*My bond with this fairy is not strange,* Abisina thought as she lay next to Neriah. *I owe so much to her! And our friendship proves that alliance is possible.*

*But will the other folk agree?* She had failed in her visit to the centaurs. Her friends had gone on the same mission to the dwarves at Stonedun, the fauns in the east, Watersmeet, and the one surviving Vranian village: Vranham. Were they also now sleeping on the hard, cold ground, having run for their lives? Or worse?

Abisina woke just after dawn. Neriah had passed a restless night, at last settling into a deeper slumber as it got light. Abisina longed to go back to sleep. She was having a delightful dream: She and her best friend, the dwarf Haret, were having an eating contest, and both had eaten thirty-six roasted blister roots, a dwarf favorite. Haret was grinning as he offered her the next root. "Can you do it, human?" he teased. Even in her dream, her belly felt full. If only she could drift off again—eat one more root!—but every creak of the forest sounded like a centaur coming for them, and she finally crawled out of their nest of wraps, empty stomach rumbling.

They would have to spend at least a day close to the Cairn before Neriah could travel, and they needed shelter. Within walking distance, Abisina found a cluster of trees growing in a lopsided circle. She and the fairy could fit among them, and the branches would keep snow from falling on the bed of pine needles and leaves in the center.

She returned to Neriah and peeled back her bandage, causing the wound to bleed afresh. Abisina dribbled a few drops of water onto the skin around the wound. It was puffy and hot to the touch—a mild infection, not enough to present real danger. Yet.

"What is it?" Neriah asked groggily.

"We need to move. It's not safe here. Can you walk at all?"

"A little."

"Let me put on a clean bandage first."

Abisina used more shave-weed and then added horse-radish from her healing pouch to help with infection before binding up Neriah's wound again. They needed water. Abisina's water skin was empty, and the fairy's had little more than a mouthful in it. Eating the snow in this cold would make them freeze, and a fire would draw the centaurs. After she moved Neriah, she had to find a stream.

"Are you ready?" Abisina asked.

Neriah tried to sit up but fell back with a cry.

"Here," Abisina said, taking the fairy's arm. "Let me help you." She lifted Neriah to her feet, and the two of them stumbled forward. The fairy was gray in the face and panting as Abisina helped her climb into the shelter, where she gratefully sank to the ground. Abisina covered Neriah with her coat and then piled more leaves over her.

"Take a sip of this." Abisina lifted the water skin to Neriah's lips. "I'm going for more. I'll come back as soon as I can. There must be water near the Cairn," Abisina explained, but Neriah had fallen asleep.

Abisina reached the edge of the trees; Irom was no longer standing sentry. Across the plain, near the Cairn, nothing moved except the wind in the few blades of grass poking above the snow. She threaded her way along the trees, listening for a trickle of water, searching for a trail from the Cairn to the centaurs' water source.

By noon, she had seen no sign of the centaurs or the water. *I have to get back to Neriah, but first I need water.* She pushed on a little longer and finally heard the burble of a stream. She crept toward the sound and found it: a small brook clogged with ice.

Abisina didn't approach the stream immediately. She followed its course away from the Cairn. The silence was eerie.

For all his appearance of madness, Icksyon knew how to track prey. He would expect Abisina to look for water. She climbed a tree to watch and listen. Nothing moved. After listening a little longer, Abisina crept to the stream, broke the ice, and filled both her water skin and Neriah's.

She had just tied off the skins when someone spoke.

"Don't move, shape-shifter."

# CHAPTER III

ABISINA RECOGNIZED THE CREAK OF A DRAWN BOW.

"Turn around."

On the opposite side of the stream, a centaur stared at her from between strands of matted brown hair, arrow poised to fly. He was so thin, Abisina could count his ribs.

"I'm not going to kill you," he whispered. "Give me the necklace, and I'll let you go."

"I don't have the necklace now. I gave it to my companion."

"I don't believe you," the centaur said flatly. His eyes roved the banks. "Just give it to me! They'll be here soon!"

Abisina took a chance.

"I need it," she said. "The necklace will convince the north to work with the south."

The centaur looked at her. "You don't know what Icksyon's like! Once he decides he wants something, he *has* to have it. If we don't get the necklace—" His voice had been growing louder, and he checked himself. "Give me the necklace, and you can still get away," he whispered. "Then go talk to your friends in the north."

"I need the necklace for that! An alliance between north and south can stop the birds!" Abisina insisted. "We fear them as much as you do—"

"We're not afraid!" The centaur stiffened. Something fought its way through the undergrowth. "Shape-shifter! I got you!" he bellowed, and his arrow flew—well wide of Abisina.

A female centaur barreled onto the bank, bow drawn, but she slid on an icy patch as she released her arrow, and it landed at Abisina's feet. Abisina transformed and galloped for the shelter of the trees.

The first centaur leapt after her.

The female yelled, "Out of my way!"

Suddenly, the wood was alive with shouts. More centaurs crashed through the bushes. Abisina ran on. She needed only a short lead to scramble up a tree. She tucked the water skins into her belt, freeing her hands for climbing.

A white pine stood directly ahead—full foliage and plenty of low branches. Abisina transformed and scurried up. She made it five lengths before the female centaur came into view. Abisina froze as the centaur hesitated and then kept going.

The centaur who had let her go followed the female. He was passing Abisina's hiding place when a drip from her soaking water skins fell on his shoulder and he looked up. Their eyes met. He trotted on. Several lengths past her, he shouted, "There she is!" and galloped off to the left. In a few moments, the forest around Abisina was silent.

Abisina waited a little longer, then climbed back down and set off for Neriah, two full water skins bumping against her waist. And one of Icksyon's herd had listened to her. It was a tiny victory. Still, as she headed through trees so thick she had to crawl under branches and zigzag around thickets, she smiled.

She reached the plain as the sun was setting. Centaurs headed back to the Cairn from the stream, and Abisina noticed with alarm that some were also coming from other directions, as if Icksyon had called the herds together. Was he sending them after her or was something else going on?

"Have I slept long?" the fairy murmured when Abisina climbed into their hiding spot.

"The whole day," Abisina said.

Neriah sat up and groaned. "We've lost a day?"

"You're hurt. You had to sleep. Here, drink this." She held a water skin to Neriah's mouth, and the fairy took a sip. "Come on," Abisina pressed. "You need more than that. I have plenty." Neriah took a second, longer drink. "How do you feel?" Abisina asked.

"Fine. I can travel."

"Well, you may be able to travel, but I can't," Abisina said with a laugh. "I've spent the day looking for water and dodging centaurs. We're safe here. We can leave in the morning—if you're really up to it."

"Of course I am."

"I'll need to clean that wound properly, then." Abisina

gathered her supplies and before the light faded too much, she removed the bandages, stiff with dried blood. Again, the wound began to bleed. "I'm going to have to stitch it," Abisina said. She pulled a few sprigs of water-dragon out of her medicine pouch. "I'm sorry. This is all I have for pain."

"I do not need it," Neriah said, jaw clenched.

"Then take it for me. I don't like folk to scream while I heal them." Abisina held out the plant with a smile, which the fairy did not return.

"I do not scream," Neriah said, but she took the water-dragon and put it in her mouth, chewing slowly.

Abisina dug in her satchel for her needle and threaded it with a long piece of sinew.

Neriah flinched each time the needle entered her skin, but she didn't even whimper. When Abisina finished, she bandaged the wound with her last strips of under-shirt. Neriah sank back against a tree and closed her eyes.

They had a meager supper of dried fruit, nuts, and a mouthful of smoked meat. *No wonder I'm dreaming of blister roots,* Abisina thought. The food revived Neriah a little, and Abisina asked the question that had been on her mind all day: "Do you know if Findlay and Elodie made it to Watersmeet yet?"

Elodie had been one of Abisina's first friends; her warmth and laughter had been a revelation to Abisina after fourteen grim years in a Vranian village. Findlay, too, had taught Abisina how to laugh. Like Elodie, he had been a true friend—but he'd become so much more.

Findlay and Elodie had left Newlyn before Abisina,

headed north to Watersmeet to bring news of the rift creatures and the need for an alliance. They had seldom been out
of Abisina's thoughts, and she held her breath, waiting for
Neriah to speak.

"I have no news of them," Neriah said. "I sent my kestrels
to watch for them at the entrance to Vigar's garden, but none
of my birds has returned to me."

"They didn't make it to the garden?" Abisina clutched
Neriah's hand.

The fairy pulled her hand out of Abisina's with a frown.

"Sorry," Abisina said, taken aback. "I—I'm just scared for
them." The garden was perched high in the Obrun Mountains, which divided the north of Seldara from the south, and
it was one of the two ways to cross the high peaks. Blizzard
had followed blizzard that winter, but they should have made
it to the garden by now.

"They may have arrived at the garden. They may be in
Watersmeet," Neriah continued. "My birds have gone missing."

"But one of your kestrels brought me the necklace?"

"That was one of the last I've seen. And that bird was
coming from the north, from Glynholly. The southern kestrels
disappeared earlier."

Abisina held on to the slim hope. *They might be fine.
Neriah just doesn't know.* Then the full meaning of Neriah's
words broke through Abisina's relief.

"Glynholly!" Abisina cried. "That's impossible! Glynholly
would never send me the necklace!"

"My kestrel showed me an image of Glynholly wrapping the chain around its legs."

"But why? What did the bird say?"

"Our birds barely understand *our* emotions, Abisina, and certainly do not understand the emotions of other folk. They can show us images of what they have seen, not explain them."

Abisina knew this was true. As a centaur, she could communicate with hoofed animals, but the communication came as a series of images and sensations. "Why would Glynholly try to get rid of the necklace? She wanted it so badly."

"Glynholly knows that the necklace belongs to you—that you are the true Keeper of Watersmeet. She is calling you back." In the increasing darkness, Abisina could hardly see Neriah, but she sounded cool, unemotional.

"You think she *meant* to send it to me? That makes no sense! She's done everything to get me away from the necklace. She hated that folk thought I should become Watersmeet's Keeper. It didn't matter that I gave her the necklace myself. I am Rueshlan's daughter, so some still felt I should have it. As more and more refugees from the south poured into Watersmeet and food supplies dwindled, they blamed Glynholly. I made it worse by going to the Fairy Mother."

If Abisina had known how badly the visit to the Motherland would go, would she have made the same decision? She wasn't sure. The Mother's plan to build a wall in the Green Man's Cleft, the main point of access from the north to the south, outraged Abisina, but when word of the plan reached Watersmeet, Glynholly leapt at it: The wall was the answer to Watersmeet's problems! Now in agreement, the Mother and Glynholly swiftly made a pact, while Abisina was exiled from Watersmeet for going to the Motherland without Glynholly's permission.

Neriah persisted. "Glynholly wanted you to have the necklace. A few days after I sent it to you, Reava found me." Abisina braced herself. She was sure that Neriah's sister had convinced Glynholly to exile her. "Reava confirmed that Glynholly knew the kestrels were *my* birds. Glynholly expected the bird to bring the necklace to me and that I would send it on to you. Because I did, the Mother banished me. You should have seen Reava's face when she told me."

"Your crown!" Abisina gasped as she realized that Neriah was no longer wearing the Obrium circlet.

"The crown means nothing," Neriah said. "Being the elder daughter does not ensure that I will be the next Mother. Reava has been waiting for a chance to win the crown, and this was it. As you said, your folk have been questioning Glynholly's ability to be Keeper, but the Mother's pact is with Glynholly. She needs Glynholly and Watersmeet to build her wall; she couldn't punish Glynholly for sending the necklace. But she saw my giving it to you as treason. Reava was only too happy to take my crown and have me banished."

Abisina hugged herself against the cold. She had been counting on Neriah to convince the Mother to bring the fairies into the Seldara alliance.

"Reava also took Vigar's box and the letter."

"No!" The letter proved that the humans in the south were Vigar's descendants as well as Vran's. The folk of Watersmeet were devoted to Vigar—they would see it as their duty to help her people. Abisina needed the letter to convince all of Watersmeet to join with the south. Now that hope was gone.

Findlay and Elodie missing. Neriah banished. The letter taken. *And I was excited to have reached one centaur. . . .*

*No. That centaur means something,* Abisina told herself. *Neriah was willing to get banished for the alliance. And Findlay and Elodie know how to survive. We'll find them as we head north.*

"I didn't even thank you, Neriah," Abisina said. "You saved my life at the Cairn."

"And you saved mine. There is no debt there."

Though there had been no humor in Neriah's words, Abisina tried to smile. "I guess both of us have to be more careful. How did you know I was there?"

"Once you got the Keeper's necklace, I knew you would return to Watersmeet. Any path you took would bring you near the Cairn. I have been watching for you."

"Well, I'm very glad you found me!"

Somewhere an owl hooted, and a small creature scuttled to its burrow.

"We should leave at dawn," Neriah said.

"You really need another day of rest," Abisina replied. "And I need to work on building support in the south." Abisina told Neriah about the centaur who had let her go at the stream. "There must be others like him. Tomorrow, I'll go out again. If I could talk to him—"

"It's not safe to stay here!" Neriah broke in. "Not for one centaur!"

"It starts with one."

"It's suicide, Abisina! I won't allow it. Even without the letter, you have a better chance in Watersmeet. You have the necklace!"

"But you're injured."

"I can travel tomorrow," Neriah insisted, "though I will have to ride."

"The trees are so dense here, I'll have to stay in human form. And it's dangerous. The centaurs will expect us to go by the dwarf road. They'll be waiting for us. With you injured—"

"We will go west to the Great River," Neriah said. She sounded like the Fairy Mother delivering a command.

"But the crossing of the Obrun Mountains is at Vigar's garden near the dwarf road."

"I know another way to the pass."

"But Findlay and Elodie are on the dwarf road—I want to follow their path," Abisina finally admitted. "They may need our help."

"By now, they are in Watersmeet," Neriah said. "I am sure."

"But you've had no birds. . . ."

"I'm sure."

Abisina wanted to believe Neriah so badly.

"We need to keep on for Watersmeet—the sooner the better," Neriah said again.

"It would be best to get there soon," Abisina agreed.

She helped the fairy to get comfortable and spread Neriah's coat over her. As Abisina lay down next to her, the fairy sat up. "What are you doing?" she cried.

"I slept next to you last night—to keep us both warmer," Abisina said.

"I must have been asleep," Neriah said stiffly. "I did not know. Of course we should sleep close."

Abisina crawled under the coat again, but the comfort was gone.

# CHAPTER IV

THE NEXT MORNING, ABISINA WOKE BEFORE NERIAH. SHE had been dreaming about Findlay. She couldn't remember the details, but something had been very wrong.

*What if he's hurt?* He and Elodie had left Newlyn six weeks before Abisina set out. She remembered standing in the snowy Seldar grove on that clear night. Abisina could hear Elodie crying as she said good-bye to Corlin, Newlyn's young leader. But she and Findlay had been silent and dry-eyed as they embraced. How do you say good-bye to part of yourself?

*If he's in trouble, how can I go west—away from the road he was on?*

The answer came to her, though it was not the answer she wanted. *Findlay would want me to. He believes—even if I don't—that I have a "special destiny."* She sighed and reached up to touch the necklace. The Obrium was warm. *He thinks I can save Watersmeet. And Seldara. He would tell me to go to Watersmeet.*

She threw off the coat, stood up, stretched, and then shook Neriah.

For the first hour of the journey, the trees were too close together for Neriah to ride. Even after Abisina could transform and carry her, the fairy had to dismount each time the trees grew dense. Neriah refused to stop or rest. At last, Abisina set Neriah down, saying, "I'm going to climb a tree to see if I can find an easier way through this forest."

Intending to give Neriah a rest, Abisina dawdled as she climbed. From the top, she spotted a section of forest that had more gaps between treetops. When Abisina came down, Neriah was sound asleep, so she had a few mouthfuls of water and bandaged the cuts on her palms, which had reopened during her climb. After an hour, she woke Neriah.

"We don't have to keep going today," Abisina said.

"Yes, we do."

When the sun was directly overhead, the trees began to thin, boulders and stones breaking through the crust of snow. They stopped to eat, but Neriah had only a few bites.

"Neriah, we don't—"

"Abisina!" she protested, and Abisina again caught a glimmer of the Fairy Mother in Neriah's tone. "I will not stop."

"Then try to sleep. If we can bind you to my torso—"

"What?" The fairy backed away.

"It works!" Abisina told her. "If you know you won't fall, you can relax enough to sleep."

Neriah frowned, though she agreed, "If it means we can keep going."

Abisina pulled out the extra bandages, brown with dried blood. In the end, they had to use their satchels to help tie Neriah snugly. When they set out again, Neriah's head lolled onto Abisina's shoulder, the fairy's breathing deep in her ear.

Abisina relaxed a little. She hadn't realized how Neriah's aloofness was affecting her. *Not like before . . .* She had felt a kinship with the fairy both times they'd met, but now, something had changed.

In some places, the snow was hard enough for Abisina to trot, and she enjoyed the speed. She ate when she needed to, without slackening her pace, and let Neriah sleep. She kept an eye out for game and brought down a few squirrels for their supper, but saw nothing larger. Evidence of the leviathan-birds was everywhere—piles of bones, skeletal trees, talon prints in trampled snow. *It's a good thing I like squirrel,* she thought.

Abisina couldn't blame the birds when she came upon a dying Seldar grove. Spying the grove through the trees, she thought it was a small one—four or five trees at most. She longed to walk among its white trunks and listen to the wind in the leaves, which the Seldars held even through the winter. In the Seldars, she felt most connected to her father.

As Abisina stood next to Rueshlan's funeral pyre, the Green Man had appeared at her side. He had not been seen in the land for generations. He towered over her, and Abisina had stared at his green skin, the vines and roots issuing from his mouth, the flowers and saplings that sprang up in his footprints. The Green Man, the patron of all that grows, had gathered the ash of the pyre in his massive hands and spread it on the wind. Wherever the ash landed, Seldars grew. Groves like the one ahead dotted the land from north to south.

When Abisina came closer to the grove, she saw that the four trees she had spotted because of their glowing bark stood among twenty or more that did not glow at all. The white bark of these trees had faded to gray, and their branches were gnarled and twisted. Even the healthy trees showed signs of disease. In winter, the Seldar leaves turned from the warm gold of summer to a soft copper color. But these leaves were brittle and brown.

"What can it mean?" Abisina said aloud.

Neriah stirred. "Mmm?"

"Look." Abisina pointed to the grove. "Have you seen anything like this before?"

It took Neriah a moment to answer, and when she did, her voice trembled. "What is wrong with the trees?" Despite the folk's suspicion about the fairies, Abisina had first trusted Neriah because of the love they shared for the Seldars.

"I don't know," Abisina said. She took a few steps into the grove and ran her fingers along the trunk of one of the healthier trees. It shivered at her touch. *What has killed these trees? Does the opening of the rift have something to do with this?*

She turned away, unwilling to stay any longer. As she resumed her pace, the cold wind cut more keenly through her cloak.

When they stopped for the night, Abisina made a fire on the lee side of a boulder. No centaurs had followed them, and the fire would keep überwolves at bay. She would take her chances with minotaurs.

Neriah sat close to the small blaze as Abisina roasted the squirrels and melted snow for the water skins.

"The alliance in the south with the dwarves and Vranham . . . have your other friends been successful?" the fairy asked.

"I left Newlyn before Haret and Corlin got back," Abisina said, turning the squirrels on the spit.

"There was another human . . . a Vranian."

"Jorno?" Abisina asked, surprised that Neriah remembered him. It was hard to talk about Jorno. In Vranille he had helped her escape from a mob bent on killing outcasts, but he had also killed Kyron, a centaur who had been like a second father to Abisina. "He never supported working with centaurs—or dwarves or fauns. The centaurs had hurt him badly once, and he couldn't get past his fear. He went crazy when he discovered I was a shape-shifter. He—he was in love with me," she said. "No, not love. Obsession. He had invented this image of me—and of our future together. Then I showed up with Findlay, and it was clear I had imagined a different future. When he saw me as a centaur . . ." That was more than she had meant to say, but it felt good to talk—even with Neriah. "We don't know what happened to him." She described the centaurs' raid on Newlyn, followed by the attack of the leviathan-birds.

"So Jorno is dead?" Neriah asked.

"We found no sign of him—dead or alive. But so many died. . . ." Abisina hated to remember the bodies strewn throughout Newlyn.

She and Neriah had settled down for the night—this time in their separate wraps with the fire for warmth—before she could speak the thought that had plagued her since seeing the dying Seldar grove.

"What if those trees are some kind of sign?"

Neriah raised her head.

Abisina sat up and went on: "At the end of his life, my father dreamed of bringing north and south together. Those trees are his legacy. But they're dying now. It makes me wonder if his dream is dying, too." When she finished, her voice was just above a whisper.

Neriah dropped her head back onto the snow, staring at the branches above them, as if mesmerized by the swirling sparks. Abisina waited, but the fairy said nothing. Eventually, Abisina lay back down and tried to sleep.

As they continued west, Neriah grew in strength, staying awake for more of the ride each day. The fairy seemed almost more eager than Abisina to reach Watersmeet: she argued with Abisina every time they slowed down to hunt, and if they hit dense sections of forest that forced Abisina to transform, the fairy stopped speaking altogether.

*I once thought Neriah was more "human" than other fairies,* Abisina mused, looking at the firm set of Neriah's shoulders as she slipped between a clump of trees. *Now she seems as much "fairy" as the Mother. Reava had better watch out—that crown may not be as secure as she thinks.*

Four days after they left the Cairn, Neriah was strong enough to leap into a tree and get their bearings. To Abisina's amazement, she came down smiling. They were within a day of the Great River.

They reached it the next afternoon. This part of the Great River was wide and gentle. Near Watersmeet, the water was too fast and rough for ice to form anywhere except at the banks, but here most of the river was covered with ice.

Across the water, the forbidding slopes of the Mountains Eternal filled the horizon, their tops disappearing in the clouds. From this far north, Abisina couldn't see the rift—or rather, she couldn't see its jagged remains. What else had the mountain unleashed? What hideous monster was now making its way through Seldara?

The urge to gallop seized her. "Hang on, Neriah!" she shouted and leapt forward.

For several minutes, Abisina thought of nothing but speed. The wind whistled in her ears, her hair and tail streamed out behind her, her hooves churned the pebbled banks, and muscles rippled beneath her shiny coat. She felt a laugh rising from her belly.

Then, above the thudding of her hooves, she heard a new sound, and her steps faltered.

"What is it?" Neriah called.

"Listen." Abisina slowed further.

The sound came again: an eerie hiss. And then a leviathan-bird soared over the trees lining the riverbank, followed by two more.

Many times larger than centaurs, the birds carried their bulk on huge wings with taloned feet tucked under them. Blistered skin covered their naked heads, and their hooked beaks jutted between narrow yellow eyes. Abisina had met one on the plain around Newlyn and killed it more through luck than skill; two other birds had almost destroyed the village.

Her hooves flew down the shore again, but now terror spurred her on. The next hiss was right on her heels, and Abisina surged forward. The second bird flew above her, its wing beats buffeting the air. The third cut off her escape to the shelter of the trees, wing tips grazing her flanks. Glancing up, Abisina saw talons reaching toward Neriah.

"Shoot for the neck!" Abisina shouted to the fairy.

The bird near the trees closed in, pushing them to the river. Abisina's strength was giving out. The expected twang of the bowstring hadn't come. Had Neriah been taken?

Abisina reared on her hind hooves, pivoting, ready to gallop the opposite way, hoping to cut back to the trees while the birds changed direction. But as she reared, a searing pain cut across her shoulder. She landed hard on her front hooves and stumbled to her knees, facing the river.

She braced herself for the stab of claws, the hammer blows of beaks.

Instead, shards of ice stung her face. A swirling column of water rose and reached toward her.

"Come to me!" a chorus of voices called; and as she knelt, motionless and staring, a storm of ice and water engulfed her. She closed her eyes. Abisina's chest contracted, forcing out her breath. The river was pulling her into its depths! She tried to scramble away, but her limbs met only the resistance of water.

*I will drown!*

Her shoulder throbbed, but what did pain matter? Abisina could no longer fight the urge to breathe.

She opened her eyes to see the world for the last time.

# CHAPTER V

HER LUNGS FILLED WITH AIR, NOT WATER. SHE BLINKED. And breathed again. Human—she didn't remember transforming—she was clasped in someone's or some*thing*'s arms, held firmly but gently in a pocket of air underwater. Heat chased the cold away, creeping up her legs and into her chest. The pain in her shoulder eased. She craned her neck to see what held her: silvery arms, thin and muscled, encircled her chest. Below, the riverbed flew by in a rush as she was carried upriver.

*Naiads?*

Abisina had heard the stories about the spirits of the river. Generations ago, the White Worm had attacked Vigar and Watersmeet for the first time. In the battle that followed, the river itself had played a role, sweeping the Worm and its army away. That was why, north of the Obrun Mountains, the Great River was called the River Deliverance.

Vigar had been caught in the flood, and the naiads had

borne her far downriver, where Rueshlan had found her broken body. He had received the Keeper's necklace from Vigar as she died.

Did these same naiads have Abisina now?

*Neriah!* Did they have her also? Abisina caught a blurry glimpse of the fairy being carried by a silvery figure.

*Where are they taking us?* For an instant, panic returned. *They saved us,* she reminded herself. She let herself relax into the warmth around her, felt it sink into her tired limbs, listened to the water murmuring in her ear. She closed her eyes.

In the grasp of the naiads, Abisina slept and woke, slept and woke. At times, the river bottom rushing below her was rocky and green with moss; at other times, it was smooth and sandy. The light changed, too, from the bright sparkle of sun through ice to the dark murkiness of shaded pools, to the impenetrable darkness of a moonless night. She woke when she was passed from one host to another, though she had no idea how often this happened. In these exchanges, Abisina caught glimpses of slender fingers, silvery hair, and once an eye as deep and black as a forest tarn. Voices babbled. Next to her, Neriah, too, was passed between escorts. She and Neriah must have eaten; Abisina's belly always felt full. The pain in her shoulder dulled to a slight ache. Had they treated her wound?

Wonder filled Abisina as she traveled north. This land had so many mysteries, secrets, and beauties! She had traversed it twice and still had so much to learn.

Hours—or perhaps days—into the journey, a deafening thunder yanked Abisina from sleep. An agonizing pressure beat down on her head. Light danced brilliantly, and blots of color flitted around her. Their pace slowed, as if the naiads were dragging them uphill.

*The waterfall!* Abisina had seen it from Vigar's garden. It flowed from high in the Obrun Mountains to the southern side. Were the naiads taking them up the Obruns?

Abisina's hopes rose. Perhaps there was a path from the waterfall's peak to the garden between Mounts Sumus and Arduus. Findlay might be there! But as the water continued to beat on them, her worries grew. How high were they? Were they moving at all? How did she know the naiads were trying to help? Just because they had helped Vigar, would they help her, too?

She didn't think she could take the pressure on her head much longer—and then it got worse. For an instant, the light dimmed, and then it was black. Abisina's scream was drowned by the water's roar.

The truth came to her: *We're going through the mountains!* Below Watersmeet, the River Deliverance disappeared beneath the Obruns and then shot out again high in the peaks, as if the water had flowed *up*. The folk believed the water was forced through a crack deep in the mountain. *And now we're traveling through that crack.* As difficult as the trip up the waterfall had been, Abisina now longed to be back in the light. The darkness, the pressure, the noise— she would suffocate. She wondered how the naiads' slender arms had the strength to swim against the current for so long.

What if they got stuck? They would be trapped in the tunnel for eternity!

She tried to make her mind go blank. Just as she had talked herself into a state of calm, rock scraped against her skin, the cold seized her, and water drenched her hair, as if the bubble of warm air surrounding her had broken.

The warmth and air returned, but at the next scrape, Abisina was drenched again. Each time this happened, fear seized her. She could not force herself to be calm. Even when air was plentiful, she braced for the next flood of water, until she wore herself out and was left limp, lying against the naiad. Then the grip across her chest loosened, and she waited for the final deluge of killing cold.

When it didn't come, her eyes flew open. Light rushed at her. They had made it through!

Abisina catapulted from the water into the dusky light of morning and landed flat on a sheet of ice ringing a pool. She relished the cold and drew stabbing winter air into her lungs. Snowflakes brushed her face. She was perfectly dry.

Neriah lay to her left, awake and wild-eyed. Abisina guessed that the fairy's trip through the mountain had been no better than her own.

"Where are we?" Abisina whispered, but before Neriah could answer, a figure rose in the open water.

Abisina glimpsed shoulders, a thin waist, and delicate fingers before the figure swung her head back to reveal her face—with the black eyes Abisina had seen earlier. The naiad seemed to be made of water. Behind her, the line of trees rippled and swayed.

"Thank you," Abisina managed, and the naiad smiled.

"I did not bring you here," she said. "My sisters did. They are resting at the bottom of the pool. We are honored to help you again."

"Again?"

"We recognized your symbol from when we carried you long ago."

"Oh!" Abisina glanced at the necklace glowing around her neck. "That wasn't me, but this *was* her necklace."

The naiad nodded. "We know you are not her, and also that you are. If you're ready, we can continue the journey."

"Where are you taking us?" Abisina asked.

"Back to where we first saw you—Watersmeet."

Abisina's heart leapt at the word. "What's happening there? Can you give us any news?"

The naiad shook her head. "We do not go into Watersmeet anymore. There's something . . . dark . . . there. We'll get you as close as we dare. The light you wear—Watersmeet needs you."

Abisina had prepared herself for bad news, but actually hearing it. . . . She glanced at Neriah, who was staring blankly at the naiad. "We're ready," Abisina said.

The naiad dissolved before them, then rose again in a shower of water. Strong arms encircled Abisina, and they dived back into the pool. The pressure and thunder of the waterfall were gone, along with the fearful rush of water. The river in her ears was now a lullaby. *Almost home,* she thought.

Late in the afternoon, the naiads delivered Abisina and Neriah to the riverbank below Watersmeet and did not wait for good-byes or thank-yous.

Abisina led Neriah to a cluster of trees and realized with a start that she had hidden in the same place before. *With Findlay.* Glynholly, led by Reava, had just outlawed her; a search party was combing the forest.

*He kissed me here.* "I thought I might never get to do that again," he had said, and pulled her to him. She had felt the beating of his heart against her cheek.

*He may be in Watersmeet even now!* She fought the excitement that would send her racing in to find him. *I may still be an outlaw,* Abisina reminded herself. She had the necklace, though she was not convinced that Glynholly had sent it. *This could be a trap.* The naiads had said that Watersmeet needed her. *But how? And for what?*

The sun was setting, and parts of Watersmeet were already deep in shadow, though light bathed the top of the Sylvyads. These trees dwarfed the pines along the banks, their roots twining together to make an island at the point where the three rivers met—the River Lesser, the Middle River, and the River Fennish. The three emerged below the island of Watersmeet as the River Deliverance.

The folk of Watersmeet had made their home on this

root-island, carving houses out of the trees' bark, using the arcing roots as bridges to the banks. Abisina's first view of Watersmeet, more than three years ago, was the same as this—the sun setting, Watersmeet dark. It had been Midsummer then; and inside the Sylvyads she had found a vibrant, welcoming community, her father at its center. What did the trees contain now? Who was in power? Who had been killed? Would they welcome her, or capture her?

Suddenly, Neriah gripped her arm. Abisina was startled by the touch. Then she saw where the fairy pointed. Near their hiding spot was a Seldar grove. While Abisina had focused on Watersmeet, Neriah had stared at the Seldars. On the edge of the grove, the trees were gray, gnarled, and leafless. Abisina's and Neriah's eyes met—and for a moment, Abisina again felt a connection to the fairy.

As the sun set, Abisina waited for the first lighted windows to emerge from Watersmeet's darkness, for a fire to be kindled in the middle of one of the wards; but no lights twinkled on the river. Her ears strained to catch a voice, the thud of hooves, or the padding of feet on the root-trails. She searched for sentries on the bridges, for refugees on the banks—but Watersmeet was silent.

"Where is everyone?" Neriah whispered.

"I don't know," Abisina said without looking away. "Did Reava say what was going on in Watersmeet?"

"No. The last I knew, Watersmeet was besieged and troubled, not deserted." Neriah stared across the water. "Despite everything, the Mother wanted Watersmeet to survive."

"Well, something's not right, whatever the Mother wanted."

They lapsed into silence, both staring into the darkness.

Neriah fell asleep sometime after midnight. Abisina kept up the vigil with a growing sense of foreboding. Even in the dead of night, *someone* would be up with a baby or a sick family member or troubled sleep. Instead, the silence and the darkness were endless. By the time dawn touched the tops of the Sylvyads, Abisina knew she had to go in.

"You can't!" Neriah insisted after Abisina roused the fairy. "You have no idea what you're walking into!"

"Something's wrong. I need to get in there. You can stay here."

"We'll go to the Motherland," Neriah argued. "The Mother will know what's happening. The folk may be there—"

"I didn't come to the shores of Watersmeet to turn back now."

They argued back and forth. Abisina would not yield. Neriah finally conceded but declared: "You cannot go alone." The fairy rose to her feet.

"You're not well. I can take care of myself."

"Like you did with the centaurs?"

Abisina started. "Fine," she said. "You can come with me." It would help to have another set of eyes and a second bow. *And company,* Abisina admitted to herself. She transformed, and Neriah leapt onto her back.

Abisina waited for a sentry to challenge them as they neared the first of the root-bridges leading into Watersmeet.

But no one cried "Halt!" and Abisina's hooves echoed dully as she crossed.

The first ward they entered—the cluster of homes where Frayda, Watersmeet's best archer, lived—was deserted. The doors were shut tight, and waxy evergreen needles coated the courtyard. At this time of morning, shouts of greeting should have rung through the ward, the doors should have stood open, a fire should have roared in the stone ring in the center.

"If they were under attack, everyone would move to the center of the community," Neriah said.

"There's no sign of attack. No abandoned weapons. No bodies," Abisina pointed out.

They left the ward and followed the root-trails deeper into Watersmeet. More wards, abandoned like the first, opened off the smaller trails. They turned a corner onto a larger trail. A satchel lay in the center of the walkway, its contents strewn about: a tangle of leggings and under-shirts, a dented and blackened cooking pot, a shattered piece of pottery, and a pair of dirty boots. Abisina bent down to pick up one of the boots. The top had been shredded, as if something had held the boot in its teeth and shaken it. *Überwolves*. It shocked her to think of them here, but, of course, with everyone gone, what would have stopped them? She showed the teeth marks to Neriah.

"Abisina, we have seen enough. I do not know what happened here, but the folk are gone. We should leave before this überwolf finds us!" Abisina could feel Neriah's legs shaking against her back.

"This is my *home*. Some folk may still be here."

Neriah's grip on Abisina tightened, though she said nothing as Abisina left the ripped satchel and continued on.

At the next turning, they found the remains of a barricade: tables and chairs piled in the junction of two trails, most of the furniture shattered. An axe and a few arrows were scattered about, and several brown stains marked where someone had been injured. Or killed.

Abisina leapt over the crippled barricade and started to trot, but Neriah put a hand on her shoulder.

"Slowly," she cautioned.

Abisina's gait slowed, but her heart raced on as she saw sign after sign of battle: more broken barricades, abandoned weapons, splotches of blood, household items that folk had been carrying when they had run from whatever chased them.

There were no bodies, no folk fallen defending their homes, no enemies—überwolf, minotaur, or troll—killed in their drive through the community.

They reached the Council House, an enormous room built into the stump of a fallen Sylvyad. The stump was twice the girth of any other Sylvyad and had splinters of wood like spires pointing to the sky. The splinters were charred, the trunk scorched. The House's doors hung off their hinges, exposing a cold, dark room that was a shell of the chamber that had stood there. Blackened bones clogged the doorway.

Abisina turned away. Whose bones were in that pile? How many of her friends had died here?

"Abisina—" A growl cut Neriah off.

A pack of überwolves entered the clearing. Some walked

on hind feet, the others on all fours. Sun glinted on the silver fur of their haunches. A few clutched rough spears in their clawed hands.

They spotted one another at the same instant. Black lips curled into snarls. Neriah already had an arrow on her string, but Abisina, distracted by the ruin of the Council House, had let her bow drop to her side. The überwolves sprang. Neriah loosed her arrow and shouted, "Go!"

Abisina spun to gallop back the way they had come when a gray shape flew out of the inky blackness of the chamber's doors, forcing her onto a trail they'd not taken yet. Behind them, a piercing howl alerted more überwolves to their presence.

Abisina raced down a wide boulevard. Gray shapes flooded in behind her, entering from side trails and wards. The überwolves had taken over this section of Watersmeet. Neriah shot all her arrows, then pulled from Abisina's quiver, though they couldn't hope to kill them all.

"Out of arrows!" Neriah yelled, and Abisina pushed for more speed. But which direction would take them to safety?

They were on an arching bridge that spanned the open water where the currents of the Fennish and Middle Rivers combined.

"No!" Neriah screamed as Abisina veered toward the bridge's edge.

"Hold on!" Abisina yelled.

They plunged off the side.

# CHAPTER VI

THEY HUNG IN THE AIR FOR A MOMENT, THEN THE FREEZING water closed over their heads. The churning river disoriented Abisina, but she forced her eyes open. With powerful kicks, she followed the rising bubbles, and the light that beckoned behind them.

Her head broke the surface. The bridge was still crowded with überwolves, but she was moving so fast downstream, she was out of range of their spears.

"Neriah!" she cried.

There was no answer at first. Then the fairy surfaced, gasping for breath. The current pulled her under again. Abisina reached out but grabbed only water.

The current rushed Neriah toward the base of a Sylvyad with a massive eddy at its roots. If the fairy was pulled under the roots, she would be trapped!

Abisina swam toward the eddy, but it was stronger than she expected, and seconds later she slammed into the roots.

Pain shot through her back, and she was sucked under.

Water buffeted her body and numbed her limbs. She beat at the current, but the water bore her down, down, into darkness and cold. She fought on, kicking and taking stroke after stroke, her air almost gone, when she surfaced into complete darkness. The water was calm around her. But *where* was she? And where was Neriah?

Something bobbed against her, and she reached out blindly to grab a handful of hair. *Neriah!*

The fairy lay facedown. Abisina yanked Neriah's head up, but she didn't hear the fairy take a breath. *I have to help her!* First she had to get out of the water. She swam forward, and, after one stroke, her knuckles scraped bark. A root or trunk of a Sylvyad. She groped along the root until she found a hold to pull herself and Neriah out of the frigid water. She pushed the fairy onto the root, transformed into a human, and hoisted herself up.

Her frigid fingers could feel no pulse in the fairy's neck.

"No!" Abisina laid Neriah on her side and drove her fists into the fairy's belly. Water flooded from Neriah's mouth. Abisina used her fists again, and the fairy vomited more water and started to cough.

Abisina fell back.

"Where?" Neriah croaked.

"I'm not sure. I think we're under Watersmeet," Abisina said, "in the roots of one of the Sylvyads. Can you see anything?"

"A little. We're in some kind of cave—safe for now."

"I thought you'd drowned."

"You saved me. I owe you a debt."

"Let's see if we can get out of here before we worry about that." Abisina heard the muffled rush of water, but around them, everything was still except for a slow *drip, drip, drip.*

"A wall of roots curves around to the right," Neriah said. "We should follow it. There may be a way out."

Abisina forced herself to her feet, limbs stiff with cold. "I can't see a thing."

"Here." Neriah took Abisina's hand, led her forward, and placed her hands on the wall. Abisina felt many roots twisting together.

"We might be able to climb this," Abisina said. "Can you see up there?"

"Not much."

They took a few more steps along the wall, but the huge root they were standing on turned back into the water, and they could go no farther.

Retracing their steps, they found no way out in the other direction, either. They stood on a loop of root that rose from the water like the back of a sea serpent.

They sat down, resting against the root-wall.

"Do you think we should try swimming out?" Abisina asked.

"I can't swim against that current," Neriah said. "We need the naiads. Can you call them again?"

"I didn't call them the first time. And they said there's something dark in Watersmeet that keeps them away."

"Let's hope we don't find it."

"Neriah, what's across this pool?" Abisina kept her voice steady, though her chest was getting tight.

"I can't tell. It feels like a closed space—no currents of air."

Abisina breathed more deeply. The smell was fetid, as if this place had been closed off for centuries. The soupy air suffocated her.

"I'll swim out of the eddy as a centaur," Abisina suggested. "Then I'll get back into Watersmeet and find a way down here from inside." She tried to make it sound like a real plan, but she knew it was useless. She couldn't fight the current, either. *Still, it's better than dying slowly here.*

"What are you doing, Abisina?" Neriah yelled.

"Help!" Something cold was gripping Abisina's leg and drawing her toward the water.

Neriah grasped Abisina under her arms; but the pull grew stronger, and the root beneath them shifted, rising and slanting until Neriah, too, slid forward on the wet wood. Abisina fought for some kind of hold and managed to wedge her foot against another root. The pull on her leg increased.

"Help me!" she cried again, and the cave filled with blinding light.

*The necklace!*

Fingers of light emanated from the pendant, illuminating dozens of white eels rising from the pool's surface. One grasped Abisina's leg, and more were coming. Their bodies—some as wide as Abisina's thighs, others as slender as twigs—ended in gaping, toothless mouths. Translucent white skin covered eye hollows on each side of the creatures' heads. Though they seemed blind, they reared back from the necklace's light. The eel on Abisina's leg released. Two of the eels, caught directly in a beam from the necklace, opened their mouths in silent screams and sank back under the black water.

For an instant, Abisina thought that they would escape the monsters, but now the root's slant toward the water grew steeper. Neriah had completely let go of Abisina, her fingers clawing the root to stop her slide. Abisina lunged, grabbed a handful of Neriah's hair, and held on as the fairy pitched forward. Then an eel rose from the pool with a smaller one wrapped around its head, impervious to the light and coming at Neriah as if it sensed precisely where she was.

A second eel shot forth with a similar blindfold, opened its mouth, and attached itself to Abisina's hand where she held Neriah's hair. The eel began to suck, and then it stung her. Abisina screamed. Her cry only drew more eels to them.

She fumbled at her waist, searching for her dagger. She had lost her bow in the river, but she found her dagger caught in the strap of her healing bag. Abisina ripped it free and attacked the eel stinging her hand, which was going numb. She was losing her grip on Neriah's hair; she couldn't hold on long enough to hack through the creature's tough hide. Desperate, she stabbed at the thinner eel shielding its eyes. The smaller eel released, and the larger one writhed away from the light and sank back into the pool.

Neriah shrieked. A cluster of eels had suctioned themselves to her waist.

Abisina stabbed the smaller eels, again forcing them to release, as the root kept rising. She freed the last eel that held Neriah and turned her dagger on the eel dangling from her own leg. The eel let go, leaving a purple bruise on Abisina's shin.

They were eel-free, but the root bucked, and Abisina lost her balance. She reached out to grab at Neriah, and her dagger went skittering across the root and into the water.

They had risen so high, the necklace lit the cave's ceiling, covered with loops of roots. Neriah grabbed one and swung up.

Abisina reached for another loop but couldn't make her fingers clutch it. She tried again. Her fingers didn't even twitch. Seeing the bruise on the back of her hand, she understood. Her bitten leg also hung limp. "Neriah!"

The fairy tried to move closer, and Abisina threw herself at Neriah and grabbed the fairy's ankle with her good hand. Two eels rising from the pool missed her.

"Hang on!" Neriah called as she swung from root to root, Abisina dangling below. The necklace cast light around the cave, and Abisina saw a gap between two of the twisting roots on the opposite wall.

Neriah had seen it, too. "Get ready!" the fairy grunted. They swung toward the hole, but Abisina's limbs hung uselessly; only the hand that held Neriah's foot could grip anything, and she crashed into the wall. Neriah had missed her target. They arced back over the pool.

"I'm slipping!" Abisina moaned as they reached the highpoint of their swing.

"Get ready!" Neriah called again. They flew toward the wall once more.

Abisina screamed as she crashed, but she clung to Neriah, who grasped the wall and climbed to the hole, dragging Abisina behind her. Abisina scraped painfully upward. Then an eel stung the bottom of her foot.

Neriah clambered into the hole and hauled up Abisina, the creature still suctioned to her leg.

"Get it!" Abisina croaked as she released Neriah's ankle. The fairy crawled forward, hitting, scratching, and kicking at the eel to no avail.

"Little one!" Abisina shouted, and Neriah attacked the smaller eel protecting the big one's eyes. Both eels fell into the water, landing with a smack.

The light of the necklace blinked out, returning Neriah and Abisina to darkness.

# CHAPTER VII

ABISINA SCRAMBLED AWAY FROM THE OPENING. HER LEGS were numb below the knees, so she pulled herself forward with her one good hand. Neriah followed.

At every moment, Abisina expected to reach the back of the small cave; but the passage kept going, sloping up and twisting to the left and right, getting narrower the higher they went. *We're between two roots,* she thought.

"Do you think they can climb?" Abisina whispered, imagining those white bodies weaving in and out of the wall of roots.

"I don't care. I have to rest." Neriah sounded exhausted.

"Are you hurt?" Abisina asked.

"I can't feel the middle of my body, but my arms and legs are fine. Just weak. And my head hurts."

"I pulled your hair. Twice," Abisina recalled. "Sorry."

"It saved me."

"And you saved me. Again."

"That debt is paid," Neriah said.

"Neither of us would have survived this journey without the other, and we're not through yet. Are you rested? Should we—"

An echoing groan cut off Abisina, and the walls around them shook.

"What was that?" Neriah asked.

Another tremor.

The tunnel shifted beneath them. "The tree is shaking!" Abisina cried. She got to her knees. Pain had slowly replaced the numbness, but she crawled anyway.

The rocking of the tree opened the tunnel more, and then the walls around them changed. Instead of the roots' rough bark, the walls became smoother. Abisina's nose filled with the smell of dampness. "I think we're *in* the tree," Abisina whispered. "Between layers of bark!"

The tree shifted again, and this time the space they crawled into grew narrower, and Abisina had to wriggle on her belly to keep going.

"Hurry!" Neriah urged, but the tunnel had ended.

"We're trapped!"

The tree rocked back and forth, and they heard the sound of splintering wood. The tunnel tipped sharply, and Abisina pitched forward. Neriah fell on top of her.

"The tree's down!" Abisina cried.

The tree continued to creak and groan. The walls tightened around them. How many eels lived below Watersmeet? Enough to fell a Sylvyad?

The tree lurched again and crashed into something else. Abisina and Neriah fell through the tunnel's floor onto a hard surface. Heavy things clubbed them on the head. Abisina tried to protect herself with her arms, but she was quickly buried.

Then, all was still. The tree had come to rest.

Abisina pushed leather bindings away from her face and smelled vellum pages. "Books!" she shouted. "We're in the library! And I can see!" A square of wan light reached her from a window in the opposite wall. The books next to her shifted, and Neriah's head poked out.

They must have climbed through the roots of one of the library's Sylvyads into the tough outer bark. Something had brought down the tree, and the landing sent them into the library. The wall across from where Abisina sat was covered with empty shelves and a hole big enough for a girl and a fairy to fall through.

Neriah was still digging through the books. Bits of parchment covered the fairy's hair. Abisina laughed, giddy with relief. "You look like a fir shedding snow!" She plucked a piece of parchment from Neriah's hair, spotted two words on it, and gasped:

—brother Vran—

"Vigar wrote this!" Abisina seized more of the scraps around Neriah, her hands shaking. What if the proof of Vran and Vigar's relationship was here the whole time?

It was possible. Vigar had started the library; Rueshlan added to it through long generations. The library contained stories from centaurs, fauns, dwarves, humans, and fairies. She had never heard that Vigar added her own papers, but Abisina had lived in Watersmeet for only a few years. She didn't know all its stories.

The parchment was brittle with age, the edges flaking off as Abisina handled the fragments. Many pieces had words on them, though some were faded and stained.

"Where are they coming from?" Abisina looked up. A sheaf of yellowed paper covered with writing was tucked behind one of the empty shelves.

"Blessings of Vigar!" she breathed.

"Abisina, I'm not feeling . . ." Neriah said softly.

"Hold on. Let me just get up there!" Abisina climbed the sloping floor on legs still weak from the eels' stings. She slipped back several times but kept trying. She had the sheaf in her grasp when she fell again, sliding down the floor, a few sheets of parchment tumbling down on top of her. She gathered the sheets; several crumbled as she touched them. Most were still wedged behind the shelf. "Neriah, help me!"

The fairy didn't answer. Her head had fallen onto her chest, and her eyes were closed.

"Neriah?"

The fairy jerked awake, but her head lolled again.

"Oh, the Earth!" Abisina shoveled books away from the fairy.

Neriah's lids fluttered. "I don't know what's wrong with me. I have such a need to sleep."

Abisina pulled Neriah from the books and laid her down. She checked her head, her arms, her legs and saw no blood, no bruises, no injury hidden in the fairy's thick hair. "Neriah!" She listened to her breathing. What was wrong with her?

Abisina yanked up Neriah's tunic, where the eels had stung the fairy on her belly, and recoiled. Around Neriah's waist, the flesh was swollen and tight, mottled gray, white, and purple. Abisina reached out to touch the skin, and it blistered beneath her fingertips and oozed a black liquid.

"Oh, the Earth!" she gasped again. Abisina's left hand was swollen and discolored, and the feeling hadn't fully returned, but the reaction seemed to be waning. Her legs were the same. Neriah's response seemed to be much worse.

Abisina reached for her medicine pouch and found only a packet of yarrow. In freeing her dagger from her belt, she had cut the pouch and lost the rest of her medicines. The yarrow would help with pain, but Neriah didn't seem to be in pain.

Abisina stared at the ruins of the library. "Come on!" she shouted at herself. Slowly, the wheels of thought began turning. They couldn't stay here. They had no water, no food, no weapons, and no medicine.

She thought of her own house. She could get medicine there, and it would feel so good to be in familiar surroundings! But it was a long trek from the library to her ward, and she had no idea what she might encounter on the way.

*Findlay's house.* Abisina's heart thumped. He lived a short distance from the library. His mother might have herbs and ointments.

She studied the room again to figure out where they were in the Sylvyad. She would need a door or a window to get out. She could tell by the slope of the floor that they were far from the ground. This room was easy to cross, but in the next room, the walls and the floor were at a much steeper incline, and in the room after that, the floor would create a treacherous slide. She couldn't make it around the Sylvyad if she had to carry Neriah.

She bent down to wake up the fairy. The bits of parchment still lay next to Neriah: *Vigar's papers*. Abisina grabbed a book and stuck the three sheets she had rescued, whole and in fragments, between the pages. There were more fragments scattered on the floor, and the thick packet was still wedged behind the shelf. *I'll try to come back. Now I need to help Neriah.* She stuffed the book down her tunic.

Neriah fought Abisina's efforts to wake her. As the light faded in the window above them, Abisina grew more frustrated. They had to get to Findlay's before dark. Finally, she slapped Neriah across the cheek, and the fairy swung her head back with a cry.

"Neriah, I'm taking you somewhere you can rest. For now, I need you to stay awake," Abisina pleaded. "We have to get out of this tree!"

"I'll try," Neriah said, but her lids were already closing. "Take . . . off . . . my . . . coat," she murmured. "The cold will help."

Careful not to touch Neriah's waist, Abisina removed the coat. The fairy began to shiver, and the shaking kept her from dozing off.

It was a painful trek. They had to climb to the doorways between the library's rooms, now halfway up the walls. And they had to contend with tables, chairs, and books that had crashed into piles when the tree fell.

In the first two rooms, the windows were too high to jump from. In the third room, they were still six lengths above the ground. Neriah had stopped shivering and started to nod off again.

"Next room, Neriah!" Abisina tried to sound hearty, but inside she panicked.

She half dragged Neriah to the next room. *At last, a door!* It fell open as she released the latch; they were only three lengths above the ground.

"Neriah," she said gently, then when the fairy didn't stir, "Neriah!" The fairy groaned. "I'll get you as close to the ground as I can. Get ready to jump."

Neriah didn't respond. Abisina picked her up, carefully lowering her out the door. "I'm letting go, Neriah!" she shouted.

Neriah fell, loose limbed, and landed in a heap without waking.

Abisina was hanging from the threshold when she heard the first growl.

She jumped down and caught sight of a large male über-wolf approaching Neriah.

Abisina transformed, ignoring the agony in her legs, and scooped up the fairy. She leapt over the überwolf and galloped out of the ward in the direction of Findlay's. The wolf howled behind her, calling the rest of its pack.

"No!" Abisina screamed. They had been through so much—and Findlay's ward was ahead.

Just in time, she saw the two beds and table barring her way. She gathered herself for a leap, knocking her rear hoof against a table as she cleared the barrier, and headed straight for Findlay's green door.

Abisina skidded to a halt and reached for the knob, but before she could touch it, the door swung open, and someone cried, "Rueshlan!"

# CHAPTER VIII

ABISINA DIDN'T MOVE UNTIL THE BLOND GIRL BEHIND THE door yelled, "Get inside!" and pulled her in. The girl slammed the door and bolted it just before an überwolf crashed into it.

Abisina transformed and sank into a chair, still clutching Neriah.

The girl peered into Abisina's face, then pulled back suddenly. "Abisina? Y—you're a shape-shifter?"

The girl's face was unfamiliar to Abisina: lank blond hair, dull blue eyes, protruding cheekbones. A Vranian refugee?

"Are you from Vranille?"

"Abisina, it's me," the girl said. The flickering light of a small fire made the hollows in her face deeper. "It's Meelah."

Abisina tried to find the Meelah she knew in this grim, wasted figure. Meelah should have thirteen winters, but this girl looked much older. When Abisina had left Watersmeet last summer, Meelah's eyes had danced, her hair shone, and her quick smile had always made Abisina smile, too. In this way, she had been a lot like Findlay, her big brother.

"What's happened to you . . . to Watersmeet?"

"I thought you were him," Meelah said as if Abisina hadn't spoken. "I thought Rueshlan had come back to put things right."

Abisina shifted Neriah. Neriah's eyes were half open; her clothing was soaked. When Abisina touched the fairy's middle, her hand came away red.

"Meelah!" She got to her feet. "I need your help! This fairy is dying! She needs—"

Meelah's face hardened. "I've lost everything to the fairies. Let her die."

"Please, Meelah," Abisina said. "I need water and medicine."

Meelah said nothing.

"This is not Reava!" Abisina protested. "This fairy saved my life. She saved Findlay, too! And look." She pulled the necklace out from under her tunic, and it lit the whole room. "Her bird brought this to me."

"Quick! Go to my mother! She needs the necklace!"

"Hesper's here?"

"This way!" Meelah urged. "Lay the fairy on my bed!"

Abisina followed Meelah through the kitchen and into her room. Tunics and leggings were strewn across the floor, a pile of bloody bandages lay in a corner, and heaps of sleeping pelts sat at the foot of the bed. The room smelled of sweat, illness, and dirt. At Meelah's insistence, Abisina laid Neriah down in the filthy bedclothes, but before she could do any-thing to make the fairy comfortable, Meelah was tugging at her, forcing her to follow. "In here!"

The next room was where the family bathed, with a wooden tub in the middle of the floor, and then came Hes-per's room. Meelah yanked the door open and pushed Abisina in.

A fire roared in the fireplace, the floor was swept clean, and a range of medicines stood in a neat line on a shelf against the wall. Candles lit the room; an animal-pelt blanket hung over the window to prevent the light from spilling into the ward. The room was spotless, though Abisina could detect the smell of rot beneath the perfume of the beeswax candles. A bed stood in the center of the room, a wasted woman almost invisible beneath a pile of blankets.

Hesper was as unrecognizable as Meelah. She had been a strong, healthy woman, with the same thick blond hair as Findlay's. She led an archery team and a foraging team. Her children had both inherited her ready laugh. But like Meelah, Hesper had aged: her hair had thinned and showed streaks of gray. A skeletal hand lay on top of the blanket. Her eyes fluttered open as Abisina entered, and a smile pulled at the corners of her mouth.

"I knew you'd come back," she rasped. "Findlay?"

Abisina crossed to the bed and took Hesper's hand. "He'll be here soon."

"You're here for my Meelah," Hesper whispered. "You must tell Findlay I love him." She closed her eyes.

"The necklace!" Meelah cried. "Show it to her!"

"It will not heal her," Abisina tried to explain.

"Show her!"

"Hesper." Abisina leaned closer. "I—I have the Keeper's necklace. Meelah wants you to see it."

Hesper's eyes fluttered open again. She looked at her daughter. "My brave girl. You are safe now. Rueshlan's daughter has returned to Watersmeet." Hesper closed her eyes and sighed.

Meelah let out a heartrending wail, and Abisina squeezed the dying woman's hand. "I will care for her, Hesper. But Findlay's coming. He would want you to wait for him," she said.

Hesper didn't stir, though her chest continued to rise and fall. Carefully, Abisina peeled back the bedclothes, biting her lip to keep from crying out at the sight of Hesper's emaciated body. Hesper's right leg was twice its normal size, her thigh torn open and lost to infection. Abisina recognized an über-wolf bite.

"I've cleaned it, put medicine on it, but it gets worse and worse," Meelah said. She sounded like a young girl again.

Abisina replaced the blanket and took Meelah's hand. "You've done all you could, dear heart. Now, we need to keep her comfortable."

Meelah searched Abisina's face. When she grasped the meaning of her words, she sank to the floor.

Abisina held her, stroking her hair.

"I did everything Lennan told me to do," she sobbed.

"Mother wouldn't let him stay. She didn't even want *me* to stay. I hid until everyone else was gone, and then there was nothing she could do."

"You've been a comfort to her," Abisina soothed. "She held on this long to know you would be cared for. Now she wants to let go."

Meelah clung harder to Abisina.

Abisina's own cheeks were wet. She had lost her mother when she was Meelah's age; not a year later, her father had died in her arms.

*And Findlay,* she thought. *How will he feel, knowing that his mother suffered and he wasn't here?*

"How long?" Meelah asked.

"Soon."

"Can I—can I hold her?"

"Of course." Abisina helped Meelah onto the bed, and the girl stretched out along her mother's body. Hesper let out another sigh. Meelah put an arm across her mother's chest and closed her eyes.

Abisina left mother and daughter together. Ignoring her own exhaustion, her aching limbs, her itchy eyes longing to close, she returned to Neriah, afraid of what she would find. She bent over Neriah's still figure, the fairy's face gray and stony, and waited. And waited. The fairy took a shallow, rattling breath.

*Alive—but not for long unless I do something,* Abisina thought.

In the great room, Abisina found a bucket of snow next to

the fireplace, half melted. As she bent to pick it up, something hard pushed against her side. There was no time for Vigar's papers now. She pulled the book out of her tunic and picked up the bucket. As she passed through the kitchen on her way to Neriah, she set the book on the table.

Back at Neriah's side, Abisina touched the fairy's neck and felt a faint pulse. "Thanks to Vigar!" she whispered. She propped Neriah up in her arms and held a cup of melted snow to her lips. Most of the water dribbled down the fairy's chin and onto the bedclothes, but then Abisina saw a ripple in her throat as she swallowed.

Bracing herself, she lifted the fairy's tunic. The fairy's waist was a swollen mass of sores, some crusted over, some bleeding. Each sting had raised a welt of skin, red and blistered. Some welts were less pronounced, more like the purple bruise on her own hand. *Like snakebites,* Abisina thought. Her mother had treated hundreds of those. Could Abisina treat these stings the same way?

She seized a small knife lying half under Meelah's bed and made a slice across one of the welts. Some viscous liquid bubbled up. She put her mouth on the cut and sucked it.

Her lips and gums burned the instant the liquid touched them. She spit and sucked again and again until her mouth filled only with blood. She moved to the next welt.

By the time Abisina finished with the seven largest welts, her mouth felt raw and her lips bled. But already the first wound she'd treated had faded from a vivid red to a softer purple.

Abisina had used all the water in the bucket; only snow was left. She returned to the great room. The fire there was almost out. Abisina grabbed a piece of wood from the pile on the hearth: a table leg, beautifully carved with vines and fruit. She pulled out several more carved pieces. What was Meelah burning? All the furniture in the great room was in place. Abisina threw the piece on the fire and set the bucket of snow as close as she could.

As soon as she got enough water, she bathed her lips and swirled it around her mouth to rinse out the poison. It did little to calm the burning.

When Abisina returned to the fairy with a bucket of warm water, Neriah's waist was a horrifying mix of colors and scabs, but the reaction to the poison was subsiding. Had Abisina gotten it out in time? She bathed the fairy, forced some more water between her dry lips, and went to Hesper's room.

Meelah and her mother were sleeping, and Abisina did not disturb them. Instead, she went to the shelf of medicines she had noticed earlier. The jars contained a variety of balms, root powders, and dried herbs. She remembered Meelah mentioning advice from Lennan, Watersmeet's most gifted healer. Most of the jars had only a dusting of medicine left. Abisina sorted through the fuller jars, sniffing, rubbing bits of herb between her fingers, sometimes putting a trace on her tongue. She took three back to the great room: garlic, wild calla root, and snakeroot—all useful for snakebites. She put together the three powders, added water, and heated the mass over the fire. She wrapped the poultice in pieces of Meelah's sheets, applied the rags to the sores on Neriah's waist, then tore the cleanest parts of the sheets to make bandages, which she wrapped around the fairy's middle. She had just finished when Neriah began to vomit.

By morning, Abisina was thankful for her own exhaustion. It made the work of the night a blur: holding the fairy as Neriah expelled whatever poison had gotten into her system, cleaning her, checking on Meelah and her mother while she waited for the next round. She quickly lost track of how many times she had mopped up. Finally, the episodes got further apart.

Utterly worn out, Abisina went into the great room. With no task to occupy her, she could not ignore the flood of memories of her earlier times in this room: sitting near the fire as Findlay held her and she sobbed out the pain of losing her father; sharing honey buns with him at the little table that looked onto the ward, a summer breeze blowing through the open window; Meelah chattering on about an upcoming celebration or festival while Findlay reminded her to take a breath; Hesper entering with an armload of cattails or pussy willows or bittersweet to decorate their home.

*And now? Hesper is dying, and Meelah is alone. I have no idea where Findlay is. Überwolves and eels have overrun Watersmeet. The folk are scattered or dead, and the rift in the Mountains Eternal has released more evil on all of us.* She touched the necklace, its glow dim. *What is my part? How can I do anything in the face of all this?*

She went to the window and lifted the blanket hung

to hide the light. Dawn was beginning to color the sky.

*I musn't give in to despair,* Abisina tried to tell herself. *I can't do anything right now except care for those here. And I will be no good to anyone if I don't rest, even if only for an hour.* She looked at Findlay's door, took a deep breath, and went to it.

She paused for a moment, then stepped across the threshold and closed the door behind her, as if something might escape.

Findlay's room was in perfect order: the animal-pelt quilt spread across the bed, the clothes hanging from their hooks, the swords ranked against the wall. But the fireplace was cold, the air stale. Findlay usually kept his room in a state of comfortable disorder. Neat, it felt . . . empty. One sword was missing—he had carried it south. *And he carries it now. Wherever he is.*

Like Abisina, Findlay had been exiled months ago. Of course his mother would have cleaned his room, though maybe not at first—unwilling to admit that her son was gone. But eventually, she would have gone in there to make it ready for his return. And now Hesper would never see Findlay again. A deeper loneliness washed over her.

She couldn't sleep here. She would take the bedding and carry it back to the great room. There was more life there, and she was closer to Neriah and Meelah. She went to his bed, grabbed the blanket and pillow, and yanked them off.

She almost missed it in the near darkness, coiled under Findlay's pillow: a green waist-cord she recognized at once. It was from the tunic she had worn to the Midsummer festival when she had first arrived in Watersmeet. She and Findlay had watched together as the fairies danced. Her father had given her the green tunic, and she had worn it until it was a rag and far too short for her. The tunic itself was hanging in her room—or it had been when she'd left Watersmeet. But Findlay must have taken the cord.

She imagined Findlay going to sleep with her waist-cord in his hand. Abisina sank down on the bed and pulled the blanket to her face, letting out the sob she had carried with her since the moment Neriah had said that she had no word of Findlay.

The room was no longer empty. She smelled his scent, the wintergreen soap his mother made, the spruce gum he loved to chew. She held the blanket to her nose and breathed in again and again, pulling Findlay's presence into her.

Abisina put the pillow back on the bed and rested her head on it, and he was there, too, in the sun and air that the pillow still carried in its fibers. She drew the blanket over her and let the warmth envelop her. In seconds, she was asleep and dreaming of Findlay.

# CHAPTER IX

ABISINA WOKE WITH A START. FINDLAY'S ROOM WAS DARK. Had she slept the whole day?

She sat up. A blanket blocked the window, though a gap allowed in a bright stripe of light across the floor. Relieved, Abisina lifted the curtain. It was midmorning. She had slept longer than she'd meant to, but much less than she needed. Rubbing her eyes, she got to her feet and stumbled to the door.

Entering Neriah's room, Abisina knew the fairy was better. Her chest rose and fell regularly, and her color had improved. Abisina checked her pulse: steady. Neriah would need to drink and eat, but first Abisina wanted to check Meelah. She did not expect that Hesper had survived the night.

Her fears were confirmed as she opened the door. The blanket on the window was tied back, flooding the room with light. Meelah sat at her mother's bedside, cheeks streaked with tears. She had already dressed her mother in

her festival tunic and laid her bow and quiver in her hands
on her chest.

Abisina touched Meelah's shoulder. Hesper looked peaceful, with the hint of a smile and her brow smooth. The pain
that had marked the wasted face last night was gone; Hesper
was once again the woman Abisina knew.

"She went at first light, her favorite time of day," Meelah
said, wiping her face. "I opened the curtain so she could see
the sun."

Abisina tried not to think of her own mother's death at
the hands of a violent mob. *If I could have been there, comforted
her as Meelah has comforted Hesper . . .*

"Did she speak to you?" Abisina asked gently.

"No, but she opened her eyes and seemed to see me. She
smiled, I think, and then she was gone."

"I can see that smile, Meelah."

They stood together in silence. "We have to make a pyre,"
Meelah said. "I want to take care of her until the end." Her
voice was hard again, her mouth a thin line.

"We will . . . somehow. . . . First you need to rest."

"I will not leave her."

"Dear heart, I'll mix you a draft to help you sleep. You've
worked so hard here alone."

"I don't need a draft."

"You need sleep, Meelah. When you wake, I will need you.
I have to know what happened here in order to know what to
do next."

*What to do next.* Abisina had thought only as far as

Watersmeet, had assumed that her path would become clear once she was home.

While Abisina mixed the draft using Lennan's medicines, she tried to focus on today. Their water was running low, so she would need more snow. And food. She had checked the kitchen during the night and found nothing. *Food and water first,* she told herself.

Once Meelah was settled in Findlay's bed, Abisina brought water to Neriah. The fairy didn't open her eyes, though she drank deeply and sighed as Abisina laid her back down. Abisina changed the bandages; the wounds around Neriah's waist seeped blood and pus, but the black ooze was gone.

Weak from hunger—when had she last eaten?—Abisina prepared to go outside. She needed a bow and a full quiver, a satchel to carry what she found, and a knife. She headed to Hesper's room to select from the bows arrayed on the wall. *I should ask Meelah before I take one of her mother's bows, but I can't wait until she wakes.*

Hesper had beautiful bows—some ornately carved, others elegant in their simplicity. Most were small for Abisina, but she picked two that suited her in weight and suppleness, then filled a quiver with as many arrows as it would hold. She found a satchel in Meelah's room. The only knife she could find was the one she had used to lance Neriah's wounds, and she didn't want to touch it. Instead, Abisina contented herself with one of Findlay's swords, though she was no swordswoman. *If überwolves get close enough that I need the sword, it will be too late, anyway.*

She approached the door and noticed its bolt. None of the folk locked the doors in Watersmeet. Before. With no one awake to lock the door behind her, Abisina left by the window.

Though all was quiet in Findlay's ward, Abisina transformed and readied an arrow. She didn't bother to check the other homes, figuring that Meelah had already raided her neighbors' pantries. She took a trail south—the part of Watersmeet that seemed to have fewer überwolves.

Her days of dodging centaurs around Vranille had taught her to be silent, and she slipped in and out of wards, in and out of abandoned houses without disturbing the Sylvyad needles underfoot. The first kitchens she searched were as bare as Meelah's. No one had lived in these houses for months. *They knew they were leaving,* Abisina thought. *How?* Then it came to her: these were dwarf houses! Like all of Watersmeet's homes, the great room could accommodate centaurs—the largest of Watersmeet's inhabitants—but in the first three houses she entered, the rooms off the great room got smaller and more cave-like, the way dwarves preferred them. The dwarves, masters of stone craft, would have been sent to build the wall in the Green Man's Cleft first. They must have prepared for their journeys, taking much of their food with them, while the hungry left in Watersmeet scavenged the rest. She needed to find the houses of those who had been the last to leave.

Abisina tried to imagine the last days of Watersmeet. The folk had been fighting for survival. She would not find these residents' homes in the quiet, deserted wards but in the ones that showed signs of battle. Entering Findlay's ward the night before, she had jumped a barricade. She returned to the trails, looking for barricades. She avoided the wards with signs of drawn-out battles—*If I have to go in them, I will*—choosing instead one like Findlay's: barricaded but clean of debris.

The first two houses she checked were dwarf houses, and she didn't waste her time in their kitchens but continued on until she came to a house with dried tree branches hung across the ceiling of the great room: a faun's house. In the kitchen, she found a few earthen jars with preserved vegetables, roots, and fruit. Too heavy for a family on the run to carry.

She broke the wax seal and opened a jar of pickled hedge-nettle tubers. *Findlay's favorite,* she thought with a pang. Then she remembered his grin whenever he bit into a hedge-nettle tuber and had to smile. "Nothing like it!" he would insist, juice running down his chin. It never failed to make her laugh.

Her own mouth was watering, and she ate three tubers before she paused for breath. It hurt to chew, and her gums started to bleed again, but it was hard to stop. *If you don't, you'll throw up the first food you've had in days,* she told herself.

Abisina loaded her satchel with the remaining jars and moved to the next house. It took three more houses to fill her satchel; no one in Watersmeet had been eating well at the end. One of her best finds was a vial of shave-weed extract at a house where a minor healer must have lived. *With überwolves surrounding us and who knows what ahead of us, there will be more wounds. I'll need all of this I can get.*

She was relieved to return to Meelah's; more than the

deserted wards, the cold, dark houses made her feel the absence of the families who had brought such life to Watersmeet. The bright day had become cloudy, and she wanted to be near her friends. On her return, Abisina saw two überwolves but silenced them with well-placed arrows before they could call the rest of their pack.

The house was quiet when Abisina entered, both Meelah and Neriah sleeping peacefully. Abisina headed to the kitchen, built a fire, and pulled out the jars she'd found: more hedgenettle tubers, orpine roots, marsh marigold roots, and hag's broom seedpods. The remaining five jars were filled with pickled leeks. Abisina groaned. *That's a lot of leeks*. She ate a few and then brought more water to Neriah.

When Abisina returned to the kitchen, she saw the book containing Vigar's papers where she'd left it the night before. She had intended to sleep, but the book was too tempting. *If I find proof that Vran and Vigar were brother and sister, it won't matter that Reava has the letter.*

She opened to the first piece of parchment. She couldn't fight her disappointment. Only curves of letters or pieces of words were legible. Water had stained everything else, though there were a few tantalizing fragments, including several that mentioned both "Vran" and "necklace."

Abisina stared at the words. Why had she never thought of it before? Vran must have *given* Vigar the necklace! That was why Vigar carried his letter in the necklace's box. She pulled out the necklace; it glowed softly in the firelight. What did it mean, if it was a gift from Vran?

She couldn't deny that her view of the necklace would change. Vran had not only hated the fauns, dwarves, and centaurs of the south—he had hated people like Abisina. He had established laws that outcast anyone who didn't have the blond hair, blue eyes, and fair skin that he did. Women, too, were second-class citizens. As a girl with dark coloring, Abisina would have been left outside the walls of the village as an infant; her mother's position as Vranille's only healer had saved her.

Abisina touched the pendant's smooth strands of metal. *What matters is that it was Vigar's necklace. And my father's.*

She returned to the parchment. The second page had broken into several fragments, and most of it was stained, but Abisina found several legible lines:

trees are weakening, the rivers no more than a trickle. The confrontation cannot be far off. I fear it and would avoid it if I could, but the gift of the necklace marked me for this destiny.

*Destiny.* That word again. Rueshlan, too, had felt a sense of destiny, especially when he faced the White Worm.

*It all comes back to the necklace.*

Once Abisina had stood in Vigar's garden and "spoken" to Vigar's spirit. Vigar had said that the "wearers of the necklace" would always be with her.

"That includes my mother," Abisina mused. Sina had worn the necklace, too—given to her by Rueshlan. But when her mother had the chance to leave Vranille with Rueshlan, she had refused. She stayed to help her people. That was how

Sina saw her destiny. And then the Worm had caused her death. In fact, the Worm was responsible for the deaths of all three: Vigar, Sina, Rueshlan.

*Is that my destiny? Will I have to face the White Worm like they did?* Abisina went cold. *Is that what has emerged from the mountain? The Worm?*

*No!* Abisina drove the thought from her mind. She had seen the Worm die, watched its body consumed by its own poison. *But folk believed that they saw the Worm killed in the floods generations ago, and it came back and killed my father.*

The floods! That's what this fragment was about. She reread it.

trees are weakening, the rivers no more than a trickle. The confrontation cannot be far off.

The White Worm and its followers had dammed Watersmeet's three rivers; as the rivers ebbed, the trees weakened. Vigar had been right: the confrontation was approaching. According to the legend, Vigar faced the White Worm in the dried riverbed until the naiads forced their way through the dams' log walls and released a torrent on the Worm, its army, and Vigar herself.

*The naiads carried her through the tunnel in the mountains— as they carried me. They recognized me as Vigar.*

Abisina smiled, imagining the words Findlay would say if he knew what she was thinking: "What more proof of your special destiny do you need, Abby?"

*If only he were here!*

A few illegible lines were left on this fragment, but at the end of the sheet, Abisina could decipher more words:

*Is my brother, too, facing a battle for his life and the lives of his people? Never again will I flee. We have been given a gift and I will—*

Rueshlan had said that when Vigar and Vran first crossed the mountains into this land, they were fleeing their own version of the White Worm. And Vigar did what she promised: she did not flee when the Worm came again.

Abisina turned to the final page, a full sheet. The side facing her was blank. With shaking fingers, she lifted it out of the book and turned it over.

Stains covered a few words, but there was more writing here than on any of the other pieces:

*not supposed to be like this. I had not wanted to flee our home, though the terrors mounted. Vran convinced me. He said that we would go together and find a new haven for our people. But that changed wh—*

A water stain made an entire line unreadable. Again Abisina wondered what had changed between the siblings. The next legible bit didn't seem to continue the same idea:

*thought so many times about standing atop the mountain as the Green Man showed us the valley*

—here a few words were smudged, though Abisina could pick up the narrative again—

my words so different from Vran's? Enough to earn
me the necklace that led us to this place the Green Man
called one of his "best creations"?

—more smudges, then—

Vran's words . . . force pushing through the mountains
. . . my word . . . smaller threads of water, weaving . . .

Abisina could make no sense of the final lines, but as she
reread the first ones, their meaning seemed clear. The Green
Man had brought them to this land—and the Green Man had
given Vigar the necklace as a reward for something she said:
her "words." Abisina clutched the pendant. A gift from the
Green Man, not Vran! No wonder it was powerful, precious.
And then the necklace led Vigar to "this place," which had to
be Watersmeet. Legend said the Green Man had brought the
Sylvyads to Watersmeet, one of his "best creations." The necklace was an image of Watersmeet—strands of Obrium weaving into one, like the rivers that came together at Watersmeet
to form the River Deliverance. Her father had pointed that
out to her once. Perhaps that last fragment—"smaller threads
of water, weaving"—referred to the necklace or Watersmeet
itself.

She read the next lines:

the only explanation I can find for why Vran left me.
And he took his mother's people with him, leaving our
father's peop—

—another water stain—

—xcept Imara. Because he took my cousin, I have to believe—

The parchment ended. "His mother," "our father." Vran and Vigar were half siblings! And she knew the name Imara. The Vranians had called her the mother of all healers, and she had long fascinated Abisina. Imara—before the green-eyed generations that followed her—was the one woman who had escaped the cruelty of Vran's laws. After Imara, green eyes marked you as a healer, indispensable to the village. Children with green eyes were outcast but spared the punishment of death. And they were powerful, in their way—they knew the art of herbs and healing. Abisina had always hated that she was related to Vran—all Vranians were his descendants. Imara was an ancestor she embraced.

And now she understood a little more of Vran's letter to Vigar. "I cannot stay," he had said. He had taken his mother's people with him when he left—and Imara.

Why?

She had learned so much from these few pages—but there was still so much she didn't understand! She thought of the sheaf of papers still behind the library's shelf.

She had to get back to the library.

# CHAPTER X

ABISINA WAS STARING AT THE CLOSED BOOK WHEN SOME-thing moved in the great room. She leapt to her feet, shoved the book under the table, and realized she didn't have her bow.

But it was only Meelah who came into the kitchen. "I'm going to my mother," she said, and then noticed the fire. "No!" she cried. "They'll find us!"

"It's okay, Meelah." Abisina tried to calm the shaking girl. "It's overcast; no one will see the smoke. You're not alone any-more, dear heart. Neriah and I—"

"Neriah?" Meelah stiffened.

"The fairy that I—"

"I want her out of my house! She's had time to recover. She's used the medicines left for my mother!"

"Meelah—" Abisina began, but Neriah had appeared in the opposite doorway, and Meelah lunged at her. Abisina just managed to hold back the girl.

"Neriah is not going to hurt you," Abisina insisted. "Let me explain."

"I know fairies!" Meelah struggled to break free.

"Reava is my sister, but I am not her," Neriah said quietly. She leaned against the doorway, barely able to stand.

"Sister!" Meelah tried again to get at Neriah, but exhausted and half starved, she was no match for Abisina.

Abisina pushed Meelah into a chair and took the girl's face in her hands. "Look at me, Meelah. You're like my own sister. I will protect you with my last breath."

"Like you took care of Findlay?"

The accusation rang through the kitchen. Abisina did not flinch. "I will find him, I promise, but you need to understand what's happened—the whole story: why we left the south, where we've been, what this fairy did for me and for your brother, why we've returned and Findlay has not. You can make your own judgments then."

Neriah took a few steps toward a chair and swayed. Abisina caught her and helped her sit across the table from Meelah. "We need to hear your story, too, Meelah," Abisina continued. "We didn't expect to find Watersmeet abandoned." Abisina cut up a hedge-nettle tuber, two leeks, and some hag's broom, filled cups of water, and set them between the silent figures, then sat down herself. "Neriah, small bites. Your stomach is weak."

Abisina spoke first to Meelah, beginning with the moment Glynholly had exiled her and the others. Meelah listened, asking few questions as Abisina described how Neriah's kestrel helped her, Findlay, and Haret down the cliff below Vigar's garden; the journey to Newlyn; the work of rebuilding it; and the attack of the leviathan-birds. The news of Vran's letter prompted Meelah to speak. "That means . . ."

"Yes. The Vranians and the humans in Watersmeet—we're all related."

"But they're so . . ."

"The Vranians are what Vran taught them to be. That's all." It had taken Abisina years to understand this herself. She needed Meelah and all of Watersmeet to understand it now.

"We've seen the leviathan-birds, too," Meelah said.

"Here?" Abisina hadn't seen any sign.

Meelah nodded.

Abisina finished by telling Meelah about Neriah saving her in the Cairn, the journey with the naiads, and the cave under the library. She said nothing about Vigar's journal. Neriah didn't seem to remember the hours in the library, and Abisina wasn't ready to share her discovery.

"Those eels," Meelah said when Abisina lapsed into silence. "We've known something was there for months, though we didn't know what."

"They're from the rift—I'm sure of it. Like the birds," Abisina said.

"The rift? That's *true*?" Meelah gripped the table. "Reava talked of a rift in the mountains. We thought she wanted to scare us into working harder on the wall."

"It's true," Abisina said. "But it's not a rift anymore. The top of the mountain has been torn off. Some final horror has arrived."

Abisina stood up, threw more wood on the smoldering fire, and lifted the blanket covering the window. It was dusky in the ward, the afternoon gone. Silence settled over the kitchen. It was Meelah's turn to speak, but the girl stared at the table, head bowed.

Then she stood up. She hurried from the room, returning a moment later with her arms full: a bag of flour, a jug of oil, and a sack of dried meat. "I'd like to sit with my mother . . . before I tell my story."

"Where did this come from?" Abisina stared as Meelah set her bundles on the table.

"There's more," Meelah said. "It was for my mother."

"Have you eaten none of it yourself?" Abisina asked.

Meelah shrugged. "I didn't know where I'd get more."

"Thank you." Abisina tried to put all her gratitude into the simple phrase. She hugged Meelah, feeling each of her bones through her tunic.

Abisina had a feast ready by the time Meelah returned: a soup made with dried meat, leeks, and orpine; warm flat bread; sliced hedge-nettle and marsh marigold roots. She had also brewed some tea using the feverfew from Lennan's stores; she thought Neriah and Meelah would appreciate its calming effect. *And I suppose I will, too.*

"Lots of folk thought Glynholly was wrong to exile Rueshlan's daughter," Meelah explained as they ate. "Even those who agreed with your exile didn't support Findlay's and Elodie's."

"Glynholly wanted to let them stay; they *chose* exile," Abisina broke in.

"She said that over and over. It didn't matter. They were gone. And then it came out that Glynholly had imprisoned Neiall, Moyla, and Anwyn for meeting with you. Their families were frantic, thinking überwolves had taken them. Everyone was so angry, Glynholly had to release them.

"The Council had agreed that Watersmeet would build the wall in the Green Man's Cleft, but Glynholly didn't call the Council or ask for volunteers as Rueshlan would have. She just named which dwarves would go."

"How did she get away with that?" Abisina asked.

"Folk were desperate. It was weeks past midsummer, and we had nothing stored for winter. They saw the wall as the key to survival.

"So many were sent, but word kept coming from the wall that they needed more. Überwolves, minotaurs, hostile centaurs, and more refugees were trying to come through the Cleft. Eventually, Reava called in other fairies—huge ones. She *said* they would provide more protection for Watersmeet—to make up for those who had gone to the wall—but we all knew they were here to force the Watersmeet folk to the wall.

"Even those fairies couldn't convince my mother to go," Meelah said softly. "She said we would go underground if we had to. With Findlay gone, there was no one to look after me."

Abisina reached out to Meelah, but she pulled away.

"Glynholly kept saying that she had worked closely with Rueshlan, and she knew his mind best. Every command came with Rueshlan's name attached to it. Glynholly had exiled you and sent the Council members to guard the Cleft. There was no one left to dispute her claims, and Reava was behind the scenes making the rules."

"How did Reava do it? How did she make Glynholly do her bidding?" Abisina asked.

"I don't know. A few times someone argued, said too many were dying. Glynholly always insisted that once the north was closed off and Watersmeet was saved, the sacrifice would be worth it."

In some ways, Abisina pitied Glynholly. They had both made decisions that put those they loved most in jeopardy. If something happened to Abisina's friends, Abisina hoped she would find comfort in knowing that they had died saving Seldara.

Neriah had sat in the shadows, saying nothing. Now she leaned forward. "Reava can be ruthless," she said. "The wall meant everything to her. She was sure that it would secure her the Mother's crown. And it did."

Meelah's mouth tightened, but at Abisina's urging, she continued: "Watersmeet got so dangerous, those left in the outlying wards moved to the center, and the divisions became clear. Some still followed Glynholly, and Neiall had his following, which we called Old Watersmeet."

Abisina knew Neiall well. He had been privy to Abisina's

plan to go to the Motherland, and during the secret meeting on her return, Neiall had allowed himself to be caught, giving the others time to escape.

"A third group grew up around a centaur called Braim," Meelah said. "Did you know him?"

"A little," Abisina said, recalling Braim's stern face.

"He wanted Watersmeet to stand alone. Expel the refugees, recall the folk from the wall, send Reava packing. Some rallied around him. His plan addressed none of the problems of food, überwolves, or refugees on the shore. It placed blame on everything that had changed since ... well, since you arrived, Abisina. His group wanted to return to the 'Golden Age.'"

*Did I bring the end of the Golden Age?* Abisina's stomach clenched. *I brought word of the White Worm, not the Worm itself.*

"Our ward supported Neiall and Old Watersmeet. Our goal was to reach out to the other factions, but it was hopeless."

"I don't understand why folk kept following Glynholly once they realized that Reava was using her," Abisina said.

"She had the necklace."

"Yes, but what about after that?"

"What do you mean?"

"Neriah's kestrel brought me the necklace several weeks before the winter solstice. According to the kestrel, Glynholly sent it."

Meelah frowned. "Glynholly was wearing it the day she

left. And I can't imagine Glynholly parting with—or I should say, Reava *letting* Glynholly part with it. Whatever power Glynholly hung on to was because of that necklace."

Neriah stood up. "Abisina, my kestrel got the necklace from Glynholly—you cannot dispute that. The kestrel *showed* me. Reava confirmed it."

"Reava's word means nothing!" Meelah said. Her chair toppled over as she stood.

Neriah turned on Meelah. "Are you saying I am lying?"

"No!" Abisina got to her feet, too, holding each of them back. "*We* can't break into factions! There has to be a logical explanation."

"Like what?" Neriah demanded.

"I don't know," Abisina admitted. "There's some piece of information we're missing. So, let's all sit back down, let Meelah finish her story." Abisina sat. So did Neriah. Meelah stared a long time at Neriah before taking her seat. When she resumed her story, she spoke only to Abisina.

"The final battle started out as a refugee attack. All the little refugee villages that had grown up on the banks came together. And in the middle of the fight with the refugees, the überwolves struck. They didn't care who they fought. We were all just food. One of them bit my mother as she tried to keep them from entering our ward. I went out to get her, and that's when"—Meelah shuddered—"I saw the leviathan-birds. They stayed on the bank, unable to fly into Watersmeet itself, but there was no escape—for the folk, the refugees, or the über-wolves. If anyone got too close to the bank, the birds would attack. Factions were forgotten. We thought only of escaping the wolves and the birds."

"How many birds were there?" Abisina asked.

Meelah thought for a moment. "Five. They controlled the area outside Watersmeet, and the überwolves gorged inside. The birds left after a few days—the wolves had established dens and were feasting in the north—and the folk slowly crept away before the überwolves emerged to finish them off. Everyone left. Reava and Glynholly took their followers to the Motherland; others sought caves in the Obrun Mountains; another group thought they should go to the wall and join the rest of our folk.

"Mother couldn't travel, and I wouldn't leave her. I found Lennan before he left, and he told me how to care for her. For a while, I expected someone to come back. No one has."

Meelah faced Neriah. "Can you blame me for wanting to turn you away? What have *you* lost? Your mother is alive—and your sister! Your home is waiting for you. But your family destroyed mine."

"This evil comes from the White Worm," Abisina said, "and the rift. It's hurt the fairies, too. If we fight against each other, we'll truly be lost."

Meelah looked sadly at Abisina. "How can we be any more lost than we are?"

She spoke Abisina's own fears—that Findlay was dead, that Watersmeet was destroyed forever, that they had already lost the fight. At a moment like this, Findlay would have held Abisina up, found the way to hope. Now she had to find it herself.

"We have this," Abisina said, pulling the necklace from beneath her tunic. It glowed in the firelight. "I will continue to hope while I have this."

"Glynholly wore the necklace, too," Meelah said dully.

"Glynholly was not chosen to lead this fight. I was."

# CHAPTER XI

THAT NIGHT ABISINA SLEPT WITH MEELAH IN FINDLAY'S room. With Meelah's warm body next to her, she slept soundly for several hours before startling awake. Meelah stood over her, the stump of a candle in her hand.

"What is it?" Abisina asked, reaching for her bow.

"I need to talk to you. Alone. I just checked the fairy, and she's asleep. Abisina, listen to me. You're making a mistake."

Abisina tried to focus. "Meelah—I—Give me a moment. . . ."

"We don't have a moment! You must do something now. While she's asleep!"

"Meelah, you can't mean. . . . I wouldn't have made it to Watersmeet without Neriah."

"I can't explain why she saved you, but she's manipulating you. Those stories you told tonight about the fairy—I dropped my guard, too. Then she talked about Glynholly sending the necklace! It's a lie! You didn't believe it, either!"

Abisina sighed. "The Glynholly I knew *wouldn't* have sent the necklace. The Glynholly you describe *couldn't* have sent it without Reava's permission, and it's hard to imagine her giving it."

"Exactly. Neriah has to be lying."

"I agree that it doesn't make sense, but that doesn't mean that Neriah is lying. She didn't understand it herself."

"You don't know the fairies like I do. They care only about themselves. I learned that in my cradle!"

"And in *my* cradle I learned that people who look like me are evil!"

"If Neriah saved you, it's because she's going to get something out of it."

"My father trusted the fairies, Meelah," Abisina countered. "And they died heroically on the battlefield against the White Worm."

"I don't believe he trusted them," Meelah said flatly. "He used their self-interest to serve Watersmeet's purpose. Glynholly tried to do the same with Reava, but it got away from her. Unless you can offer the fairies something they want, they aren't interested in alliances or the greater good or anyone except themselves."

Abisina shook her head. "I *need* Neriah or I have no hope of getting the fairies to help us fight whatever is coming from the rift."

"You sound like Glynholly. She *needed* Reava."

"I understand what you're saying, but I'm not going to send Neriah away."

"You can't see what's right in front of you, Abisina." Meelah blew out the candle, plunging the room back into darkness.

When Meelah finally fell asleep—now on the far side of the bed—Abisina lifted the quilt and tiptoed into the great room. She stirred the coals and threw some more wood on the fire. She huddled on the hearth as close as she could get to the tiny flames and tried to think: The folk of Watersmeet were scattered throughout the north. Even if she could bring them together, they hated the fairies. She had to convince them to work with the very folk they blamed for the destruction of their home. And then she had to convince them to work with the south.

*Who am I to think I can make an alliance when so many others have failed?* She listened to the hiss of the fire and held her hands to the glowing coals. *It doesn't matter,* she realized. *Alliance is the only way to survive. Someone has to make it happen, and I'm the one with the necklace.*

Abisina went into the kitchen and groped under the table for the book with Vigar's papers. She held it in her lap, staring at it. Meelah's misgivings had rattled her. She reminded herself of the times Neriah had helped her, the fact that she loved the Seldars. *And how can I build an alliance without trust?* she wondered.

*It's not worth the risk.* She stood up. *Neriah had the letter from Vran, and now it's gone. For now, Vigar's papers are my secret.* She returned to Findlay's room, stopping first to bury the book in her satchel.

"We leave tomorrow," Abisina announced as the three sat at their morning meal. Meelah and Neriah looked up.

"Where are we going?" Meelah asked.

"East. You said the folk went to the wall, the Motherland, or the mountains. We'll find them. But first, we'll go to Vigar's garden. There's a chance Findlay and Elodie will be there, or that we can learn something about them."

"It will cost two days," Neriah said.

"We have to go!" Meelah cried. "If Findlay's there—" Her blue eyes pleaded with Abisina.

"We may learn something," Abisina repeated. "And some of the folk might have gone that way."

Neriah frowned, and Meelah looked smug.

Abisina knew Neriah was right. If her goal was to bring the north together, Abisina should go where she might find the most Watersmeet folk. But Hoysta, Haret's grandmother, was at the garden; she might have seen what came from the ruined mountain. *I have to think of Meelah, too. And I owe it to Findlay and Elodie.* Abisina was justifying what she longed to do, and she knew it, but she didn't change her mind.

"From the garden to the Motherland—it will take about fourteen days," Neriah said.

"Yes . . . but I'm not going to the Motherland," Abisina said evenly. "I'm going to find the folk."

"You *must* go to the Motherland!" Neriah struck the table. "The folk are there, and you need the fairies!"

"We do need the fairies," Abisina agreed. "You can go and convince the Mother yourself that we must have a full—and equal—alliance. The old pact between Watersmeet and the Motherland is broken."

"I am exiled," Neriah protested. "*You* have the necklace. You can make this argument much better than I can."

Meelah looked at the fairy with narrowed eyes. "Why do you want to get Abisina to the Motherland?"

Neriah hardly glanced at Meelah as she said, "I know you do not trust me"—Meelah sniffed—"but I am thinking of everyone's survival." Neriah leaned toward Abisina. "Most of the folk *are* in the Motherland. More importantly, the Mother will have news of how the others are faring at the wall. We can plan together."

Abisina pushed back her chair and picked up her plate. "We have work to do. We do not need to decide now. After the garden, our path lies east. We can decide then."

They divided the work: Abisina would find more food and medicine in the abandoned wards. Neriah, still weak, would use the rest of the flour to make flat bread. Meelah would go through Hesper's and Findlay's clothes to find some things for Abisina; she would gather the household's satchels, water skins, and weapons; and she would drag the furniture from the house into the center of the ward, where they would light Hesper's funeral pyre before they left.

Abisina worried about leaving the other two alone together, but they seemed resigned to being in each other's company—for now.

Abisina stepped out into the ward. It felt good to have a plan—even a desperate one.

As she combed through the wards, the library was never far from her mind. *What else might I learn there?* But it would be difficult—if not impossible—to get back into the fallen tree. And it would take time. Once or twice, her steps turned in that direction, but she stopped herself. *I'll be back. Those papers have been in that tree for three hundred years; they can wait a little longer.*

Abisina did allow herself a detour to her own ward. She told herself it was practical: she could get one of her bows, which were much better suited to her. But it was more than that. She wanted to be *home*, if only for a minute.

Once she stood in her ward, she wondered if she'd made a mistake. Scene after scene of her life in Watersmeet rose before her eyes—storytelling around the central fire, bonfires for the winter solstice, suppers laid out in the summer evenings—images filled with faces now lost. Ulian, killed on patrol, played his pipes here; Frayda, Rueshlan's companion driven mad at his loss, visited daily; and Kyron, slain at Newlyn, had provided constant companionship.

Findlay had stood there, right outside her door, when he first kissed her. She had been about to leave for the Motherland, and he had taken her hands—his own were shaking—but before he could speak, Hoysta padded through the ward. He started to go, then rushed back to kiss her before dashing out. She smiled at the memory—how young they both seemed, still full of hope.

Her door opened at her touch. The dust lay thick on the floor, on the mantel, on the backs of the chairs, but nothing else had changed. After her father's death, Hoysta and Haret had moved in with Abisina. Even now, Hoysta's rocker sat close to the hearth, her own favorite chair on the other side. She could see the old dwarf—as much a grandmother to Abisina as to Haret—sitting in it, chattering away over her knitting. *Haret would sit there,* Abisina thought, turning to a stool set closer to the window where the light was better. She could see him shaping an axe handle with a chisel or leaning against the wall and smoking his pipe, grumbling responses to his grandmother or directing a more pointed "Human!" at something Abisina had said. For all his gruffness, Haret was her best friend, and she didn't know where he was. The sense of emptiness was unbearable.

"I came to get my bow," she whispered to herself. But her feet didn't move toward her room. Instead, she headed to the doorway that led to her father's room. After he had died, Abisina left his room untouched. She visited at times—as the pain of losing him faded to a dull ache, it comforted her to feel close to him.

*That's where I'll leave the book.*

The instant the thought came to her, she knew it was the right thing to do. Once she left Watersmeet, she could be captured by fairies or überwolves or leviathan-birds or some other enemy. She could find herself in the middle of a war. And despite the desolation around her, she believed that Watersmeet would survive the coming storm, if anything could. This was the safest place to leave Vigar's words.

She passed through a sitting room Hoysta had converted to her sewing room, then through a smaller room that Rueshlan had used for meetings with dwarves, and then, finally, Abisina pushed open the door to Rueshlan's bedroom.

The sun was close to setting; the shadow of evening touched the window. Rueshlan's enormous bed dominated the room, but two chairs were pulled up to the hearth. The few weeks Abisina had lived in Watersmeet with her father, he had been readying for war. Most of the time she had alone with him was spent in these chairs, late at night, when Rueshlan had returned from meetings and strategy sessions and weapons surveys. But he always made this time for her—enough time for a cup of mint tea, his favorite, and some conversation. In those moments, he seemed to think of nothing except her.

Abisina sank into the chair that had been hers. It was too short for her now—her knees rose above her lap like hills rising from a low plain—but she still felt small as she faced her father's chair with its broad seat, high back, and solid legs.

*Who am I to do something my father couldn't? Something Vigar couldn't?* The same question had plagued her the night before, and she came to the same answer: *I am the one who has the necklace.* But she didn't feel any real certainty or strength coming to her from this gift. Like the chair facing her, the necklace felt too big for her, too heavy.

She drew the book out of her satchel, rubbed her thumb across the soft leather cover, and, without opening it, placed it on a table in an alcove. She should have tucked it underneath the feathers of Rueshlan's mattress or behind his stand of swords and bows. But there on the table, it seemed as if Rueshlan had just been reading it, as if he had stepped out for a moment and would be right back to pick up where he left off. It made it seem as if they were all there together—Rueshlan, Vigar, and Abisina—wearers of the necklace. It didn't feel like an ending.

Abisina walked out of the room and then the house. She did not get the bow she had come for. She wanted to be on her way—to pack the gear she needed and head out to the east and make her attempt, no matter how inadequate, to fulfill the destiny that Vigar and her father had left her.

# CHAPTER XII

THE EVENING'S FIRST ÜBERWOLF HOWL ECHOED THROUGH Watersmeet as Abisina entered Findlay's ward. The evidence of Meelah's work stood in the center: a huge pile of beds, tables, chairs, and stools. Hesper's pyre.

*I guess we begin sleeping on the ground tonight,* Abisina thought, spotting Findlay's bed at the bottom of the pile. She touched the green waist-cord curled in her pocket, glad she had rescued it before Meelah burned it.

The house was cold when Abisina walked in, the travel supplies laid out in the now bare great room. "Hello?" she called, suddenly afraid. She had been gone for hours.

Meelah came from the kitchen, dirty and tired, but with a tentative smile. "You've found food then," she said as Abisina set down the heavy satchels. "I'm about to start a fire for the loaves Neriah made and to heat water for baths."

Abisina didn't mention the pyre or her visit home. "Where's Neriah?"

"Asleep in Findlay's room. I was making too much noise out here." Meelah headed back to the kitchen.

Abisina tiptoed into Findlay's room, bracing herself for more emptiness. But only the bed was missing. Findlay's swords, his work tunic, his presence still hung in the air.

*We leave tomorrow,* Abisina thought, and it felt as if she were saying good-bye to Findlay again.

"Abisina?" Neriah lay on a pile of pelts with her coat on top of her. She rolled over and blinked sleepily.

"How are you feeling?"

"All right," Neriah said, closing her eyes again. Abisina turned to leave. "You went home."

Abisina froze. "H-how did you know?"

"You've been gone so long. And something's changed in your face." Neriah didn't open her eyes. "He's there, isn't he? The way Findlay is here?"

"Y-yes." The fairy's insight shook her.

"I know how that feels—visiting the places where loved ones have been, that they still inhabit. I find him in the Seldars."

"Rueshlan?"

"Yes."

Neriah had once told Abisina that she had known and respected Rueshlan, and Abisina had seen her love for the Seldars as part of that. "I feel him there, too," Abisina said.

Neriah resettled herself on the pelts, and her breathing became deeper and more even. *Was she awake at all?* Fairies were so mystifying! Abisina backed out of the room and returned to the kitchen.

Neriah woke for dinner and had a bath while Meelah baked the last loaves of bread and Abisina, clean after her own bath, checked the weapons. Each of them had a bow and a full quiver of arrows. Meelah had two daggers, but Abisina decided to keep Findlay's sword. *His other one may be damaged by now. I'll have this for him when I find him at the garden.* Neriah and Abisina bedded down on a pile of pelts in the great room. Meelah would sit her final vigil with her mother's body.

Their activity in the ward had not gone unnoticed. When Abisina woke at dawn, she pulled aside the blanket over the window and saw thirty überwolves prowling around the pyre. "The Earth!"

Neriah sat up. "What is it?"

"Wolves. They're all over the ward. I don't know how we're going to get out."

"I won't give up my mother's pyre." Meelah had joined them, pale, exhausted, and determined.

To Abisina's surprise, Neriah agreed. "The pyre will drive the überwolves out of the ward. I can take your mother's body to the top of the pyre. Abisina, you shoot a lit arrow from the window to start the fire."

"With you on the pyre?" Abisina asked.

"I can get into the lower tree branches and move through them to the ward's entrance. The wolves will flee the flames, and you two can get out."

"Where the wolves will be waiting! Neriah, this is crazy!" Abisina said.

"It is out best option. Eventually, the wolves will pursue us, but we will have a head start."

Abisina glanced at Meelah. The girl was staring at the fairy. "You're helping me?"

"It helps us all," Neriah said simply.

Abisina and Meelah watched from the window as the fairy leapt—burdened with Hesper's body—from the doorsill to the top of the pyre. Used to landing on the thinnest of branches, Neriah chose the arm of a chair as her landing place, but she hadn't considered Hesper's weight. As she landed, the chair tilted. Other pieces of furniture shifted. Neriah tried to get her balance, dropped the body, and slid half a length before grabbing hold of a table leg. She dangled just out of reach of the wolves' teeth. She groped with her feet but couldn't find a solid surface. Then the wolves' spears began to fly.

"Light it!" Meelah yelled at Abisina.

"Are you trying to kill her?"

"No, the wolves!" Meelah shot arrow after arrow at the wolves, but there were too many. Abisina shot her lit arrow into the tinder; the flames caught and spread up the leg of a bed, leapt to a chair, and ran across a tabletop.

As Neriah tried to get into a better position, she kicked another chair and dislodged more furniture. Her feet dipped lower, a hand's breadth from the wolves' snouts. But the fire had caught, and the wolves began moving back. Tears streamed from Neriah's eyes as the smoke billowed over her.

"It's time!" Abisina called as she transformed, and Meelah climbed on. They charged out of the door to Neriah. "Let go!" Abisina shouted as she neared the pyre. Neriah obeyed instantly, falling into Abisina's arms. Snarling überwolves blocked the ward's exit.

"Knock it over!" Neriah rasped between coughs.

Abisina galloped around the pyre, staying close to the flames. No überwolves challenged them. At the back, the space between the pyre and the Sylvyads was narrow, and the wolves had retreated from there as the heat intensified. Neriah leapt from Abisina's arms onto her back behind Meelah. A table provided some shield from the scorching flames. Gritting her teeth, Abisina put her shoulder to the table and pushed as hard as she could, bracing her hooves against a trunk. The flaming furniture rocked dangerously above them.

"One more push!" Neriah shouted.

Abisina drove her shoulder into the table again.

As the pile toppled forward, Abisina leapt to the right. A stool crashed close to them, and then more debris rained down, but most of the furniture fell toward the ward's exit, driving out the wolves.

Abisina dashed for the exit, jumping the pyre's wreckage. The screams of a burning wolf, trapped under Findlay's bed, pursued them out of the ward.

The wolves scattered in every direction. Abisina knew where she had to go. Meelah's fingernails dug into her waist as they careened around corners and leapt barricades.

"There's one on your heels!" Neriah yelled as Abisina's rear hoof connected with something big. "You got it! But here come two more!"

Abisina put on a burst of speed. A bridge to the bank was ahead. *It's not safe out there either!* Once in the trees, she would have to slow down, but the wolves would not. *I'll stop and fight!* she thought, reaching for Findlay's sword.

She crossed the bridge, her hoofbeats echoing loudly. She had Findlay's sword in her hand, ready to turn and face the wolves, when Neriah screamed, "Run for the trees!"

The terror in the fairy's voice sent Abisina straight for the forest, crashing into branches and running through any opening that led them away from Watersmeet.

"Stop! It's okay now," Meelah said.

"Is Neriah all right?" Abisina said. They were deep in the forest.

"I—I think so," Meelah answered. "It was the eels."

Abisina stopped, and Meelah slid off her back and then helped Neriah down. The fairy huddled on the ground, rocking, arms wrapped around her waist.

"I think they heard your hooves on the bridge," Meelah explained. "They surfaced as the wolves crossed. The wolves never had a chance."

"How—" Abisina began, but Neriah interrupted her.

"Came from the water, wrapped around the wolves' limbs . . ."

"In the daylight?"

"They—they had smaller eels around their eyes, like in the

cave. There were hundreds of them...." Neriah rubbed a hand over her own eyes as if trying to erase the image.

Abisina transformed and sank to the ground, still breathing hard. Meelah sat next to her and took her hand. "Thank you," she said. "Both of you." She glanced at Neriah and then back at Abisina. "My mother had her pyre. The flames had reached her."

"And we're out of Watersmeet," Abisina said, giving Meelah's hand a squeeze.

They'd shot half their arrows, and one of the satchels was badly singed, but it had stayed together. Neriah looked worn-out, and her wounds had started to bleed again; Meelah was strangely bright eyed. "I haven't been out for so long," she said, staring up at the trees. "I don't need to sleep yet. Shall I walk?"

Abisina wanted to go faster than walking would allow. She transformed, and the others rode, Neriah closest to Abisina so she could rest on her back. Meelah and Abisina had arrows ready as they turned south.

# CHAPTER XIII

WHILE THEY TRAVELED, ABISINA OFTEN REACHED OUT with her mind for any hoofed creature that could give her news about trolls or überwolves—none answered. The only überwolf tracks they found were several months old. The signs of trolls, minotaurs, and leviathan-birds were even older.

"They've lost their food source!" she said suddenly.

"What?" Neriah asked. It was afternoon. Meelah had finally gotten tired and gone to sleep, so it was the fairy's turn to keep an arrow ready.

"I've seen no fresh evidence of überwolves, and I just figured out why. The food is gone. I've seen only a few squirrels." One of them hung off her belt to supplement their supper.

"They've all gone east," Neriah said. "The Motherland is besieged."

Abisina stopped. "Did a kestrel come to you?"

"Reava told me," Neriah explained. "It made my treason worse, she said. I didn't tell you that?"

Abisina resumed her trot, glad that Meelah had slept through this exchange. *Why didn't Neriah mention it before?* "Even to the east, the food must be getting scarce," Abisina added, trying to draw Neriah out. When the fairy didn't respond, she said, "I wonder what the wolves in Watersmeet are eating."

"Bodies?" Neriah suggested.

Abisina winced.

Night fell, and Abisina could no longer see the path. They got what rest they could and woke at moonrise to continue their journey.

Abisina preferred moving. Despite her insistence that there were good reasons for going to the garden, she knew it was costing them time. She had hoped to find some evidence that the Watersmeet folk had come this way, but she saw no tracks.

On the evening of the second day, they arrived at the cliff below the garden. Abisina had worried about this moment. Twice before, she had struggled to get into the garden. The necklace should help her as it had before, though once, even with the necklace, the garden refused to open to her. *The necklace was black then,* Abisina reminded herself. *And I was running away from my father.* She had eventually found a way in, but she didn't want to lose the time it would take to search. In human form, she stood before the wall of stone and drew the shining necklace from beneath her tunic, knowing the others were watching.

At first nothing happened. Then an archway glowed in the rock face. Abisina waited for the wind that had accompanied this archway in the past, but the mountaintop remained still. Instead, a dark figure appeared in silhouette: short, round, and with a rolling walk that Abisina would have recognized anywhere.

"Haret!" she cried, and ran through the archway to meet her best friend.

He stood in the room that was at the center of the garden's tunnels, with trails spiraling off it like spokes in a wheel. He had lost weight; the skin on his cheeks sagged. More alarming was the axe he had slung over his shoulder. What had he expected to meet in the tunnels?

"Human," he growled. His typical gruff manner didn't fool Abisina. His hug was warm, his smile real.

"Meelah." He smiled at the girl, too, but his brow creased as he took in her haggard face. Then, stiffly, "Neriah, is it?"

Abisina was anxious to smooth over Haret's reintroduction to Neriah. They had first met when Neriah had given Abisina the Obrium box. Haret, like so many of his kin, had a weakness for the powerful dwarf metal, and the box had driven him out of his mind. He had been ready to attack Abisina, and Neriah had forced him away. Abisina knew the memory still embarrassed Haret.

"Is Findlay here?" Meelah asked.

"He's not in Watersmeet?" Haret stared.

A hole opened in Abisina's chest. The garden had been her last hope. Findlay and Elodie had left Newlyn thirteen weeks ago. The journey from Newlyn to the garden—even with the blizzards—should have taken ten. Something had happened to them.

Meelah fell to her knees with a sob and though Abisina wanted to weep, too, she bent next to her, rubbing her back and searching for comfort she did not feel.

"We'll talk more in the garden," Haret said. "It's safer." He glanced warily around the room. "Arrows out."

Abisina helped Meelah to her feet. *More bad news,* she thought. The garden was a haven, but back when the White Worm was on the rise, a minotaur had broken in and defaced Vigar's grave. *Has something come here since the mountain exploded?*

While Neriah put an arrow on her string, Abisina kept an arm around Meelah and slipped her hand into her pocket where she still carried the green waist-cord. They both needed comfort. Haret hurried them down a tunnel, red lights in the ceiling glowing to meet them and then fading after they passed.

When they stepped into the garden, peace settled around Abisina like a mantle. Ripe fruit perfumed the air, and water gurgled in the distance. The garden was still a refuge. But then Haret mumbled, "Watch it, human," and swung a stone door closed behind them to shut off the tunnel. After he bolted the door, Abisina caught his eye; he gave a slight shake of his head. He would explain later.

An ancient dwarf emerged from the orchard. Abisina had once thought her hideously ugly: she had long thin white hair, which barely covered her scalp; she had no teeth; and she was missing her left hand, lost to an infected überwolf bite. Now Abisina saw only the beauty of Hoysta's brown eyes as she beamed at her.

"Dearie!" Hoysta limped toward Abisina, arms outstretched. She had also lost weight, and one side of her face drooped. "Oh!" Hoysta cried, dropping her arms before she got to Abisina. She had caught sight of Neriah.

The fairy bowed. "Hoysta. I hope you are well."

"Do you have it?" Hoysta whispered. Abisina stared. *She found Vigar's Obrium box in the garden,* Abisina remembered. Unlike many dwarves, Hoysta had resisted Obrium's call, but the box proved too strong for her. She had dug it up and was close to madness when Neriah arrived at the garden and wrested the box from her.

"I do not," Neriah replied.

Haret looked sharply at Abisina. Now she shook *her* head—something else for them to talk about later.

Hoysta's gaze turned to Meelah, and she seemed to come back to herself. "My dearest Meelah! So thin!" She embraced the girl. "Come to the table and let Hoysta feed you up. Then I'll tuck you into bed for a good sleep. Come, come," she said. As the old dwarf led them into the trees, her steps faltered, and Haret was quick to take her elbow.

They came to a table in the center of the orchard, where the odor of fruit and the rustle of leaves surrounded them.

Frayda was there, too, though Abisina hardly recognized her. The last time Abisina saw her, Frayda had looked like a hunted animal, completely undone by the death of Rueshlan and the many others lost in the battle with the Worm. Now, after her time in the garden, she was again the lithe archer who Abisina had met on her first night in Watersmeet. Her limbs were muscled, her blue eyes were clear, and her beautiful hair had begun to grow back in the patches where she had pulled it out.

Frayda rose from the table. "Abisina, I'm glad to see you." She took Abisina's hands. "Thank you . . . for saving me."

Abisina could only nod.

"You must eat!" Hoysta interrupted. "Frayda picked some fruit when Haret said you were coming." She set a dish in front of Meelah.

"You knew?" Abisina asked Haret.

"I've been walking in the tunnels. I was on that side of the mountain as you climbed. Not taking much care to disguise yourself, eh, human?"

"We've seen no überwolves or leviathan-birds."

"Don't ever think you're alone," Haret warned.

As they enjoyed the succulent fruit and the cold, clear water, some of Abisina's worry and exhaustion fell away. It was the effect of the garden, and though she knew her worries would return, she was relieved.

Hoysta talked as she patted Meelah's hand and continued to feed her. "To know the snow is piled outside while here fruit blooms and buds still open! This garden is wonder enough to make even a dwarf like me consider living aboveground. Of course, I do need time in the tunnels to keep my head." She chuckled. "And not all the trees are as healthy as these around us. It's why we moved the table here, isn't it, Frayda? The winter has touched some of the trees. The ones closest to the wall have dropped their fruit, and their leaves are turning. They'll have just finished with autumn when spring returns."

Haret frowned as Hoysta spoke.

"And the Seldar?" Abisina asked quickly.

"Such trees! We visit the one that's here whenever I can make the walk, don't we, Frayda?" Hoysta replied.

"The Seldar helps me," Frayda said, looking at Abisina. "I feel close to him when I'm near it. . . ."

Across the table, Neriah's hard features softened.

"Bedtime!" Hoysta announced as soon as Meelah had enough to eat. "You, too, Neriah." Abisina stifled a smile at Hoysta's daring to command the fairy. "You need the sleep of the garden."

"We go to the sleeping alcoves early here," Frayda added. "And we're up with the sun—or I am. Hoysta doesn't sense the day like I do."

"The sun does not call a dwarf," Hoysta said. "But I need more sleep than I used to. You two, stay up yet." She winked at Abisina and her grandson. "You have a lot to talk about."

"I will stay, too," Neriah said.

"They will tell you all tomorrow," Hoysta said. "You're asleep on your feet! Never seen a fairy so droopy!"

*Thank you, Hoysta,* Abisina thought.

Frayda helped Hoysta to her feet and then back to the tunnels. Meelah and Neriah followed.

Haret watched them go. "The garden has been good for Grandmother, but she can't stay."

"What's happening here?" Abisina asked.

"I don't know." Haret ran his fingers through his bristly dark hair. "I've been in the garden for twelve days now, and in that short time I've seen changes. I put up the door after I found tracks in the tunnels."

"What kind of tracks?"

Haret shook his head. "Don't know that, either. Something with claws and a long tail. Nothing I've seen before. I've been patrolling the tunnels, but I haven't found it. I think I was close last night. Heard some strange rustling."

"And the trees?"

"Grandmother says they're in autumn, but they're dying. Just on the edge of the garden, though every day another one . . . fades. I have to get Grandmother and Frayda out of here," Haret concluded. "I'll take them back to Watersmeet. Glynholly will have to accept that. Breide will care for Grandmother and— What?" Haret broke off as Abisina clutched his hand.

"Haret—there is no Watersmeet," she said gently. "The birds have been there, and the folk have fled—or died. It's overrun with überwolves. We had hoped to find Findlay and Elodie. They came north, but no one's seen them! We plan to head east. That's where Meelah said the folk have gone."

"Breide?" he asked, after a stunned silence. The two dwarves had fallen for each other during Haret's time in Watersmeet.

"I don't know anything about Breide or Alden or any of the other dwarves," she admitted. "They were all sent to work on the wall soon after we left Watersmeet."

"It wasn't their choice?"

"I think they wanted to go at the time . . . though that may have changed. Meelah says the fairies forced them to go."

"Fairies," Haret spat.

"Rueshlan trusted them. And Neriah is different—at times."

"Do you trust her?"

"I—I think so. Yes, I do," Abisina corrected herself.

"Human . . ."

"Neriah says that Glynholly sent me the necklace, but Meelah swears that Glynholly was wearing it when she left Watersmeet—weeks after I received it," Abisina confessed. "And there have been other moments, little things, that don't quite feel right. Still, I wouldn't have returned to Watersmeet at all if it wasn't for Neriah." Abisina told him how Neriah had taken so many risks to save her. "And she lost the crown. She was the heir, but when she helped me, the Mother banished her. She's given up everything to help us."

"What happened to the box?" Haret asked.

"Reava took it—and the letter inside. The Mother has it now." Abisina picked up a slice of fruit, then set it back down. "I know I sound like I'm defending her. But something's coming from the rift, Haret. These eels, this thing in the tunnels—they're all part of it. The fairies are at risk, too.

Even if their motives are entirely selfish, they'll ally with us to save themselves."

"Maybe." Haret scratched his bearded chin. "But the fairies won't see it that way. If something is coming from the rift, they'll want the wall more."

"A *wall* will not keep out something like the Worm! And the eels, the birds—they're already in the north."

"The wall is better than an open Cleft," Haret replied.

"Why are you here, Haret?" Her distress at not finding Findlay and Elodie had kept Abisina from wondering why Haret had come to the garden. "You were supposed to be with the dwarves at Stonedun."

"They wouldn't listen to me. Well, not many. I told them about the birds' attack on Newlyn. They didn't care."

"Hadn't they seen the birds?"

"They'd seen them—but Stonedun is built underground. They don't fear the birds, so they saw no reason to work with us. And they care even less about Vran and Vigar. A few—mostly the young ones—were intrigued. And when the mountain exploded, I got a few more. I took about twenty back to Newlyn. They're our best hope, I guess, but there aren't enough to make a difference."

"Twenty! That's something," Abisina said. Haret's morose face had prepared her for less, though it was a tiny portion of the dwarves at Stonedun.

"I haven't told you the worst of it," Haret continued. "Corlin hasn't come back from Vranham yet. They assume he's been captured—or killed."

"Corlin killed. . . ." Even the peace of the garden couldn't erase Abisina's shock. Corlin had saved her from the mob in her home village. Even though he was Vranian, he had fought *against* the Worm. And when the people in the south were struggling for survival, he had come north to get Abisina's help to rebuild Vranlyn into a village more like Watersmeet. Vranlyn, now named Newlyn, had grown stronger through Corlin's leadership.

More than that, Corlin had been a friend. *And Elodie's love.* Abisina had tried to imagine what it would be like to lose Findlay. *That's what Elodie will feel now.*

"It's a huge loss for Newlyn, for all of us," Haret said. "And you see what it means. Theckis and his Vranians weren't interested in learning about Vran's family, either."

"You sound like you think this is all a mistake!" Abisina cried. Abisina had been sure that news of Vran's relation to Vigar would convince the Vranians to work with Newlyn, especially with the threat of the birds.

"Abisina, I don't doubt the need to ally. It's why I went to Stonedun in the first place. I expected them to listen. I'm amazed at how blind they are to threats so obvious to me."

"The centaurs were the same," Abisina said. "But I think I reached a few." She told him about the centaur who had let her escape with the necklace. "One centaur, twenty dwarves—they matter. They're the beginning. Tomorrow, we go east. Vigar willing, we'll find Findlay and Elodie and whoever is left from Watersmeet, even if it means going into the Motherland."

"No, human!" Haret got up from the table and started to pace. "You should not go in there. You'll be at the Mother's mercy—and Reava's!"

"Neriah won't let them hurt me." She smiled at his scowl. "No—I'm not defending her or being ridiculously optimistic. Every time I rescue her or heal her, she says she's in my debt. At the moment, she owes *me*. That will keep me safe."

"Trust a fairy's word?"

"It's not her word, Haret. It . . . it's something else. I can't explain it. It's like a rule she can't break."

"Maybe you can trust Neriah, maybe you can't. But we *know* you can't trust Reava or the Mother, and they may have more power over Neriah than you suspect."

"I'll avoid going there if I can. But we can't fight this battle without the fairies, and I can't get to them without Neriah."

"Human—"

"I will take *any* risk to save this land, Haret. I am Rueshlan's heir, and I wear the necklace. It responds to me. What choice do I have?" Abisina picked up the same piece of fruit from the table and studied it. "At least you're with me now."

Haret sighed and sat down again. "I can't leave Grandmother. And for now, if Watersmeet is abandoned, she has to stay here. She's dying, Abisina." He put his head in his hands. "You saw her stumble, how shaken she was at seeing Neriah. Some days she doesn't even get out of bed. Until she leaves this world, I have to care for her as she has cared for me. I owe *her*, human."

Abisina could see the scars on his hands from when Haret

had attempted to dig into the Obrium Lode beneath the mountains, unable to resist the metal's call. Hoysta tried to stop him, but he was too far gone. He almost killed her before he regained his senses.

For a moment, Abisina and Haret had been a team again. She'd been so relieved to see his silhouette in the archway! She would have someone to help her plan, someone to weigh the competing demands from Neriah and Meelah and her own heart. But she knew Haret had to stay with Hoysta.

Abisina reached for Haret's hand, smiled, and touched the rough scars.

"I'll follow when I can," he said.

"I know."

# CHAPTER XIV

THEY SET OUT LATER THAN ABISINA HAD PLANNED. Like Haret, she owed Hoysta a debt: Hoysta had saved her life, too—when Abisina escaped from Vranille. More than that, Hoysta first showed Abisina how to love those she had been taught to hate: the dwarves, the fauns, and eventually, the centaurs. Abisina couldn't leave without saying good-bye, but she didn't want to wake the old dwarf too early.

Neriah chafed at the delay. She spent the morning stalking through the garden, returning at regular intervals to the table where Abisina, Haret, and Meelah sat. She would stay for a moment before resuming her agitated walking. She was more distant—more fairy-like—than ever. Haret watched Neriah's every move.

"You're leaving today?" Frayda asked shyly when she joined them at the table.

"Yes," Abisina answered. "We're going east to find

Watersmeet's folk. I have this now, Frayda." She pulled out the necklace from beneath her tunic.

Frayda stared. "It was his." She reached out and touched the necklace tentatively.

"Rueshlan's folk are scattered," Abisina said. "I'm going to bring them back together—or try to. Will you join me?"

Frayda dropped her hand. "Leave here?"

"I could use your bow," Abisina said. "You were Watersmeet's champion."

"No," Frayda said, moving away from Abisina. "I—I know it's not safe here anymore. But I can't go back."

"Watersmeet needs you!" Abisina said more forcefully than she intended. Her anger surprised her. *It's because I cannot make the same choice,* she realized. *I wear the necklace. I can't refuse to help.*

"I understand," Abisina said. "I—I shouldn't have asked."

Frayda stepped closer and laid a hand on Abisina's shoulder. "You carry him in you, Abisina. You are the one who can do this." She kissed Abisina on the cheek and retreated back into the garden. She did not appear again.

There was another reason Abisina didn't leave at first light. She had to visit Vigar's grave. Twice Vigar had spoken to her there, and Abisina hoped she would again. She had so many questions: about the papers she'd found, about what was coming from the rift, about where she should go next. *And about Findlay.* But she had learned that Vigar could not be commanded. She spoke only when *she* decided to. And sometimes her words raised more questions than they answered.

Abisina walked slowly to the circle of white stones that marked the grave. It was here that Hoysta had dug up the Obrium box, and Abisina worried that the grave would still show signs of damage; but the stones were in place, the grass smooth and tall. The rowan tree stood at the top of the ring. Though she had never seen it without white blossoms till today, it looked healthy enough—leaves green, new growth at its top. Even in the garden, trees couldn't always bloom. The well that bubbled near the grave was also undisturbed, its music whispering along with the rustling leaves.

Abisina sat against the rowan and waited. She didn't *feel* Vigar as she sometimes did; still, the garden was mysterious.

After an hour, Abisina admitted that Vigar was not there—had not been there for some time. *Maybe it's the box,* she thought. *Did she leave with it? Is she with it now?* Abisina tried to remember holding the box in her hand. Had she felt a presence then?

No. She had felt a power, certainly, but not Vigar's presence.

Abisina returned to the others. Hoysta had joined them. She shuffled to Abisina, smiling her toothless smile, her rheumy eyes swimming with tears. "Dearie," she said, enfolding Abisina in her arms. Abisina's eyes were misty, and she could feel Hoysta sway against her. "My grandson thinks I don't know what's happening, but I do. I wish my strength had lasted a little longer so that we could go with you. But you don't need us." Hoysta touched the lines of doubt on Abisina's forehead and smiled. "We've already given you what you need." The dwarf pulled Abisina to her again. "Trust yourself."

They left at midday. Haret took them through the tunnels, axe on his shoulder. He discreetly pointed out to Abisina the tracks he had found, but she could make no sense of them.

They reached the mountaintop. Haret had refilled their quivers with his arrows. "I prefer an axe for tunnel fighting," he grumbled when Abisina protested that he might need them. "And I'll have time to make more."

Haret accepted Meelah's warm hug but only nodded when Neriah said good-bye. To Abisina, his good-bye was brusque, as she had expected. "I'll come when I can!" he called after them as they picked their way down the gravel slope.

Abisina felt exposed on the mountainside until they made tree line, but she was glad they had waited to leave. They were better rested, and, even if she remained human, they could cover many leagues before dark.

When they reached the Obruns' foothills, Abisina turned to follow the mountains east, the fastest route to the wall. Neriah stopped. "We should go to the Motherland."

"Meelah said the majority of the folk would have gone to the wall," Abisina began patiently. "That's where I'm going."

"There will be constant travel between the Motherland and the wall. If we go northeast, to the southern side of the Motherland, I can find out how things stand at the wall *and* in the Motherland."

"Even though the Mother banished you?" Meelah asked.

"I'm still her daughter; fairies will give me the information I request." Neriah turned back to Abisina. "We have already lost two days looking for Findlay. We will do more for him if we build the alliance that will stop Seldara's destruction."

Abisina sighed. She knew Neriah was right again. "We'll go northeast *for now*," she said curtly. "We can always turn to the wall later." No one spoke as they altered course.

They traveled for four days through eerily quiet forest before they found the ruin of a Watersmeet camp. The amount of trash, the shelters, and the number of tracks suggested that the folk had lived at the camp for a week or more. Skimpy huts of evergreen branches were built in a depression of land that was cold and hard to defend. Most had blown down or been crushed by snow. It appeared that some fifty or sixty folk had camped here. The pots and satchels and intact weapons left behind indicated a hasty departure, though Abisina saw no sign of attack. What had made them camp for so long in an ill-suited place and then abandon it suddenly?

Beyond the camp, they found the remains of a big funeral pyre. If there were sixty in the camp at the beginning, less than half left here alive. Abisina transformed to human shape and leaned down to study the ground. The melted snow around the pyre had refrozen, catching bones, sword hilts, arrow-heads, and an Obrium ring in the rutted ground.

"Were the folk sick when they left Watersmeet?" Abisina asked Meelah.

"Some. All were starved and exhausted."

"Well, something killed large numbers here—and I've seen no predator tracks."

"The fairies?" Meelah whispered, scanning the trees

overhead for Neriah. The fairy had gone to see where the folk's trail led. "If they were in the trees, they would not leave tracks."

Abisina frowned. "That doesn't make sense. These are not fairy arrows." She kicked one embedded in the ice. "And from what you said, Reava *wanted* folk to go to the wall."

"Refugees?" Meelah suggested.

"There was no fight. They built this camp because they couldn't go on."

"I wonder who died here. . . ." Meelah's voice broke.

They had come upon the camp late in the afternoon, and they pushed on far into the night, helped by the light of the almost-full moon, trying to put distance between themselves and the wretched scene.

They followed the trail of the survivors from the blighted camp for a few more days. At one point, tracks from another group joined them, then split off to go south. "Must be a group headed to the mountains," Meelah noted. "These tracks go to the Motherland. Perhaps this was Glynholly's group."

Even facing cold and disease and hunger, the folk hadn't come together. Seeing those second tracks leading away reminded Abisina that the folk in the north were as divided as those in the south, and her task of bringing them together seemed more impossible than ever.

They traveled on. Abisina appreciated having Meelah to talk to. Whenever she indulged herself and talked about Findlay, she was sure of a receptive audience. But when Neriah and Meelah were together, Abisina got worn out trying to keep peace between them. She was glad that Neriah chose to spend most of her time in the trees, leaping from branch to branch.

The fairy seemed more distracted and uncomfortable the closer they came to the Motherland, and she often met Abisina's attempts at conversation with disdain. Abisina recalled the nights she had curled up next to Neriah for warmth. She couldn't imagine doing that now.

Abisina continued to reach out with her mind for hoofed creatures, though she had seen no tracks since they'd left Watersmeet. She stopped in surprise when she sensed an answering mind.

"What's happening?" Meelah asked from Abisina's back.

Abisina held up a hand, her consciousness flooded with impressions that made no sense. Was the animal young? Or mad? *Or in pain?*

That was it: the creature was in pain, and something was hurting it more.

"There's someone over here!" Abisina said, wheeling to her left.

The wild donkey was lying on its side in a clearing. An überwolf hunched over it, jaws buried in its belly while the creature kicked feebly. In an instant, the überwolf lay dead with Abisina's arrow in its back. She reached out to the donkey with thoughts of fresh grass, clover, and sunshine as it died.

Neriah landed next to Abisina and Meelah. "Did it tell you anything?"

"No, it was in too much pain." Abisina noticed shreds of leather on the ground. "It wore a harness. It must have been from Watersmeet." Watersmeet never used wild donkeys as beasts of burden without their consent. "Some of the folk may be nearby."

Without another word, Neriah leapt into the trees and a moment later called, "Smoke to the east!"

"Let's go," Abisina said.

Neriah landed again. "I will go ahead, find out how many there are."

"They're *our* folk," Meelah said acidly. "We have nothing to fear. If they see you, they won't trust *us*."

"I can get close without being seen," Neriah said. "What if it is Glynholly's group? If you show yourselves to the wrong folk—"

"There are no wrong folk in Watersmeet," Abisina said firmly. "But, Meelah," she continued, "we should know what we're walking into. Neriah, take care you're not seen." The fairy disappeared into the trees.

"Meelah, she is the only way I have of getting to the Mother," Abisina said.

"The Mother will not work with you," Meelah replied.

"She will if I convince her it's in her interest. But I'll never get the chance if I don't have Neriah to help with the boundary trees."

Strange and threatening trees surrounded the Motherland in an impenetrable ring. The fairies controlled them. The last time Abisina had traveled to the Motherland, roots as strong as steel whipped from the ground to bind and imprison her friends as they approached. Once she was among the trees, vines entangled her feet and branches shifted to block her way if she did not go where the fairies wanted her to. Abisina didn't know if Neriah still had the power to control the trees, but she was sure that she wouldn't get through them without her.

After an hour of trudging through drifts of thawing snow, Abisina could smell the camp's fire. She stopped and waited for Neriah to return, while Meelah ate a few mouthfuls of travel bread. The smell made Abisina's mouth water, but she took none for herself. Their food was running low, and Meelah, after months of near starvation, needed it more than she did.

Neriah leapt from the trees. "There are three of them. A centaur and two fauns. One of the fauns is injured; the other is on guard with about half a quiver of arrows and a sword. The centaur has a sword. He's tending the faun."

"And do they have a donkey?" Abisina asked. "I thought I sensed one."

"Yes. The creature can barely stand."

Abisina considered. "I'll get the donkey to divert them. Then we can approach the camp."

"All three of us?" Meelah asked.

"Not Neriah. Not until we've talked to them. And maybe not even then."

To Abisina's relief, Neriah agreed. "I will stay in arrow range," she said.

"Meelah, you should ride," Abisina told her. "No weapons out."

Neriah looked startled. "They could attack!"

"We'll invite their arrows if we have ours out," Abisina said.

When they could see the camp's fire flickering through the trees, Abisina reached for the mind of the donkey and nudged it awake with thoughts of warm dens crowded with fellow donkeys. She hated to mislead the poor creature, but if she got into the camp, she could help it.

The donkey started toward Abisina.

"Hey!" the centaur shouted, and Abisina broke through the trees. She held up her hands as the faun raised her bow, and the centaur got to his hooves. The second faun huddled under a cloak. The donkey stopped, confused.

The faun lowered her arrow. "Rueshlan?"

"Anwyn!" Abisina said.

Abisina's voice was not Rueshlan's, and Anwyn raised her arrow again as the centaur drew his sword. "I don't understand. . . ." Anwyn said.

"It's a fairy trick," the centaur warned.

"It's me! Abisina." If Anwyn didn't lower her weapon, Neriah would shoot from the trees. "Meelah's here with me." Meelah leaned around Abisina to show herself. Anwyn's arrow held its aim. "Please," Abisina urged. "You know us. Look!"

She moved to pull out the necklace, but Anwyn cried: "Hold! Ready, Erith!"

"If she even flinches . . ."

"This is not a trick, Anwyn. It's me," Abisina said again, hands raised. "I last saw you in the wood outside Watersmeet.

We met there with Haret and Findlay, Kyron and Moyla." She groped for details. "Elodie stood guard and told us to run. Glynholly captured you. Findlay, Elodie, and Kyron escaped."

Anwyn's arrow drifted lower, but Erith stayed tense.

"How—How is this possible?" Anwyn said. "You look so like him. . . ."

"I have the necklace, too. I can show you if you let me."

"But you're a centaur," Anwyn said with wonder.

"Don't trust it!" Erith said. "We don't know what the fairies can do. It's some kind of illusion."

"Anwyn, could an illusion name who was at that meeting? Would an illusion shake as I am?" Abisina held out a trembling hand. She longed to signal Neriah to stay back, but she didn't dare.

"Tell me more about that night," the faun demanded. "Tell me something that Glynholly and Reava wouldn't know."

Abisina tried to recall more details—it felt so long ago. "Haret and Elodie brought me and Kyron to a circle of rocks. There were old fire pits. Others had met there before." Anwyn tensed. It was not enough. "Kyron was angry. He thought more centaurs should have come . . . and Findlay!" How could she have forgotten that moment when Findlay appeared from the darkness? "W-we ran to each other. . . ." Abisina's throat closed around her words.

She had said the right thing. Anwyn dropped her arrow. "It *is* you! How?" Erith did not sheath his sword, but the tension went out of his shoulders.

Abisina exhaled. Behind her, Meelah did the same. "I'm a shape-shifter. Like my father."

"There were rumors," Erith said.

"Rumors?"

"From Findlay and Elodie, I think."

Abisina's mouth went dry, so Meelah spoke for her. "Did you see them? Did you see Findlay?"

"A dwarf at the wall talked to them," Erith said. "Or maybe it was a faun."

Meelah jumped to the ground. "Where is Findlay?"

"I don't know for sure," Erith said heavily. "They took so many—most of the guards from the wall, many of the dwarves, all of the others who had come from Watersmeet. My brother. Findlay and Elodie must have been with them."

"Taken?" Abisina asked.

Erith nodded. "To the Motherland."

# CHAPTER XV

*FINDLAY'S IN THE MOTHERLAND. HE'S ALIVE!* ABISINA THOUGHT. But Erith had said, "They took so many." *As if they were prisoners.* She touched the waist-cord in her pocket. *Why do the fairies want them?*

"We have to go!" Meelah pulled at Abisina.

"We wanted to go after them, too," Anwyn said. "But it's going to take the army."

"*The* army?" Abisina asked.

"Neiall's army. They say he's out here with his followers, getting ready to attack." Anwyn's drawn face lightened a little. "*You* can lead us! We have a chance now!"

Abisina glanced warily at the trees.

"Anwyn!" Erith called. He was bent over the injured faun. "Callas is hardly breathing!"

Abisina transformed. In two strides she was at the side of the faun, feeling her pulse, checking for wounds. "Where is she injured?"

"In the leg." Erith pointed.

Abisina tore off the cloak that covered the faun. She saw the blood in the snow before she saw the protruding bone. She ripped some shave-weed from her pouch. At her touch, the faun's eyes fluttered open. "You're going to be all right, Callas," Abisina said soothingly. "But this is going to hurt." Abisina pushed the bone back into place, and Callas passed out again.

"What are you doing?" Erith demanded.

Abisina ignored him. "Get the bandage in my satchel!" she yelled to Meelah. Still holding Callas's leg, she said, "I need two straight branches—two fingers' wide. Now." Anwyn and Erith turned to the trees around them.

"Got it," Meelah announced, holding the bandage roll to Abisina.

"Start wrapping," Abisina commanded. "Begin at the hoof." Abisina held Callas's bone in place and talked Meelah through the bandaging. By the time Meelah had wrapped the leg, Erith returned with branches, and Abisina put the splint in place. The faun's breathing was shallow, her pulse rapid, but Abisina had done all she could for now. She pulled the cloak back over the faun and put her own on top of it. "Build up the fire," she told Anwyn, but the faun was already throwing more wood on it.

"Will she live?" Erith asked.

"She has a chance," Abisina told him.

"She's just mated," he said. "Right before the birds came to Watersmeet. We don't know where her partner is."

Drained, Abisina fought the desire to sink onto the

ground. If only she could rest. *Findlay is alive!* she told herself, and turned back to Anwyn.

"Tell me whatever you can about the situation, here and in the Motherland. Yes, Meelah," she said as the girl opened her mouth to speak. "I promise I will try to find Findlay, but I have to figure out how to get past the boundary trees first."

"That's easy," Erith said. "The trees are dying."

Neriah dropped to the ground. Erith drew his sword.

"Wait!" Abisina screamed, getting between the fairy's arrow and the centaur's blade. "Leave her alone!"

"You want me to leave a *fairy* alone?" Erith didn't take his eyes from Neriah.

"She's with me," Abisina said. "You can trust her."

"Never. The fairies have destroyed everything."

"Please, Erith. Put down your sword. Let me explain. I swear this fairy won't hurt any of you. I swear on the Keeper's necklace!" Abisina drew it out for the first time, and Erith glanced at it before staring again at Neriah.

"I swear on the necklace that I will do nothing to this fairy—for now. But I will not put my sword away," Erith replied evenly.

"What did you say about the trees?" Neriah still pointed her arrow at Erith.

"He will tell us, Neriah. You don't need that arrow here. Your sister mistreated these folk. You know what Reava's done—"

"Sister!" Erith had taken a step back, but now he came at Neriah again.

"Erith!" Abisina put up her arms. "Neriah's been banished. She's no more welcome in the Motherland than I am! Please, step back. Both of you."

The fairy and the centaur glared at each other. Then Erith took a small step backward, muttering, "Because you're Rueshlan's daughter." Neriah aimed at the ground but left her arrow on the string.

"Sword away, Erith." Abisina kept her arms raised. Erith dropped the sword to his side but did not sheath it. *Good enough.* Abisina lowered her hands. "Now, tell us about the trees."

"They're down all along the boundary," Erith said. "We can't get close enough to see more."

"Those trees have been there longer than the fairies," Neriah said. "The Green Man gave them to us."

"The Seldars and the trees in Vigar's garden are dying, too," Abisina said. *And the Sylvyads?* she wondered. Vigar had said that Watersmeet was the Green Man's "creation." *Are all of his creations in trouble?*

"Erith," Abisina went on, "you said that the fairies had taken the folk to the Motherland."

"The fairies *forced* us to go," Erith spat. "The wall's almost complete. Anwyn, Callas, and I were in one of the last groups to go. We ran away in the night. We knew that once the fairies got us to the Motherland we'd be no better than slaves."

"We planned to join Neiall," Anwyn added. "All our hope is in him and Old Watersmeet, but we're not sure where they are. We've been searching these woods for days—until Callas got hurt."

"And when we find Neiall, we'll need you," Erith said. "You're Rueshlan's heir, and you have the necklace! It changes everything."

"What about Findlay?" Meelah demanded, as if Abisina had already agreed to join them. "Will you abandon him? He went south for you, Abisina. He gave up his family for you."

"I agree with Meelah, Abisina. You have to go to the Motherland. You came north to work with the fairies," Neriah broke in.

"I don't want to work with the fairies!" Meelah protested.

"I know the Mother has broken promises," Neriah said. "But if the trees are dying, she will see that the fairies cannot survive without Watersmeet. We will convince her, Abisina."

Abisina looked at each of them. Her instincts told her to go to the Motherland, but she wasn't sure. *Findlay's there.* She forced herself to think slowly.

Neriah had a point. If the boundary trees were dying, the Mother needed to join with Watersmeet more than ever. Would Watersmeet agree? Neiall and his followers planned to *attack* the Motherland.

But Neiall's army was all rumor. She could waste weeks searching for an army that didn't exist!

*And something's coming. Whatever blew the top off that mountain is coming north. If I go to find Neiall now, the wall and the Motherland could fall.*

"What have you decided?" Anwyn said. "I can see it on your face—you know what you're going to do."

"I'm going to the Motherland," Abisina said.

"Then you're a traitor to Watersmeet—and to your father," Erith declared.

"My father would do the same thing, Erith. So would Vigar. I want to save this land, just as they did. The rift in the mountain has released its final evil. We all need to come together."

"Since Rueshlan's death I've stood by you, Abisina. I was wrong. If you can go into the Motherland with *her*"—he tipped his chin at Neriah—"you are not Rueshlan's heir." Erith sheathed his sword and walked over to Callas. "Come on, Anwyn. I'll carry Callas. We're going north."

"No," Abisina said. "We'll leave. Callas should not be moved. Here—I'll give you the medicine you need." She dug through her packets and pulled out a second vial of shaveweed—her last one—and some herbs for fighting infection. "Do you know any healing, Anwyn?" she asked, handing the herbs to the faun.

"Erith knows a little," she said.

"Poultice these herbs and leave them on the wound. Change the dressing and the poultice daily. She shouldn't move for two days. Keep her warm." Erith gathered Abisina's cloak, but she stopped him. "She'll need that more than I will. We're almost to the spring equinox."

"Thank you, Abisina," Anwyn said. Erith had turned away.

"And your donkey," Abisina added, digging in her satchel

again. "It needs the herbs in this packet. It's eaten something bad, and this will help. In two days, it can carry Callas." She sent the donkey the feeling of a sound stomach, and it whickered with contentment.

"Erith," Abisina said, speaking to the centaur's back, "we are each doing what we think is right. Tell Neiall you've seen me, and what I told you about the mountain. The wall will not hold for long, and we will need his army."

Erith didn't turn, didn't speak.

"Come on, Meelah," Abisina said, transforming back into a centaur so that Meelah could ride. "Due east, Neriah. We'll stop at nightfall for a brief rest. Then we go on."

Neriah nodded and took to the trees.

Through the next days, both Meelah and Neriah tried to convince Abisina that she had made the right decision, but their reassurances irritated her. Meelah was thinking of Findlay, and the news about the boundary trees had shaken Neriah.

Erith's accusation rang in her ears with every hoof-fall: *You're a traitor to Watersmeet—and to your father.*

As Abisina galloped across snowy fields, softening with the approaching spring, she replayed their argument again and again. Should she have told Erith and Anwyn about Vigar's papers? That Vran was Vigar's brother? She had planned to tell the folk when she found them. But she also remembered Haret's words: the dwarves and the Vranians were not interested in Vran and Vigar's family tree. They were interested in survival.

If she was honest with herself, Abisina had to admit that

Findlay was never far from her mind, either. Erith had said the folk would be no better than slaves in the Motherland. What were the fairies forcing them to do?

Abisina didn't know if she'd been right to continue east, but she had needed to make a choice. She only hoped that the choice hadn't cost her Seldara.

# CHAPTER XVI

As they neared the Motherland, the numbers of überwolves increased. They also saw a couple of trolls; but the trolls, loud and very smelly, could be avoided. Abisina and her party traveled by day and slept in the trees at night. Skirmishes with the starving wolves slowed them. Twice Neriah spotted packs of wolves fighting each other.

Abisina worried most about crossing the plain that surrounded the Motherland. From the moment they left the forest, they would have no cover until they reached the boundary trees. They had few arrows left. Findlay's sword would only be useful in close fighting—and close fighting would mean they were done for. They decided to cross at the plain's narrowest point along its southern border, near the Cleft—a journey of two hours.

Abisina arrived at the edge of the plain and knew they had underestimated the time. Ridges and mounds of drifted snow stood between them and the Motherland. Abisina would have to wade through the wet, heavy piles. They had planned to wait until the sun was directly overhead, when the wolves were least likely to be on the prowl, but Abisina urged them to leave much earlier. "If we don't, night will catch us in the open."

"The snow will slow down the überwolves, too," Neriah pointed out, but Abisina felt little comfort as she stepped onto the plain.

By noon, Abisina doubted they would reach the Motherland before midnight. Though no überwolves had attacked them, she was worn out from forcing her way through the larger drifts, her ankles were cut and bleeding from breaking through crusts of snow, and she could barely go faster than a walk. They had just glimpsed the boundary trees between two drifts when the first wolf howled.

*It's a matter of time,* Abisina knew. She tried to pick up her pace. Soon she was breathing so hard, she had to slow down again. To relieve Abisina of the extra weight, Meelah walked in the path Abisina cleared, but it wasn't enough.

Another howl, closer.

Neriah leapt to a drift and gazed off into the distance. "I cannot see them," she whispered, coming back down to where Abisina and Meelah waited.

"Do we keep going, or will that draw attention?" Abisina asked. "We could hole up in one of these drifts. . . ." *But then what?* Meelah was white with fear.

"Keep going for now," Neriah said. "I will stay on top of the drifts and signal if they get too close." For days, she had been nervous and jittery, but just before they left the forest, her mood had shifted. She seemed settled—even content—though she kept an arrow always on her string, pausing to listen to the increasing howls.

Abisina watched Neriah go, her own fear growing. *We've left quite a trail. And with the sun going down, it's getting cold and slippery. If another pack comes from the east or from behind . . .*

And then a wolf howled from the opposite direction—another pack.

"Neriah!" Abisina called, as loud as she dared. There was no answer. "Where is she?"

"Don't you know? She's gone to her folk," Meelah said, again on Abisina's back, armed and ready. "She's probably already safe in the boundary trees. The Mother is congratulating her for getting us here so that the überwolves can tear us apart."

"She hasn't abandoned us, Meelah," Abisina maintained, but her fear grew.

They kept struggling forward, Abisina calling out for Neriah now and then, ears strained for the next howl. The packs were getting closer on each side, while the boundary trees still looked far off. *And how will we get into them without Neriah?*

Meelah, focused on the pack to the east, missed the überwolf hurtling at them from the west, but Abisina saw it. "Meelah!" She fumbled for Findlay's sword, the wolf too close for an arrow.

The wolf leapt on Meelah before she could shoot. Freeing

the sword, Abisina stabbed behind her but was afraid of hitting Meelah. The wolf and Meelah tumbled off her back, the wolf on top of the girl, teeth sunk into her arm. Abisina drove her sword through the wolf's back, and it went limp, trapping Meelah under its crushing weight. Abisina kicked the wolf off her. Blood dripped onto the snow; the wound on Meelah's arm was deep.

"Did it get you anywhere else?" Abisina asked, scanning the drifts for the rest of the pack.

"I don't think so."

Abisina ripped her last bandage from her satchel. *And I've no shave-weed!* She had only moments to bind the wound and slow the bleeding before more überwolves would be on them. And Meelah could no longer shoot. *We cannot survive this,* Abisina thought as a wolf howled from behind the next drift.

Abisina pulled Meelah onto her back. "Grip with your knees. Don't worry about hurting me. Just stay on. And take this." Abisina put Findlay's sword in his sister's right hand. "I'll get us out of here."

"I'm going to fall!" Meelah shrieked as Abisina readied an arrow.

"Your knees!" Abisina called, and Meelah squeezed. "Good girl! Now grip tight!" She jumped a few lower drifts, the impact sending ribbons of pain up her tired legs, and then wove between some valleys in the snow, turning left and right. She was searching for the next low drift when she saw them: three überwolves blocking her way, teeth bared. Abisina pivoted to turn back when the second pack arrived:

at least ten. More wolves joined the first three. Abisina couldn't shoot so many, and if she reared to lash out with her hooves, Meelah would fall.

Abisina sent arrow after arrow into the packs, but the hungry wolves came on. She backed into a snowdrift to protect her sides.

"Give me the sword!" Abisina shouted. Meelah thrust it into her hand as the packs attacked from both directions.

Abisina slashed out at fur and teeth and eyes. Meelah did what she could with her dagger. Abisina pulled her sword from one überwolf, but another snarled on her right. Meelah's dagger struck its throat. It fell back, taking Meelah's dagger with it. Abisina gathered herself to leap among the wolves, hoping the surprise would give her time to gallop down one of the snow valleys.

A shadow passed over the sun. Instantly, the wolves cowered on the ground, tails between their legs, and then scattered.

"A leviathan-bird!" Meelah screamed. Abisina took off, heading west, ready to leap over the first low drift. A wolf ahead of her yipped and fell, an arrow sticking out of its haunch.

Neriah stood on a high drift above them, another arrow on her string.

"Keep going!" she called. "There's a stretch of clear ground to the north. I will meet you!"

Abisina obeyed, mind racing along with her hooves. *Where did Neriah come from? Where has she been?*

Abisina cut north, and her way opened—a section of

snow only as deep as her ankles. A second and third shadow crossed the sun. Abisina kept running until her breath was gone and her legs felt as if they would collapse under her.

The birds did not come after them.

"Are you all right?" she called back to Meelah.

"I think so."

"Is your arm still bleeding?"

"A little."

Abisina wanted to clean and treat it, but she couldn't risk putting Meelah on the ground. She slowed to a trot.

"That was Neriah?" Meelah asked. "I didn't imagine it?"

"She was there." Abisina stopped to look back. A dark figure ran in their direction: Neriah.

"What do you think happened?" Meelah whispered.

Abisina stared toward Neriah. "I have no idea."

"I killed most of the wolves." The fairy panted as she ran up. "The birds terrified them. And you left quite a feast of dead wolves to hold off the birds."

"What happened to you?" Meelah asked coldly.

"I am sorry," Neriah said. "I saw how much it was costing you to wade through those drifts. I knew we would not make it to the Motherland by nightfall if I did not find a better way. I lost track of where I'd left you. The howls started to move together, and I knew I had to come back, but I had traveled farther than I realized."

Abisina didn't respond. Neriah had said she would stay close. She *knew* they were headed into danger.

"I need to tend to Meelah's wound," Abisina said.

Neriah glanced around her. "We should keep going. The fairies have gifted healers."

"Meelah?" Abisina asked.

"I'll be fine," Meelah said curtly. "But I'd like a *Watersmeet* healer."

"As you wish," Neriah said. "There is a deep drift coming up. To the left is another open area, which will take us close to the Motherland."

Neriah started forward.

"I don't believe that fairy," Meelah whispered.

Abisina whispered back, "I know you don't, dear heart. But right now, we're stuck with her."

As they crossed the final drift before the smooth halo of snow that circled the Motherland, Abisina was shocked at what she saw. Erith had said that the boundary trees were failing, but the trees had fallen three or four deep in some places. Farther into the Motherland, more sick trees leaned against ones that still stood strong.

Neriah crouched on the ground, staring at the heaps of trees, tears streaming down her face. Abisina transformed and approached, leaving Meelah a few paces back. She put her hand on the fairy's shoulder.

"So many," Neriah sobbed. "So fast. What will become of us?"

"All the work we've been doing—this is why," Abisina said. "The whole land is diseased. We're all living behind walls and boundaries when we should be joined together."

"It hasn't worked! The centaurs, the dwarves—they are not joining us. You have failed, Abisina."

"As I always said she would."

Abisina looked up.

Reava stood on the edge of the boundary forest, curly black hair hanging past her waist, blue eyes glinting, hands on her hips. Four large fairies surrounded her, with arrows trained on Abisina and Meelah.

Neriah got to her feet, wiping her eyes. "I am sorry, Abisina," she said. "We have to take you to the Mother now."

# CHAPTER XVII

ABISINA STARED AT NERIAH. "THE MOTHER?"

Reava laughed.

"Quiet!" Neriah commanded. "This will be easier if you do not fight, Abisina. Take her sword and her bow," she said to the other fairies.

"Neriah! You can't do this!" Abisina shouted.

"One of you bring the child," Neriah said tersely, and turned to the trees, which parted at her approach. Meelah fought like a cat, kicking and scratching, landing a strong blow on one fairy's mouth with her good arm before another fairy grabbed her from behind. Abisina transformed and reared, slashing out with her hooves at one of the guards, but the fairy jumped aside before she could strike.

She heard a bow go taut, and Reava said, "Keep fighting, Abisina, and two arrows will fly right into her chest."

Abisina landed hard. One fairy held Meelah while two

others had arrows trained on her. Another had an arrow on Abisina.

"Fine," she said through clenched teeth. "I won't fight, but Meelah rides."

At a nod from Neriah, a fairy placed Meelah on Abisina's back. Neriah led the way, followed by Reava. Two fairy guards walked on either side of Abisina, arrows ready, and two more brought up the rear.

The trees parted easily as they walked through the boundary, threading their way carefully around trees that had fallen against others. Abisina was hardly aware of her surroundings. She watched Reava in front of her. She was not wearing the crown.

*Another lie.*

There had been so many! Neriah's claims about the necklace; her knowledge of events in the Motherland, though she had said she'd had no messages from her birds; her strange vacillation between the almost friend Abisina recognized and the commanding, remote heir of the Fairy Mother.

*We were friends!* Abisina wanted to cry out. *She sent me the necklace, brought me the box. She saved me at the Cairn and with the eels. I would never have gotten out of that cave if she hadn't been there.*

*She was bringing me here,* Abisina realized. *But why? The necklace? Why not just take it?* The Mother needed her for something. That was the only explanation. She blinked away her tears. She had to be on her guard.

They walked for more than an hour before the trees

opened up, the slender trunks and bare branches of beech, aspen, and birch replacing the thick trunks and heavy evergreen foliage of the boundary. Ahead, Abisina could make out the silhouettes of the fairy houses high in the trees: woven of twigs, like huge beehives, dark against the red sky. They headed away from the houses, to the east. *To meet Lohring,* Abisina thought. *The Mother.*

*When did Neriah stop helping me and start using me?* Abisina wondered. *Or was she always using me?*

Neriah stopped. "Here we separate," she said. "Meelah will join her folk. I will bring Abisina to the Mother."

"No!" Abisina cried. "Meelah stays with me."

"We will not harm her. She will be with Findlay."

"You *knew* Findlay was here?" Somehow this, of all Neriah's betrayals, was the worst.

"I did not know for certain until a few days ago. By then we were already going to the Motherland."

"The Mother has been sending you birds this whole time. You knew Watersmeet was deserted, that the folk were here, and you said nothing." Abisina stared into the fairy's eyes— the eyes flecked with brown rather than the blue of the other fairies'. Like a Vranian, Abisina had fallen prey to prejudice. Neriah looked like her; therefore she must *be* like her. Abisina couldn't believe she still hadn't learned her lesson.

"Do you think I planned to be attacked by those—those *things* under Watersmeet? Yes, I have been supporting the Mother, the fairies, trying to bring you here. But there is much I did not know. The boundary trees! I learned about them from Erith, like you. Please try to understand, Abisina. *These* are my folk." She gestured to Reava and the other fairies. "Like the folk of Watersmeet are yours."

"Your pain is touching, Sister," Reava cut in. "But the Mother is waiting for the shape-shifter." Reava pointed to the guards. "Take this girl to the enclosure. We can handle the shape-shifter."

"Meelah's hurt," Abisina said. "She needs a healer. A *Watersmeet* healer." Abisina parroted Meelah's words.

Neriah flinched. "The fairies want the folk of Watersmeet healthy," she said. "It is in our interest, too."

Neriah's discomfort—even hurt—surprised Abisina. "If it's in your *interest*, I can believe you," she said.

Meelah slid off Abisina's back, and Abisina transformed and pulled the girl to her. "Go to Findlay," she said. "It's going to be all right . . . somehow." Meelah clung to her, shaking.

"Go," Reava ordered.

Abisina watched as the guards led Meelah off through the dark trees. She looked frail next to the large somber fairies. Abisina remembered her young friend Thaula, left in Newlyn. Like Meelah, she was small and struggling to survive. But she fought as if she were mighty. Abisina straightened her shoulders. These two girls—Thaula and Meelah—one a Vranian, one from Watersmeet—*they* were Seldara. And they deserved whatever fight Abisina had left in her.

"This way, shape-shifter," Reava said.

Abisina turned away from Meelah and followed the sisters to their mother.

Neriah led them on a zigzagging path that Abisina could never retrace. *Which is the point.* For all her resolve, Abisina was sore and weak. She stumbled once but caught herself before she fell.

Neriah noticed. "You have not eaten since morning, Abisina. There will be food at the Mother's."

Abisina said nothing, but when they resumed their walk, Neriah took a straighter path. They stopped in front of an enormous tree that blazed in the night as if each branch, twig, and leaf were on fire. Among the branches, Abisina saw turrets and towers, arches and doorways—a palace built with woven twigs like the fairy houses. The tree that cradled this castle was an oak—the first one Abisina had seen in the Motherland. With massive girth, towering height, and wide-spreading branches, the oak had to be hundreds and hundreds of years old. Had the Green Man given the fairies this tree, too? Was it dying?

Neriah led Abisina to a ladder that disappeared into the oak's branches, but this was not a ladder like the ones from Abisina's last trip to the Motherland: it was strong enough to hold her weight, as was the floor of the room they climbed into. Clearly the room was built to receive nonfairy guests. Had her father come here on his trips to the Motherland?

The room was spacious. On the ceiling, woven branches of varying colors created an image of a fairy standing on a treetop, wind whipping her long hair, staring coldly into the distance. *Not designed to put visitors at ease,* Abisina thought.

Except for a small table, chair, and candle sconces, the room was empty. Someone had put bowls of fruit, nuts and berries, a loaf of bread, and a pitcher of water on the table. "Abisina, you must eat," Neriah said.

Abisina considered refusing. She didn't want any kindness from Neriah, but she had no idea when she might eat again.

Once Abisina had eaten, some of the heaviness in her limbs was gone, and her head cleared. She stood up and faced Reava and Neriah.

"Do you need to rest?" Neriah asked.

"I'm ready to talk to the Fairy Mother," Abisina said. She would not give them the satisfaction of her anger or her fear.

"Yes, but if you need to rest first—"

"I'm ready now. I would like to return to my folk as soon as possible."

Reava began to speak, but Neriah cut her off. "The Mother is ready. Reava?"

Reava leapt up through a hole in the ceiling. Neriah and Abisina were left in silence.

Neriah spoke first. "Abisina, you must understand. I—"

"I understand." Abisina didn't intend to speak, but the words tumbled out. "'The crown means nothing!' you said. And all the time—"

"I didn't do this for the crown! I had no choice. Your folk left me with no choice."

"*My* folk?"

"After I sent you the necklace, I came back to the Motherland."

"So it wasn't Glynholly who'd sent it. And you were never exiled. More lies."

"I don't know who sent it. It came on my kestrel, and I sent it on to you. I came back from Newlyn full of your story of unity and togetherness, ready to show Vran's letter to my mother, to convince her to stop building the wall." Her tone grew bitter. "The Mother punished me at once for sending you the necklace. I lost the crown. That was true, though Reava didn't get it. The Mother wanted the necklace—and you. I refused to help her. She shut me up here for weeks." Neriah stared around her as if they stood in a dungeon. "But then I learned the truth about Watersmeet. They don't want unity! That's the real lie. I thought you were like them, but on this journey I realized that you are as naive as I was. This world is full of anger, hatred, and death, Abisina. Unity?" A bark of harsh laughter. "That's the biggest lie of all."

"That's not true! My father—Vigar—they built Watersmeet, brought the folk together! They're not like the Vranians! The Watersmeet folk—they've lost their way, but—"

"Lost their way?" Neriah's voice rose, close to hysterical. "They're murderers, Abisina! They kill innocent children!"

"No! I don't know—"

"They killed my cousins—two of them! The fairies have done everything, risked everything to save our children. But *your* folk slaughtered them."

"That isn't true, Neriah!"

"I saw them myself!" Neriah seemed to tower over Abisina. "My cousins wanted to see the wall, and my aunt"—she laughed again with no humor—"she is too indulgent. She took them, heavily guarded. Überwolves and centaurs attacked the wall. Our guards tried to protect *your* dwarves. While we shot the wolves and centaurs, other Watersmeet folk took the fairy children and slit their throats."

"No. They wouldn't do that!" Abisina insisted. "They'd never kill children."

"I *saw* their bodies!"

"It—it can't be true," Abisina said. But she heard Erith calling her a traitor when she'd said she would go to the fairies, heard Meelah's words the night that she and Neriah arrived at her door: "I've lost everything to the fairies. Let her die." Could this hatred become a willingness to punish, to kill? *Even children?*

Reava dropped through the ceiling and landed between them. "The Mother is coming." Three more fairies dropped in after her.

Neriah paced away, only turning back when the Mother leapt from the ceiling.

The Mother wore her Obrium crown, much larger than the circlet of leaves Neriah had once worn. She was a striking figure: her light eyes stood out against her midnight skin; silver streaks wove through her ebony hair; and her proud bearing spoke of her power and expectation of obedience.

"We are together again, Rueshlan's daughter," Lohring

said. "You have continued to dream of unity among the folk of this land—I understand you have decided to call it Seldara now?" She paused. "I have pursued the only solution for the fairies: control of the north. The Mother before me was willing to ally with Rueshlan and Watersmeet—a sentiment I understood when I was young. But facing the Worm and becoming Mother changed my perspective." Her eyes were on Abisina.

"You have something I need," she went on. Abisina's hand twitched, wanting to reach up and touch the necklace. The Mother saw. "Do not worry, Abisina. You have given nothing away. I know you wear the necklace." She glanced at Neriah, who studied the ground. "My daughter paid with her crown, but she has done well in bringing you here. It has not gone as we planned, has it, Neriah? We sent the rift birds to bring you here. We didn't expect the naiads."

"You—you can control the leviathan-birds?" Abisina gasped.

"It is not easy, and it gets harder each day. But yes, we had sent them after you at the Great River."

Abisina remembered Neriah's insistence that they go west. "You sent them to Watersmeet, too."

The Fairy Mother smiled in agreement.

"Why? You need Watersmeet! The folk are building your wall!"

"From the beginning we intended to keep Watersmeet from holding equal power in the north. The war with the Worm cost us too many lives. If we cannot ensure the survival of our children, the fairies face extinction. I will not let that happen."

"Watersmeet wants the fairies to survive!" Abisina protested.

"I do not care what Watersmeet wants. My concern is the Motherland. I could not have you spread that story of Vran and Vigar's relationship, convincing others of your dream of a united land. We burned Vran's letter. I planned to gather all those who supported you here where I could control them. I used the birds to be sure that your friends did not make it to the garden. The birds forced them to cross the Obruns at the Cleft. I sent Neriah after you, and she sent birds telling us that Corlin was captured and—who was the other?"

"Jorno," Neriah supplied.

"Yes, Jorno. The chaos of the south took care of him, and the dwarf—well, the letter was found in an Obrium box. Who would believe a dwarf when there's Obrium involved? I know now that I overestimated the threat of the letter. From what Neriah has told me, the south is no more interested in your plans than we are. Still, I have not forgotten your victory at Newlyn. You *do* have a power, Abisina. I see your father in you. And with the necklace . . . well, I thought it best to bring you to me."

"Why let me live?" Abisina asked. "Neriah could have killed me so many times! Instead, she worked to save me!"

"I wanted you alive. I thought I might need you to control your folk. But our situation has changed. When the boundary trees began to fail, I knew the wall would not be enough to protect us. We can no longer stay in—Seldara."

"What are you saying?" Neriah stared at her mother. "Leave the Motherland? The wall has been built; Watersmeet is destroyed. The wolves are starving to death, and *we* have the birds. Even without our trees, what threat is left?"

"The mountain," Abisina said.

Lohring nodded. "Across this land, the gifts of the Green Man are dying: the Seldars, the Sylvyads, our boundary trees. The rift birds are shaking off our control. We've lost two entirely. This afternoon I needed all of my power and Reava's to get the three we have left to go after those wolves without also attacking you." She touched Neriah's cheek, while Reava glared.

"My eagles have shown me three armies moving to the wall," the Mother continued. "Icksyon leads herds of centaurs; the Vranians have left their remaining village; dwarves have emerged from Stonedun. What drives them with such purpose and speed to our wall in the north? I cannot say. *Something* is there, something is forcing these armies this way. By the new moon, the armies will converge. They will pull down the wall and come north. But they will not find the fairies here. We will be out of this land, and safe from whatever the rift has sent."

"Mother, where will we go?" Neriah asked.

"The Fens, deadly to all our enemies, will be our savior. While other creatures would drown in the mud and marsh, we fairies can skip across on blades of grass. And that's why

I still need your folk," the Mother said to Abisina. "I need them to protect us—particularly our children—as we make the journey from the Motherland to the Fens. Once we're there, you may have them, Abisina. They may follow you as they would not follow Glynholly. Of course, you will not have the necklace."

Now Abisina's hand went to her throat.

"The necklace was nothing while Glynholly wore it. In fact, the foolish faun removed it each night. She knew she was an imposter, and the cold black thing constantly reminded her of that. She would have stopped wearing it altogether, but Reava forced her. It kept the folk listening to her. One of your supporters slipped into the faun's room at night, replaced the real necklace with an iron one. I assume the moment you put on the necklace it returned to its former luster."

"Yes! In Watersmeet—" Neriah started.

"We will discuss it later, Neriah." The Mother cut her off. "Once we get to the Fens. And then, I hope, *you* can show me what the necklace can do."

"Me?" Neriah looked startled.

"Her?" Reava shouted. "Mother, you said I could have it!"

"Reava, it would lose its power as quickly on you as it did on the faun," the Mother said dismissively.

"I am nothing like Glynholly!" Reava declared. "You did not give me the crown, but you promised—"

The Mother simply raised a hand, and her daughter fell silent.

*She uses them against each other,* Abisina realized. *And they dance to whatever music she plays.*

"You are Rueshlan's heir," Lohring said to Abisina, leaning close until her lips almost touched Abisina's cheek. "But Rueshlan," she whispered, hot breath against Abisina's face, "has another daughter."

# CHAPTER XVIII

ABISINA JERKED AWAY FROM THE MOTHER. "WHAT ARE YOU saying?"

"What daughter?" Reava cried, but the Mother ignored her. She went to Neriah and took her hand.

"Think, Neriah. Rueshlan's other daughter! His *older* daughter! Another heir who could wield the necklace more powerfully than the shape-shifter ever could. Because this second daughter is a *fairy*."

It all made sense to Abisina. Neriah's straighter hair, brown eyes, love for the Seldars. Abisina's feeling that Neriah was like her.

"Rueshlan was my father?" Neriah said, eyes wide.

"Rueshlan loved *you*?" Abisina stared at Lohring.

"Ah, poor Abisina," Lohring crooned. "She thought her own mother was Rueshlan's true love. But he loved me, too—long ago. I shared his ideals then. I pushed *my* mother to build a relationship with Watersmeet, though by the time we needed their help, Rueshlan had long spurned me, and I had spurned his ideals."

"How could you keep this from me?" Neriah said.

"Neriah, I want you to have the crown. If you are to be Mother, you must think like a fairy."

"Mother!" Reava shouted.

"Your desire to know your father—it is not the fairy way," Lohring said without a glance at Reava. "Your sister does not know her father. It is the *mother* who matters! You have done well these last months, Neriah." Lohring's voice was soft. "You have shown you can devote yourself to the fairies. And now we have this!" Lohring turned back to Abisina and reached for the necklace. Abisina didn't struggle. The Mother lifted the Obrium chain over her head.

Lohring caressed the necklace before she placed it on Neriah, letting the pendant settle on her daughter's chest. "We need this, Neriah," she said fervently. "The Fens are our answer, but the way will not be easy. *This* can help us!"

Neriah picked up the pendant and stared at it—the strands of Obrium woven together.

*It represents Watersmeet!* Abisina thought. *It represents my destiny.*

But who had told her that?

Vigar implied it. Rueshlan, too. He had refused the necklace when Abisina offered it back to him. He had said he wanted her to have it. That did not prove she was *meant* to have it.

"Can you feel its power, Neriah?" the Mother asked.

Neriah's eyes flicked to Abisina's. "Yes, Mother," she said. "Yes, it's . . . alive." She dropped the necklace quickly beneath her shirt.

*She's lying.* In the glimpse Abisina had caught of the pendant, it had already dulled.

"I *am* like you, Mother," Neriah said. "When you need me, I will have the strength to lead the fairies."

Reava stepped forward. Her fists were clenched, her movements stiff.

The circlet of Obrium leaves must have been hidden in the folds of Lohring's coat, because she now had it in her hands. Neriah trembled as her mother placed it on her head.

*Neriah said the crown didn't matter.*

"Reava," the Mother said, never taking her eyes off Neriah, "take Abisina to her folk. We leave for the Fens in the morning."

Abisina could see the rage flowing through the fairy: her shoulders hunched, her arms and legs shook, her beautiful, smooth face bent into an ugly grimace. And then Reava controlled herself. She straightened, gave a quick bow to the Mother, and grabbed Abisina's arm. "This way, shape-shifter," she said.

Reava didn't bother to take a circuitous route away from the Mother's house. It took all of Abisina's effort to keep up. Reava muttered to herself as she hurried along.

". . . promised me," Reava hissed. ". . . I stayed with Glynholly despite . . . After what I have done for her . . ." The fairy's voice dropped, then rose again. "She did not see their faces!"

The fairy started to sob. "They expected me to save them . . . begged me. So much blood . . . They were *children*. . . ."

Abisina's foot jammed on a root, and she sprawled at Reava's feet.

"Get up!" Reava screamed.

Abisina got to her knees, tasting blood. But no pain could drive Reava's words from her mind. "She had *you* kill the children?"

Reava's foot caught Abisina under the chin and sent her crashing backward. Then she was in Abisina's face, hissing and spitting as if she was choking on her anger. "You listen to me, shape-shifter!" Reava slapped Abisina hard. "Whatever the Mother does—whatever I do at her command—it has to be done—to save us! She *will* give me the crown! She needs Neriah for now. But she will make good on her promise to me!" She slapped Abisina again, and warm blood dripped from Abisina's nose. "It was necessary!" With a final slap, Reava stood, breathing roughly. "Now get up," she said.

Abisina rose slowly, wiping the blood from her nose and mouth, keeping a wary eye on Reava's twitching foot.

"I would kill you now, but the Mother may need you." Reava drew a dagger from her belt, and Abisina tensed. "In front of me!" Reava snapped. The sharp point of the dagger pierced the back of Abisina's tunic, but Reava did not push the point any farther. "Walk!" She thrust Abisina forward.

Abisina stumbled on until, without warning, Reava shoved her at a solid line of trees. *The boundary forest!* she thought, and shielded her face. The trees shifted. The ground rushed up to meet Abisina, and the trees snapped together with a loud *crack!*

Abisina lay still, relishing the cold snow on her aching face. When nothing else happened, she lifted her head.

A row of trunks surrounded her. Pressing her face to the narrow gap between the trees, she saw more trunks. The Mother had said to bring her to the Watersmeet folk, but she was alone. *Reava wouldn't give me that comfort.*

"Hello?" The voice was low and weak. "Is someone there?"

"Yes," Abisina whispered back. "Are you from Watersmeet?"

"Abisina?"

"Yes! It's me!" she called. "Who's there?"

At first no one responded, and Abisina panicked. Was this a trick of the fairies? Then, finally: "It's me, Glynholly."

"Glynholly! Are you all right? Where are you? Are the folk with you?"

"Some . . . We're held in a pen. Like animals."

"I'm in a pen, too. Is there any way between the trees?" Abisina stuffed her fingers in the cracks between the trees and tried to pull them apart. She only managed to make her hands bleed.

"Do you . . . have the necklace?"

"Not anymore," Abisina said, sinking to her knees. "The Mother took it."

Glynholly's laughter sounded like a cry of pain. "It will do her no good. She is no Keeper. And neither was I. I knew I was a pretender—from the moment I put on the necklace."

Glynholly paused. "It was yours, Abisina. I'm—I'm sorry I saw that so late. Neiall sent it to you. He never wavered. I wish it had been me . . . but my pride blinded me—until I saw the rest of the folk, saw Breide. . . ." Glynholly's voice faded away.

"What happened to Breide?"

With a deep sigh, Glynholly continued: "Reava brought us here. She said the Mother would help us, protect us. We met up with dwarves from the wall. They were injured, half-starved. The fairies kept them working night and day. Breide was bent over like an old woman. Dragging her left leg. It was mangled. She'll never walk without pain.

"At the end, when so much of Watersmeet had turned against me, Breide still invited me to eat her stews, to join the folk always gathered at her hearth. Breide's house was the one place that Watersmeet felt whole again. Watching her struggle to take a step, I saw for the first time what we had become. It was too late. The folk were scattered and weak. I tried to do right, Abisina," Glynholly pleaded from the darkness. "The überwolves and the refugees threatened to destroy the home I loved. Now the überwolves are dying off. The refugees have been killed or have joined with us—we are all so desperate. The problems I worried about are solved—but so many more have replaced them. Watersmeet is gone. Abisina, I don't know how to apologize. . . ."

"Glynholly, please." Abisina's voice shook. "I have done no better."

The dark silence pressed around them.

"Is Findlay with you?" Abisina asked.

The answer seemed to come to her from across an eternity: "Yes. He's with Meelah."

Something in Glynholly's tone made Abisina shiver. "Is he—is he all right?"

"Y—Yes," Glynholly said, and her hesitation increased Abisina's dread.

"Can I speak to him?"

Another frightening pause before Glynholly said: "I'll see if he'll leave Meelah."

"What's wrong with Meelah?" Abisina asked, but Glynholly didn't answer.

Abisina crawled as close to the trees as she could. She touched the green waist-cord in her pocket.

The shadows behind the trees shifted, and Abisina knew he was there.

"Fin?"

"Yes."

One word. It chilled her more than Glynholly's despair.

"Fin, what is it? Are you all right? Is Meelah?"

He said nothing. Then, "I need to get back to my sister."

"Was her wolf bite worse than I thought? Has a healer—"

"You want to know how she is?" His voice was so hard, so cold. "She watched our mother die. She nursed her alone while überwolves prowled in our ward. She starved herself. And where was I?"

*With me.*

"I—I got caught up in the cause," he went on. "I went south sure that we could save Newlyn—and save Watersmeet. I thought we were on some great adventure! But while I helped people I hardly knew, my home, my family, everything that mattered to me was destroyed. Meelah is all I have left, and I will do whatever I can to protect her—as I should have all along."

Findlay's words were like a sword slicing away Abisina's illusions. She'd thought she understood how different her life had been from Findlay's. Now she realized that she had only *known* that the differences were there. She hadn't understood what they meant.

She had lived through things Findlay could hardly imagine: she had seen children chase their mother—accused of some imagined crime—out of the protection of the village. She had seen innocent babes—guilty of having dark eyes or being a girl or exposing birthmarks their mothers had not managed to hide—left to die outside the village walls. She had seen the one Vranian girl who tried to befriend her beaten to death for suggesting that widows had a right to eat the food they helped grow. She had watched her own mother pulled from the wall by a murderous mob.

While Abisina had fought for survival in Vranille, Findlay had known the warmth, love, and support of Watersmeet. He was brave, honorable, and loving—and unprepared for the hatred and violence that surrounded him now.

"Fin," she said numbly, "go to Meelah. She needs you. Before your mother died, I told her that you would be with

Meelah soon. You can do what she wanted." It was the only comfort she could offer him.

"What are you going to do?" Findlay said, his voice softer.

*I don't know, Fin!* she wanted to cry. Instead she said, "I have a plan. Please don't worry about me. It's your sister who needs you."

"I'm sorry, Abisina." His voice broke.

Abisina heard him move away. She had no tears. She was empty.

But after a time, a horrible anger grew in her chest. She had been tricked into a beautiful belief that she, of all the folk, should have seen through. She had been so desperate to put her past behind her, she had followed a dream. The dream had led her to Watersmeet—to Rueshlan and to Vigar.

*Father! Vigar!* she cried in her head. *You made me believe unity was possible! Look at Watersmeet now! I should have known! In peace and plenty, unity might be possible. In danger and conflict, it gets ripped to shreds.*

*You fed me these illusions. Where are you now?*

Her anger consumed her. She had lost everything: her father, her mother, her dreams of a future with Findlay, her best friends, her home.

She had been alone before. But after three years of feeling that she belonged, that she could be loved, being alone was so much worse—*Vigar said that the wearers of the necklace would always be with me. Where are they?*

*Vigar, I was in your garden, and you weren't there! I've stood in your groves, Father, waiting.*

She blamed Rueshlan and Vigar, but the other folk hadn't followed only *them*. They had followed *her*. How much had her own desires cost Watersmeet?

*I pretended I didn't want it, that I didn't believe in this special destiny. But really I wanted to believe that there were "signs" pointing to me. How greedily I read Vigar's papers, finding myself in every line. When I found the name Imara and knew I was a descendant of Vigar's people, I was so proud. It was proof I was her heir. But Vigar's had thousands of heirs. Little Thaula back in Newlyn is as much Vigar's heir as I am. She, too, has green eyes. Every time the necklace sparkled, I saw proof of my power. Now it's gone, and I'm alone again.*

*Deceptions and dreams,* she realized. *That's all Seldara was. It's time to face reality.*

# CHAPTER XIX

ABISINA LAY IN THE SNOW, FOCUSING ON THE COLD AT HER back, the dark above her, the ache in her feet, legs, and nose—those were *real*. Her senses, her body—she had to rely on them.

A voice came out of the darkness.

"Abisina?"

She didn't answer.

"Abisina?" A little louder.

Images came to her: curly dark hair framing a beautiful, dark face.

"Elodie?" The name was dragged out of her.

"Thank Vigar! You *are* alive."

"Yes," she said, because she was. That was real.

"We were so worried about you!"

"And I was worried about you." She had been.

"Please understand about Findlay, Abisina. He's been through so much. He didn't tell me all that he said, but—well, I'm sure he didn't mean it. He loves you, Abisina!"

She had felt his arms around her, his lips on hers. Her skin had tingled beneath his touch. She had felt his absence—like she had felt the absence of her toe, long after Icksyon had taken it. And she had longed for him—the pressure in the center of her chest which had come so often on the journey north. But didn't that only mean she loved *him*? How could she know if he loved *her*?

"Abisina!" Elodie's sharp tone startled her.

"Yes," she said. She *was* Abisina.

"Are you all right? You don't sound like yourself."

She frowned. This was an impossible question. She answered Elodie with what she was sure of: "I'm tired. Hungry. Most of my body aches."

Elodie sighed behind the trees. "I know. And we're helpless! If we knew what was next, what the Mother was going to do with us—we could plan."

"The Fairy Mother will let you out," she said mechanically. "The fairies are going to the Fens. They want the Watersmeet folk to shield them from überwolves and minotaurs and whatever else comes after them. They're leaving this land for good."

Then Abisina remembered: she could not trust the Mother.

"Let them go!" Elodie said. "The land will be better without them! Will they arm us?"

Abisina closed her eyes. A pain had started behind them. But she had been through battles and journeys and so much more with Elodie. The habit of answering her, of planning, was hard to break. And there was a logical answer to this question. Logic was like reality. "I think they must arm you," she said slowly, "if you are to protect them."

"Fine. Once we're armed, we turn on them—kill them, if we have to. They're no longer allies. Then what?"

Elodie's conclusion also seemed logical, but the Mother had said something. The ache in Abisina's head grew. "The fairies control the leviathan-birds. They will try to use them to make you go to the Fens."

Elodie gasped. "All this time? Of course! How stupid of us not to realize! They're *birds*."

"Yes."

"Will they take the birds with them when they leave?"

"I don't know. . . . Something is coming from the rift. The birds are harder to control."

"What are you talking about? And what's wrong with you?" Elodie's voice got sharper.

Abisina avoided Elodie's second question: what's wrong with you? It seemed dangerous. She described the three armies converging on the north, the Mother's belief that the land was dying. The fear about what the rift might bring.

Elodie said, "We've fought before. We'll fight again."

"It's impossible."

"What?"

She had been speaking to herself, but why not tell Elodie the truth—as no one had told her?

"It's over. Watersmeet is destroyed. We're all imprisoned. And—" She could hardly make herself speak the next words. "The Vranians captured Corlin, Elodie. We don't know if he's alive. Newlyn, too, may be in ruins. It's over," she said again.

Elodie didn't respond right away. When she did, her voice was steely. "So that's it then? You're giving up?"

"*How* can I fight, Elodie?"

"How can't you? How can you turn your back on everything we've worked for? Everything we believe in?"

She was so tired. And her head hurt so much. "All that we believed, all that we were taught, it was a lie."

"I believed no lie."

"A dream then."

"Watersmeet was *not* a dream. Newlyn was not a dream. I don't know what's happened to you, Abisina, but we need you. Lots of us are here. Friends you know and love. Findlay, Meelah, Breide, Lennan. Gilden is here, old as he is. You're going to give up on him? Let the fairies use him to keep the überwolves at bay? You owe them more than that. Whatever you may believe now, they believe in *you*. They know you have the necklace."

"I don't have the necklace. The Mother took it," Abisina whispered.

"Well—that doesn't change what you owe us. What you owe *me*."

Elodie's words hammered on Abisina's aching head. She couldn't sort through them fast enough. But she could not ignore that one word—*owe*. Abisina did owe the folk, did owe Elodie, something.

She thought of Gilden. She had met him her first night in Watersmeet. An ancient dwarf, bent with age, silver beard trailing to the floor. He wouldn't last a moment against an überwolf.

Now she didn't speak from logic or reality or dreams or wishes. She spoke from fear. "What if there is no fighting this, Elodie?"

"So?"

"But—"

"No! There is no 'but'! You said once that I can make you laugh even at the most serious times. Well, I'm not sure I can laugh now, but that doesn't keep me from hoping—however foolish those hopes might be. I hope that somehow we will survive and find a haven to continue Vigar and Rueshlan's beautiful dream—to make it real. So," Elodie said, "if you've given up, then I have to do it."

*Find a haven.* In her papers, Vigar had said that she and Vran had fled their own land to find a haven for their people. Could they do that now? Get out of this land? Away from the armies in the south and the monsters from the rift?

"There's one possibility . . ." Abisina said.

"I knew you wouldn't give up!" Elodie cried.

"It's *you* who's not giving up," Abisina warned. "I found some writing . . . of Vigar's. Something like this happened to her people. That's why they fled across the Mountains Eternal. There might be a chance like that now. You could go east— away from this land and start over."

"W—what's east?" For the first time, Elodie sounded scared.

"I don't know. It can't be worse than here. The folk must

get away as fast as they can. When the fairies give you weapons, the folk will want to fight. You have to stop them. Tell them you have a plan."

"I'll tell them *you* have a plan."

Abisina waved this away, though Elodie couldn't see her. "You'll have weapons and a head start. Once the fairies enter the Fens, go east."

"Abisina, you're talking as if you're not going!"

"The Mother will leave me here," she said.

"Then we'll come back for you."

"No!" Abisina was on her feet, pressing her cheek against a tree to get as close to her friend as she could. "Elodie—this is very important. I'm not giving up when I say we can't win. It's true! But Watersmeet can survive—if you leave." She glanced around. She could see the trunks now, distinguishable from the dark sky. Dawn was near. "The fairies will be here soon. You need to get everyone ready. And there are others," she said in a rush. "Anwyn and Erith. Neiall and his army near the Fens. Look for them and tell them to go east with you."

"What if they won't go?" Elodie said. "Neiall's sworn he will not let Watersmeet die."

"It won't die! It will survive! You need to tell him that!" There was so little time now, and so much to say. "And Elodie—one more thing. Tell Findlay—tell Findlay that I'm sorry. Tell him that I love him." She shouldn't have said it. She should have just let him go. . . .

"Abisina—" Elodie may have argued more, but a low, throbbing groan echoed around them.

"The trees are moving!" Elodie said.

The trunks around Abisina were as still as stones. "The fairies are coming! Get the folk ready! Hurry!"

"Are you sure we should leave, Abisina? There's no chance?" She sounded young and scared again.

"This is the only chance, Elodie."

"I can't leave you!"

"I'll come," Abisina said. "I'll do what I can here, then I'll find you." She didn't believe it, but Elodie needed to.

"Promise?"

"Promise."

It was enough.

"Until then—take care," Elodie whispered, and she was gone.

Abisina listened as the camp awoke. The murmur of voices—some afraid, some resigned—the rustle of cloaks, a few shouts, and then silence. Somewhere, far above the canopy of gloomy trees, the sun had risen, and the fairies had come for the folk of Watersmeet.

Then a voice spoke from within her head. *Lohring.*

"You have realized by now that you cannot come with us," the Mother said. "Neriah is having second thoughts about the necklace. She owes you a debt, she says."

"I saved her," Abisina whispered.

"That is why I cannot kill you. I will leave you here among the trees. The forest is dying, but it will outlive *you.* Still—"

An unbearable pain ripped through Abisina's skull.

# CHAPTER XX

HOW MUCH TIME HAD PASSED? ABISINA CRACKED OPEN HER eyelids, checked the angle of the sunlight. Afternoon. *Of the same day?* She was thirsty, hungry, and tired, but she forced herself onto her knees—she didn't think she could stand yet—and pried her eyes open.

Nothing had changed: The trees encircled her, the trunks unmoving. Bare branches rattled in the wind. She sank back onto the snow. Her clothes were damp. She would freeze to death if the temperatures went lower. "You were supposed to kill me," she said, her voice deadened by the quiet around her.

If she could stay warm, she could survive three days with no water. If she was lucky enough to get a thaw, she could drink the melting snow. The spring equinox was days away, but the cold might linger in the north. If she ate the snow, the cold would kill her.

*I want death,* she thought. *Though I was hoping for a quick one.*

She lay still, watching the shadows lengthen. *I should sleep. And then the cold will take care of me. Painlessly.* She shut her eyes.

She opened them again. For all she said to Elodie, giving up did not come easily.

She stood. Despite the pain, she made her way from tree to tree to peer through the cracks.

When she had completed the circle, finding nothing new, she stopped. She didn't want to lie back down in the snow. As a centaur, her skin would be less exposed. Or she could stay human and build a snow shelter. She picked up a handful of snow, and it crumbled in her hands: too dry.

She idly wondered if one of these trees was about to come down like so many in the boundary forest. She told herself she was simply trying to pass the time as she transformed and pushed each of the trunks with her shoulder. All were solid.

Abisina turned back into a human and ran around the circle of trees to warm herself. *Why am I working to survive?* she asked as she fought to keep her feet moving.

*Because they're out there. Findlay, Meelah, Elodie—all of them.* She imagined the folk crossing the plain that surrounded the Motherland, then fighting their way through the forest to the Fens. It would take at least two weeks. *How close are the southern armies? Will they get away in time?*

*And what about those on the wall?* She stopped jogging. *I have to warn them—tell them to go east! They're my responsibility, too.*

She suddenly pitched forward. The ground was bucking

beneath her. The roots of the boundary trees boiled up. She had seen the roots break the necks of überwolves with a quick yank. Were the fairies going to kill her after all?

The ground rolled more violently, and the trees that had been so solid moments before swayed. Then, with a deep groan, two trees in front of her began to pull apart until a face peered through. The creased brow, the fingers nervously twining in the hair, the tremulous lower lip were familiar.

"Erna!" There was no one in all of Seldara who could have surprised Abisina more. Erna was one of the most timid fauns she had ever met. Erna squeaked when someone spoke to her above a whisper and cried at the possibility that someone was cross with her. She was also extremely fond of Abisina and fiercely loyal. Most remarkable of all, she had the very rare gift of communicating with trees. While all fauns had an affinity for trees, Erna could actually *talk* to them.

"Hurry!" the little faun said. "I don't know how long they'll listen to me!" She dropped her voice. "These are *not* nice trees. More room, please!" she added louder.

With cracks and pops, the trees pulled farther apart. The curly head of the faun ducked out of sight, and Abisina climbed through the opening. The second she had passed between the trees, they snapped back together with a crash.

Erna hugged Abisina. "We've been so worried about you! We must leave the forest at once." She lowered her voice again. "Some of these trees will not behave, but most will let us pass. I think I'd better ride." Abisina transformed, and two roots flew from the ground, grasped Erna under her arms, and set her on Abisina's back.

"I'm sorry we didn't come sooner," Erna said. "I refuse to travel at night. It started after that fight in Newlyn. I won't even sleep without a light!"

Abisina leapt forward, and the trees allowed them to pass. Erna called out directions to Abisina: "Left here! Now bear to the right! There's a patch of ivy that will give you trouble ahead—can you jump it?" Their path jagged this way and that, and Abisina lost track of where they were. When they broke out onto the open plain, another surprise waited for her.

Two figures stood with their backs to the boundary: a tall, blond man and a female dwarf. Each carried weapons, though they didn't need them at the moment. In front of them, roots darted back and forth, attacking a cluster of überwolves.

The man turned around as Abisina and Erna emerged. "Landry!" Abisina cried. She knew him well. His mother, Ivice, had worked with Abisina in the healing house in New-lyn, and Landry had often joined her at Abisina's hearth in the evening.

"It's good to see you." He grinned before turning back to the wolves.

The dwarf was also familiar; Prane was one of the first three dwarves that Haret had convinced to leave Stonedun to help repair Newlyn's wall.

"How—how did you get here?" Abisina managed.

"The Newlyn Council sent us," Prane said simply, "with a lot of urging from Erna."

"I don't understand." Abisina looked from one to the other.

"The south's in trouble. Theckis is mobilizing his people at Vranham," Landry said.

"And a new dwarf has appeared in Stonedun," Prane added. "He's clad from head to foot in Obrium armor, and they say he's come to return the dwarves to the ancient city that once flourished below the Obrun Mountains. They think he's Ulbert."

"Ulbert?" Abisina didn't recognize the name.

"In dwarf legend, Ulbert was the hero who discovered the Obrium Lode and started to build the Obrun City." Prane frowned. "That was over five hundred years ago. It was a *story*! And Ulbert was known as the Peacemaker, but Stonedun is preparing for war."

"The centaurs are preparing for war, too," Abisina said.

"We thought so," Landry told her. "The herds hardly bothered us as we came north."

"The Council wanted you to take Corlin's place, Abisina," Prane said. "He never came back from Vranham."

"But I told them we had to think of *Seldara*, not just Newlyn," Erna said proudly. "'The battle will be wherever Abisina is,' I said. So our army is coming north. We went on ahead to look for you and tell you help was coming."

*More folk are risking their lives.* Erna, the faun who lacked the courage to sleep without a candle, had traveled north through überwolf-infested forests and carnivorous trees to rescue Abisina from a fairy stronghold and bring an army to her aid. Landry—a former Vranian—had come to rescue someone he would have once called a demon. And while the other dwarves gathered behind an ancient hero, Prane had risked her life for Seldara. How could Abisina tell them that she had lost the necklace? That Watersmeet was destroyed? That their folk should give up on the dream?

"These other armies," she began, "I don't think we can fight them."

"So what's the plan?" Prane asked. Erna and Landry looked at Abisina expectantly.

She tried again. "The fairies have left, and they've made the folk of Watersmeet go with them as protectors, as far as the Fens. The fairies control the leviathan-birds. And I don't have the necklace anymore."

Erna gasped, but Abisina hurried on. "I've told the Watersmeet folk to go east—away from this land—once the fairies release them. You should go, too. It's the only way anyone will survive."

"We can't leave our folk!" Landry said. "And you'll need us."

"You don't understand," Abisina said. "We will lose this battle."

"I don't think *you* understand, Abisina," Erna said, tugging on her curls. "We believe in Seldara. So does Newlyn."

"And those at the wall will not flee," Landry said.

"You crossed at the wall?" Abisina asked. "It is down?"

"I found the gate," Prane explained. "Only a dwarf would see it—a thing of beauty. It opens only from the north side. I was searching for the trigger to open it—there wasn't one, as it turns out—when a dwarf called Alden showed up and—"

"I knew him!" Erna jumped in. "He let us through."

"Alden was there?" Abisina said. Alden was Breide's father and one of Haret's best friends.

"And Neiall," Landry said.

"Neiall was supposed to be at the Fens," Abisina told them.

"He has lots of followers with him—folk you know," Erna said.

*Thank Vigar! I can tell him to take his army east!*

"Neiall came to fight the fairies," Prane explained, "but all the fairies left the wall sometime last night."

"They're on their way to the Fens with the rest of the Motherland," Abisina said.

"The folk at the wall are readying for battle," Landry went on. "The wall is the easiest place to defend with a small force. We told them about the Vranians; they need to hold them only until the Newlyn army arrives. Then we'll have the Vranians between us!"

"The Vranians are not the only threat!" Abisina had to make them understand. "There's something from the rift—I don't know what. We have to send someone to warn Newlyn, tell them to flee!"

"We'd walk right into the arms of the Vranians," Prane said. "And those who are following us won't flee."

"You said we had to work together," Erna reminded Abisina. "We stopped at my community on the way north. My mate, Darvus—and my mother's new mate"—Erna added in a lower tone, still angry that her mother had re-mated "only" fifteen winters after her father died—"are rallying the fauns."

"Look, Abisina," Landry said. "Come to the wall. Talk to Neiall. You'll see the preparations and understand."

"We cannot leave tonight," Erna said, pointing at the darkening sky.

Abisina had no other choice. And if those at the wall refused to go east, she would join them. Delaying the enemy armies bought time for the rest of the folk to get out of Seldara.

They settled in with their backs against the boundary trees. Erna passed Abisina some bread and a portion of cheese, then dug the stump of a candle out of her bag and lit it.

"It's what we've been working for," Landry said quietly, as if he sensed Abisina's doubt. "North and south working as one."

The night grew very cold, but Erna refused to build a fire. "How long do you think the trees will support us if we burn their brothers?" she asked. Even with a fire, they wouldn't have shut their eyes. All night the überwolves attacked in wave upon wave. They were kept awake by the howls, the roots whipping through the air, and the wolves' strangled cries as the roots pulled them underground.

By dawn, not a single überwolf waited on the plain. Erna calmed the vicious roots, and they set out in patrol forma-tion. They didn't have a bow for Abisina, so Landry gave her his sword. The drifts that Abisina had waded through as she crossed the plain had hardened to mounds of slick snow and ice, too slippery to climb. They wove back and forth through the valleys, trying always to head south. For the first hour, they were left alone. Abisina knew the quiet couldn't last, so they made the best time they could, Abisina carrying Erna.

The first attack came suddenly—a pack of eight über-wolves racing down a high drift. Erna drew her dagger in a shaking hand while Abisina drew her sword, fingers longing to grip a bow. They made short work of the wolves; Landry wielded his spear so skillfully that only three wolves got close. Abisina brought down one wolf with an awkward thrust of her sword, while Prane felled the others with axe blows as powerful as Haret's.

The next attack—two packs, one from either side—came as they were hurrying toward open ground. The wolves on Abisina's side struck first. As Abisina and Prane fought, another wolf leapt over the backs of its mates, jaws open. Abisina had just stabbed a wolf and had nothing but her bare hand to ward it off. Then Erna's small blade flashed, and she caught the wolf under the chin. Erna shrieked as it fell. Abisina freed her sword and spun to protect Prane from a wolf about to sink its teeth into her shoulder. Again, Erna's blade slashed as a wolf lunged at Abisina's exposed flank. The faun didn't kill it but sent it reeling, a deep cut across its snout.

The wolf had bitten Prane on her arm. She managed to wield the axe with her other hand, but her left arm, covered with blood, dangled uselessly at her side.

Abisina transformed and dropped Erna. Then she and

Landry moved so that they stood back to back, with Prane and Erna in the middle.

"Help Prane!" Abisina shouted to Erna. "Bind the wound tight." She heard cloth ripping as she brought her sword down on the head of a wolf, then raked the belly of another on her counterstroke. She was getting the hang of the sword.

The wolves formed a snarling ring around the fighters.

"Now what?" Landry asked.

"They couldn't do this if we had bows!" Abisina said in frustration. "Erna, how's Prane?"

"I can speak for myself," Prane snapped. "And I'm fine."

"Her color is *not* good," Erna put in.

"Slip your knife into my belt, Erna," Abisina said softly. Überwolves did not understand speech, though their eyes missed little. Abisina felt the dagger slide into her waist-cord. "At the count of three, everyone yell. I'll throw the knife into that big male to the right. Do you see it, Landry?"

"Hard to miss the brute."

"You take the one on the left with your spear, and I'll take the smaller female to its right. Prane and Erna, head for the drift. Landry and I will keep the wolves busy. Got it?" Landry grumbled his agreement, and Abisina started the count. "One . . ."—she put her sword into her left hand—". . . two . . ."—she grasped the dagger with her right—". . . three!" She let the dagger fly as the big wolf lunged. Her dagger flew past its head. Then the wolf was down. Abisina just had time to register the arrow in its chest before she turned her sword on the next target.

"Watersmeet!" came the cry from behind them. Several more wolves fell beneath a volley of arrows. The rest were in retreat.

Three figures stood on the drift above them: A red-haired dwarf who Abisina recognized as Alden; Alden's brother, Waite; and, in the center, a thin man with long white hair and equally white skin. As his eyes met Abisina's, the man smiled.

"I wasn't sure I'd ever see you again," he said.

Abisina couldn't help but smile back. "It's good to see you, too, Neiall."

# CHAPTER XXI

NEIALL THUMPED LANDRY ON THE BACK AND GRINNED AT Prane. When Neiall smiled, it was clear that despite his white hair, he was only a little older than Abisina. "I shouldn't have doubted, but I didn't think you could do it, Abisina—transform a Vranian village. These three told me how much you'd accomplished. I should have expected it. You're Rueshlan's daughter!"

Abisina met Neiall's smile, but inside she quailed. How could she convince him that, unlike her father, she could not save Watersmeet? That the only option left was to flee?

Alden and Waite slid down the drift. They welcomed Abisina heartily and asked about those taken to the Motherland.

"Glynholly told me about Breide's injury, Alden. I'm so sorry," she said.

The dwarf coughed gruffly. "Breide's tough. They have Lennan with them. He'll heal her."

"How do we get them out?" Neiall asked, gripping his sword.

"They're not there anymore." Abisina explained what was happening. "Once the fairies get to the Fens, they'll cross them and leave this land. And . . ." She took a deep breath. "And I told our folk to do the same, flee east, once the fairies leave. It's what you and the folk at the wall should do. Get out of this land. It's the only chance for survival."

Neiall brushed this aside. "They'll never go—any more than we would. Findlay? Leave Watersmeet? Leave *you*?"

Abisina's face grew hot. "Findlay blames himself for his mother's death. He thinks only of Meelah now."

"Findlay was serving Watersmeet, Rueshlan, and Vigar," Neiall said. "We all would have done the same. Some have forgotten what Watersmeet is, but *we* remember. And now we have you!" He put a hand on Abisina's shoulder. "The folk headed to the Fens—the instant the fairies leave, they'll turn back for the wall. You'll see."

Abisina shook her head but didn't argue. She expected this from Neiall. *He'll stay and fight,* she thought.

"We need to get going," Waite interrupted, "if we plan to make it back before dark."

"Right," Neiall agreed. "Waite, why don't you and Alden take the rear guard, while Landry takes the front." He looked at Prane's bloody arm.

"I'm fine," the dwarf insisted, though her face was drawn.

"I'll carry you," Abisina offered.

"It's true then?" Neiall asked eagerly. "I was afraid to believe it, but you *are* a shape-shifter?"

"It's true," Abisina said. "I don't know how much difference it will make."

"It will make all the difference," he said.

Abisina transformed. Alden gaped, and Waite gave a low whistle. Neiall raised his arms and whooped. "It's like Rueshlan's returned to us!"

Prane was not impressed. Like all dwarves, she preferred to be on the ground, and it took a lot of coaxing to get her onto Abisina's back.

As they set out for the far trees, Abisina prodded Neiall to tell her about the wall. He didn't deny that the situation was dire, but it wasn't as bad as Abisina had expected.

"We have about fifty dwarves and twenty more folk sent as guards: fauns and humans. Centaurs can't make it to the top of the wall. By the time I got to the wall, I had about three hundred and fifty with me."

"So many!"

"We told you, Abisina!" Erna chirped from her back.

"Fifty have been working with me since—well, since you were exiled," Neiall continued. "More joined through the months of Glynholly's and Reava's madness." He broke off. "You would not have recognized what Watersmeet had become!" He had to command his emotions before going on. "Some of those with me are refugees. We met up with another fifty or so down near the mountains. They had a vague plan for living in caves, but when I explained that my force was headed to the wall to release the dwarves, they came with me."

"Over four hundred," Abisina calculated.

"You can fit twenty-five on the wall at a time," Neiall said. "Thirty if you don't care about them using bows or swords. Mind you, the enemy can come at us with only twenty-five at a time—more like twenty if they've got centaurs—"

"They will," Abisina cut in. "I heard it from the Mother. Icksyon's herds will join this fight."

Neiall shrugged. "I assumed they would. Centaurs will be useful for bringing down the wall. As the dwarves will tell you, no wall will hold forever. And this one has a huge flaw. Once their fairy captors began to mistreat them, the dwarves sabotaged it. The final third—the western end—is little more than a facade."

"The dwarves *wanted* the wall."

"At first, but the fairies made clear that the pact with Watersmeet was a sham. The dwarves figured their lives would be worth nothing once they finished building. The only way to fight back was revenge. By weakening the wall, they'd take down some fairies with them."

"And to think I went to the fairies in the first place!" Abisina said bitterly.

"You were right to try." Neiall stopped and laid a hand on her arm. "If anyone could have brought the fairies into an alliance, it was you."

Abisina gave a rueful smile. "You tried to warn me. You said that only Rueshlan had a connection to the fairies. You were right. The Mother wanted to be the only power in the north."

They resumed walking. "When word came that the rest of the folk had abandoned Watersmeet, the dwarves changed their plans," Neiall said. "If all of Watersmeet rose up, there was a chance they could defeat the fairies. The dwarves figured they would need the wall to keep the southerners out, so they've started to reinforce the wall's weak section."

"I thought you were working *with* the refugees."

"We are! But the leaders at the wall thought—and frankly, I agreed—that we would have to compromise for the present and focus on saving the north. Before we could try to work with the south, we needed to be reasonably safe. And we had to get some food stored. All that changed when the folk from Newlyn arrived. It's what we've been working for—it's Rueshlan's vision! And now you're here—the very image of your father!" Neiall had grown loud in his excitement.

"I am not my father," Abisina said firmly.

"You have the necklace! I sent it to you."

Abisina bit her lip.

"You didn't get it?"

"I did," Abisina said. "The Mother took it. It seems . . ." She glanced back to Erna and Prane. Prane had nodded off, but Erna was listening. Abisina decided there was no point in keeping secrets. "It seems Neriah is my half sister—"

"What?" Neiall's cry startled the others. Prane mumbled in her sleep.

"She is Rueshlan's older daughter," Abisina said in a

lower voice. "The Mother thinks that Neriah can use the necklace."

"I thought Neriah was on our side." Neiall frowned. "I sent it right to her! The necklace responds to her?"

"I . . . I don't think so," Abisina admitted. "I saw it on her briefly. The light had started to fade. But it hardly matters. By now, the folk have seen it on Neriah. The Mother will be sure they do. They're so broken already; when they see that the fairies have the necklace, they won't return to the wall."

"They have to!" Neiall persisted. "We have a decent force at the wall. And Newlyn is on the way."

"They don't know that. They think your army's up near the Fens. They know nothing of Newlyn at all."

"They'll come back," Neiall said, as if that ended the conversation. "We just need to hold off the southern armies until Newlyn and Watersmeet arrive."

Abisina said no more. If Neiall insisted on fighting, she would fight with him. Every centaur, Vranian, or minotaur they killed, every hour they delayed the armies, would give the folk of Watersmeet a better chance to escape.

In the early afternoon, they reached the end of the plain, paused for a moment to share some food, and pushed on through the forest, hoping to reach the wall soon after nightfall.

After her father's funeral pyre, Abisina had traveled through the Green Man's Cleft, but she had noticed little on that journey. Now, she studied the Cleft closely. The road ran straight before them until it disappeared into the darkness. Sheer rock walls rose from the ground on either side of the narrow road, starting low and quickly rising to dizzying heights. In the twilight, the walls glistened as if wet, but it was the rock that shone—black, smooth, and hard.

The wind had picked up while they'd been trudging through the forest. Abisina had been relieved to get out of the chill, but she soon longed for open air. The sides of the Cleft penned her in. When she thought about a battle at the wall, she felt more confined than ever. The road was wide enough for twenty centaurs to walk abreast, but four hundred folk in full retreat . . . they'd be caught in a narrow corridor with only one way to run. Once they left the Cleft, they could regroup in the forest and fight from the protection of the trees, but getting to the trees would be tricky.

"What about an avalanche?" Abisina suggested. "Could the dwarves create one to block the road behind us after the wall falls?"

"Not enough rock up there for a full avalanche," Alden answered. "We've already brought down what loose stone we could get for the wall, though we would have rather mined for it. We did a little mining, but we didn't get too far into the ground before we hit that cursed black rock. These mountains beside us are made of it, the same rock that closed the dwarves out of the Obrun City during the earthquake."

Abisina nodded. Once, the dwarves had lived in a magnificent city below the Obrun Mountains. The precious Obrium Lode brought the dwarves wealth and power, but an earthquake hundreds of years ago had destroyed the city. The black rock of the Cleft's walls thrust the Obruns higher and made returning to the city impossible. Generations of dwarves had died trying to dig through that rock, but the rock broke their tools and defied all their stone craft.

"We've gained a new respect for the Green Man because of the Cleft," Waite said. "We grow things, of course, but we're *stone* folk. The Green Man's attention to plants—it didn't seem as important before. Now . . ." He cast an admiring glance at the walls around them. "If the Green Man cut through that rock when he'd built his Cleft—well, I want to know all I can about him."

"I wish he were here to build us a wall with that rock!" Abisina said. "I don't see any way to get out of the Cleft unless we abandon the wall *before* it falls."

"I haven't come up with anything, either," Neiall said, "but the dwarves won't go for it. Abandon stone for trees?"

Alden snorted.

"We will have no choice if the time comes," Abisina said. "This battle cannot take place in the Cleft. The sooner we fall back to the trees and set up defensive positions, the better. If we ask the dwarves to dig some trenches, they'll agree."

Neiall was smiling.

"What?" Abisina asked.

"It's like talking to your father again," he said. "Planning the next battle . . ."

Abisina stopped. She hadn't realized what she was doing. "Neiall," she said seriously, "I hope there will be no battle. I'll do everything I can to save the folk, but I will convince as many as I can to go east."

"And when they won't?"

"I'll fight," she said.

"I told you—it's like talking to your father again." He grinned.

# CHAPTER XXII

AFTER AN HOUR IN THE CLEFT, ABISINA NEEDED TO GALLOP, but once the wall was in sight, she stopped to wait for the others to catch up. Tents stood in rows on either side of the road. Campfires burned at intervals, and dark shapes sat around them. Except for a few hammers clicking against stone, the camp was silent. Beyond the array of tents was the massive wall.

"No one challenged us," Abisina said.

"There are sentries close to the tents in case of überwolves, but they fear what's coming from the south," Prane explained.

Abisina and her riders were shivering when Neiall and the others finally caught up. "Where have you been?" Abisina grumbled. Now that it was time to meet the folk, she was nervous. "We need to gather," she said. "Who is the camp leader?"

"That'd be Neiall," Waite said. "But I suspect the folk will gather quite naturally once *you* show up."

Abisina's stomach tightened. "Lead the way."

"I will *not* be carried into a gathering of dwarves!" Prane cried out. "Put me down!"

"I was going to transform," Abisina said.

"No!" Neiall protested. "They need to see you like this."

"I told you—"

"I know what you said, Abisina. You don't have the necklace. You are not your father. But they need to be reminded of him—badly."

"Fine," Abisina said.

Neiall gave Prane a hand as the dwarf jumped from Abisina's back, groaning and clutching her arm as she struck the ground.

Abisina followed Neiall into the tents, and the camp began to stir. Folk rose from their seats around the fires, heads poked out of tents, and an excited buzz spread.

A centaur named Salat approached Abisina first. She had lived near Abisina's ward and, after Rueshlan's death, had often come to visit. She extended her arm—straight, in the traditional centaur greeting. "I'd heard about you, but—" She smiled as she looked down at Abisina's legs and hooves.

Abisina grasped Salat's arm. "It's good to see you."

Then Farron approached—a faun Abisina had once argued with about the future of Watersmeet. She saw dwarves she had eaten supper with in her own house and two fauns she knew were distant cousins of Glynholly. Soon Abisina stood in the center of a crowd, clasping hands, embracing, calling out greetings to those she knew or recognized. She hadn't expected their joy at seeing her, or her comfort in seeing them. *I will not be with them for long,* she reminded herself. *I must convince them to go.* But she was with them for now.

A whistle cut through the greetings. "Are we all here, then?" Neiall called. "It's time to gather, now that Rueshlan's daughter is back among us."

"Hi-yah!" the crowd responded in unison, their cry echoing off the Cleft.

Abisina held up her hands to stop them. Neiall ignored her: "Rueshlan's daughter!"

"Hi-yah!"

Then, with a wink at Abisina, he cried: "Abisina!"

"Hi-yah!"

It was the traditional opening of a Watersmeet Gathering. Abisina stepped forward. "Watersmeet—"

"Hi-yah!" the crowd thundered. She gave in, letting the cheers roll over her.

"I am happy to be among friends again," she said as the cheers died down. "I wish we stood in our own Gathering place among the Sylvyads, but I thank you for your welcome." She paused. When she continued, she was grave. "We face the most serious challenge of our history. Worse than the White Worm." She paused again. All here had lost loved ones to the Worm. "I've talked to a few of those held captive in the Motherland." She explained the fairies' decision to flee and the folk's plan to go east. Whispers rippled through the crowd. "You must join the rest of our folk—your children, mothers, fathers, and friends."

"We want to fight!" someone called.

"We can't win this fight," she said.

"What will *you* do?" another voice said.

Abisina had worried about this question. "I will stay," she said, and the silence erupted into cries. Abisina held up her hands. "Neiall tells me that some of you will want to stay. I hope he's wrong. The folk need you. We don't know what challenges lie to the east. Joining the rest of our folk is a *heroic* choice. If a few of you stay, I will fight with you. We'll give those who leave more time to get to safety."

"We cannot abandon Rueshlan's daughter!"

The crowd started to shout again.

*No! If they see me as my father, they'll think there's a chance.*

"I urge you *as Rueshlan's daughter* to go!" she cried in desperation, and the crowd quieted. "In the end, he faced the Worm alone—to save you, to save Watersmeet! Vigar created our home as a haven. You'll honor my father and Vigar by surviving!" She stopped and surveyed the faces before her. "Please. Think about what I've said. Talk to one another. You need to decide by dawn."

She stepped back, and Neiall came to her. "Can I go to your tent?" She was suddenly drained. Neiall led the way. She transformed and entered his tent as the crowd exploded into debate.

"Abisina—I need to go out there," Neiall said.

"Please, Neiall—let them make their own choices. It's what Rueshlan would have done."

————

Abisina slept for several hours and woke before dawn. The camp was silent. The folk had made their decisions.

She got up and headed to the eastern side of the wall, where she found uneven, hastily made steps. She met the first sentry—a faun she knew by sight—at the top.

"Abisina!" the faun said in surprise.

"Do you mind if I walk here?"

"Of course not. I'm alone right now. I've got my pipes, though, should anything happen." She held them up.

"They should be for dancing," Abisina said.

"They will be again."

Abisina walked out to the middle of the wall, leaned against the parapet, and stared north. Out there, somewhere, the fairies were forcing Elodie, Findlay, Meelah, Breide, and so many others to the Fens. Would any survive to go east?

*Findlay.* She called to him in her mind as she touched the waist-cord in her pocket.

She faced south. The dwarves built the wall a quarter of a league from the southern opening of the Cleft. The moon had set, and she could see nothing in the land beyond. One day's travel would take her to the plain where her father had faced the Worm.

Who had come to that plain already? The centaurs? The dwarves? The Vranians? Or whatever was coming from the rift? The Mother had said they would be assembled by the new moon. Twenty days away. How strange to know the entire compass of your life. She would cease to be in twenty days.

As a healer, Abisina had sometimes welcomed death as a relief for those whose pain and suffering could end no other way. She herself had wished for death before—countless times when she lived in Vranille. And yet, imprisoned in the Motherland, she had fought to survive; she couldn't *let* herself die, lying in the snow, waiting to freeze.

*In twenty days, it will be easy. Someone will take care of it for me. And like Vigar and my father, I will die for a good reason. I thought I would save Seldara. Perhaps my death can save a little of Watersmeet.*

Abisina paced the wall until the sky began to grow gray. She was sure she imagined it, but the growing light did not seem to penetrate the landscape south of the wall.

Finally, as the sun peeked over the horizon, she headed back to the stairs, with an understanding nod from the sentry as she passed.

Neiall met her at the bottom. "They're all waiting for you. We didn't know where you were." Two fauns hurried up the stairs, ready to take their turn as sentries.

"Is anyone staying?" Abisina asked.

"Anyone? Most!"

"Neiall—"

"I let them make their own decisions!" he insisted.

Neiall led her through the tents to a cluster of folk standing a little apart. "They're the ones who are leaving. While you say good-bye, I'll gather our leaders. They'll want to hear your plan and—Abisina?" She had stopped moving.

"*My* plan? You're the leader here."

"Not anymore," Neiall said, flashing a grin that Abisina didn't like. "They're calling you Keeper!"

"No, Neiall!" she said, almost shouting. "I will not be the Keeper! I don't even have the necklace."

"Rueshlan did not wear the necklace in his last years as Keeper. And the necklace did nothing to make Glynholly a good Keeper."

"Well, I'll say no," Abisina said. "They'll understand."

Neiall pulled her behind a tent. "No. They won't understand. They need a hero right now. They need *you*. These folk are willing to *die* beside you. With or without the necklace, you have to be the hero they need."

*He sounds like Elodie.*

Neiall looked out at the waiting crowd. "I'll leave you here to gather yourself."

Abisina tried to recall the certainty she had felt on the wall. *Like me, these folk want to fight for Watersmeet.*

"Wait, Neiall," Abisina said. "I'm ready now."

# Chapter XXIII

Twelve or thirteen humans, fauns, dwarves, and centaurs with satchels at their sides stood apart. *So few.* Neiall had said that Findlay, Elodie, and the rest of the folk now going to the Fens would never abandon Watersmeet. What if he was right? Abisina pushed the thought aside. *They must!*

"You are doing the right thing," she said as she approached the group, grasping their hands, hugging them. "You will carry on the idea of Watersmeet. Go with Vigar's blessing!"

An olive-skinned woman with short dark hair held on to Abisina's hand longer than the others. "Here," she said, thrusting a bow at her. "My husband used it until . . . Well, you need a bow, and this served him well. It's made of ash; he did the carvings himself."

Abisina took the beautiful bow in her hands and ran her fingers along the smooth wood. She tested its weight, the tension of the string. The bow seemed to be made for her. At the top and bottom, carved figures danced. They were naiads, hair flowing and mingling with swirling waves.

"Thank you," she said, embracing the woman. "The naiads have saved me before."

A crowd had surrounded those who were leaving, and Abisina left them to their good-byes.

Neiall waited for her with Alden, Waite, Farron, and Salat. There was a second faun, Kerren, and a second centaur named Ravinne.

"Northern wards," Ravinne said as she greeted Abisina in the traditional way. "I know you, of course, but I had a big family and didn't get to the southern wards often."

Prane and Landry were also there.

"I thought you needed someone from Newlyn," Landry said.

"And Stonedun," Prane added.

"Of course," Abisina agreed. "You'll know the strengths and weaknesses in the Vranian and dwarf armies."

"I can tell you about the southern fauns!" Erna squeaked, dashing up.

The group crouched on the ground, and Abisina used a dagger to sketch a diagram of the wall, the Cleft, and the forest at its entrance. A man of about thirty winters also joined their group. His blond hair, blue eyes, and fair skin marked him as a Vranian refugee.

"This is Hain," Neiall said.

Abisina stared at him, battle plans and strategies forgotten. "You're from Vranille."

Hain smiled awkwardly. "I didn't think you'd remember me," he said. "Or I hoped you wouldn't. It was, uh, not easy for you and your mother there, and I was as bad as the rest. If you want me to leave . . ."

"No," Abisina said. He was haggard, like most of the refugees, but she saw the strong jaw and slightly crooked nose that were etched in her memory. Abisina's mother had been helping Hain's wife through a long labor when the White Worm had come to Vranille.

"Sina delivered all five of my children," Hain said, looking at the ground. "She had just brought my first son into the world when the Worm came. I never thought I'd get to tell you I'm sorry—you may not believe me—but I am. Your mother was a good woman. Most of us thought so."

"Your children, Bryla"—the name of his wife came to Abisina—"did any of them . . ."

"Two made it," Hain said. "The eldest girl and my son. The fairies took them to the Motherland. I'm here for them."

"We're all here for them," Abisina said. She turned back to the leaders. It was time to tell them the plan she had begun to form as she walked through the Cleft. "I know the dwarves' stone craft is unmatched," she began.

"You don't have to flatter," Alden said. "The wall will fall. Any of those Stonedun dwarves will know after one look that the west end is weak. We've shored it up, but they'd have to be blind to miss the problems." Prane nodded in agreement.

"How long will it stand?" Abisina asked.

"With centaurs and a battering ram?" Alden scratched his beard, a gesture that made Abisina think of Haret.

"And trolls," Hain added. "We had trolls when the Worm led us." He blushed.

"With trolls, half a day at the outside," Alden said.

"A whole day! Day and a half if we're here to make it a bit more difficult," Waite said.

"They'll have leviathan-birds, too," Abisina said. Brows furrowed. Some of them had not considered the birds. "The fairies worked the dwarves hard," Abisina continued. "Do they have the strength to dig trenches where the Cleft meets the forest?"

Alden was scratching his beard. Waite answered. "Dwarves unable to dig? Never!"

Abisina had to smile. She remembered now that Waite was the younger brother, and known for being hasty. "And there's not too much of the black rock?" she asked.

"Hmm," Alden considered.

Again, Waite jumped in. "Spots of rock, but plenty of dig-gable ground."

"Good," Abisina said. "Here's what I'm thinking: Most of us will abandon the wall. The birds make it impossible to defend, but it will keep the army out for a time, and that's something. We have to plan for the moment when the army breaches the wall. The trolls will come through first, then the centaurs." She leaned over the diagram and drew an X on the western end of the wall with the dagger. "We'll keep some of our centaurs here—"

"The centaurs can't climb the wall," Kerren noted.

"They won't have to. We'll also have archers—those who are small enough for the centaurs to carry easily. The archers will do what damage they can, but once the wall starts to go, they'll retreat with the centaurs to the forest, where the rest of the folk will be waiting." She drew a line through the Cleft.

"And where we'll have dug trenches!" Waite exclaimed.

"Exactly."

"Waite," Prane said, "have you tried digging in the Cleft's floor?"

"A little. We got some of the stone for the wall from the floor," Waite said. "Why?"

"If we could dig some pits in the floor, slow them down . . ." She made a few circles on Abisina's map with her finger.

"Yes!" Waite looked as if he was going to kiss Prane. Alden was frowning at his brother.

"If there's time," Abisina said. "The Mother thought the armies would gather on Rueshlan's plain at the new moon. We need to dig trenches first. This force will be too big for us to confront in open battle."

"Until Newlyn arrives," Landry said. "Then—"

"We can design the trenches," Waite interrupted.

"What about the wall?" Prane said. "Shouldn't we work on that, too?"

"Stop talking all at once!" Abisina cried.

Silence.

"Sorry," she said. "The Keeper role is new for me. First

to Prane's point: we know the wall will fall fast. I think we should—" Neiall coughed. "What we'll do," Abisina corrected herself, "is pull the dwarves back to the forest to dig trenches and perhaps lay some traps in the Cleft itself." Prane grinned. "In terms of the trenches," Abisina went on, "I don't pretend to advise dwarves about digging." She shot a look at Neiall to warn him that he should not argue with this. "I do know we need them here, among the trees." She pointed again to the map.

"Roots in the soil," Alden grumbled. "And frozen ground."

"We can use the burrowing technique," Waite countered.

"Not burrowing!" Prane argued. "We used that when—"

"We need a general plan first!" Abisina broke in, and Neiall smiled.

The three dwarves looked up sheepishly.

"Right."

"Sorry!"

"Little carried away when it comes to digging," Alden added.

"We will also need some kind of bulwark for the fauns and humans who carry spears or swords—" Abisina continued.

"Which you can also plan later!" Neiall said as the dwarves started to speak again.

Abisina persisted: "All the archers who can climb will be in the trees." The three dwarves shuddered.

"What about the centaurs?" Ravinne asked.

"They, too, can go behind the earthworks."

"Can other folk be useful for digging?" Neiall asked. Waite grunted, but Neiall kept on. "None of us can match the dwarves' artistry and know-how, but if we organized labor crews that the dwarves directed . . ."

"We worked on the wall at Newlyn," Landry noted.

"Some of it was comical." Prane smiled at Alden and Waite. "This one time—"

"But did they *help*?" Neiall asked.

"Yes, they did," Prane admitted.

"We should move today," Abisina concluded. "How many centaurs do we have?"

"About a hundred," Salat said.

"And we can place twenty-five archers on the wall?" Abisina asked. Neiall nodded. "We don't want to keep too many from the trenches because the bulk of the battle must take place there. But the longer we can hold the wall and the more we can bring down here, the better chance our folk have. We'll keep only a few here now," she decided, "and no dwarves. They are more valuable as builders. As the time nears for the armies to arrive, we'll pull back all the best archers and fastest centaurs to defend the wall."

"Salat and I can select from among the centaurs," Ravinne offered, Salat nodding beside her.

"Kerren and I are archery captains," Farron declared.

"I've been working with the spears since I joined up with Neiall," Hain said. "We can put them in the trenches and behind the earthworks."

"I can speak for the swordsmen," Neiall added.

"And the dwarves have their axes," said Alden.

"Yes, and . . . Erna," Abisina turned to the faun, "the folk at the trenches will need to eat, and your ability to speak to trees makes you the best forager we have."

"She can speak to trees?" Kerren stared at Erna, who basked in the attention. "I've heard that a few fauns have that ability."

Erna slipped her hand into Abisina's. "You'll be with me, right, Abisina?"

"When I can," Abisina said gently. "I'll need to be here, too."

"I'd be honored to look out for you," Salat offered.

"Thank you. That would be lovely," Erna said, as if accepting an invitation to tea. But she cut her eyes to Abisina as she dug her hands nervously into her hair.

"Abisina, you're not thinking of staying at the wall during the battle?" Neiall said.

"Of course I am. I am both an archer *and* a centaur who can carry someone else to the trenches. I'm perfect for the wall!"

"But if you're—"

"Neiall." He said no more; she knew he would talk to her later.

The meeting broke up. Salat and Ravinne went off to choose the centaurs who would serve as messengers between the wall and the trenches, Farron and Kerren to choose a few archers as guards, and the rest to break camp and move the folk to the mouth of the Cleft.

Abisina watched the others rush off to their tasks. *They're preparing their own graves,* she thought. *No. Their sacrifice will save the lives of their loved ones. That's why we're doing this.*

As she followed to start moving camp, she couldn't help wondering, *What if Findlay and the others make the same choice? What will I do if they return?*

Suddenly, the loss of the necklace took on a new importance. It wasn't just a connection to her father and mother or a symbol of authority. If the folk returned, Abisina would need its *power*.

After the death of her father, the necklace had stopped a battle that would have destroyed Watersmeet. The White Worm and Rueshlan lay dead, but their armies still faced each other. It seemed inevitable that the war would resume—until Abisina stepped between the enemies, holding the necklace aloft. Its light reached trolls and fauns, centaurs and fairies. Even the überwolves had paused and then disbanded.

If the Watersmeet folk returned and the southern armies came, there would be no necklace to stop the bloodshed. The massacre would not have been prevented—it would simply have been delayed.

# Chapter XXIV

By noon the camp was on the move. No donkeys survived to carry gear, so the folk loaded their tents and belongings on their backs. Abisina carried Prane and Erna again. Their presence comforted her, one clinging as if to a branch in a flood, the other chattering on about digging techniques and stonework.

When they reached the mouth of the Cleft, a pack of überwolves waited for them. They lost no one in the ensuing melee, but that night they posted a large watch and camped inside the Cleft, where the walls sheltered them.

The folk built a fire for protection from the wolves, but also for the reassurance of its light. Through the evening they turned anxiously away from the fire to stare into the gaping blackness behind them, wondering if they heard the galloping hooves of centaurs, the slow tread of trolls, or perhaps something worse, something not yet imagined.

The morning broke bright and clear, with a touch of spring

on the wind. The drip of water accompanied Abisina and the other leaders as they scouted the area around the northern entrance to the Cleft, planning trenches and earthworks and archer placement. The Cleft opened into a long, narrow glade. The dwarves would dig trenches among the trees. Once the enemy had come into the glade, those in the trenches and behind earthworks would charge the armies' flanks while the archers in the trees would rain down arrows. Abisina couldn't have asked for a better battle site.

Since they could be here for as long as three weeks, Abisina also scouted the best place to make camp. They would stay in the Cleft at first, but eventually, they would have to move. She found a stream nearby, and though the folk at the wall had been foraging here, Erna assured her that she could find enough food. The warmer air would make for a muddy camp, but that seemed a small price to pay for the bright sun. *And the thaw will make the digging easier.*

Abisina's steps were almost light as she helped plan. She had a purpose, and there were no decisions left to make. She knew how the battle would end, but she had chosen the terms. *As long as the rest of the folk head east . . .*

Others shared Abisina's mood. The idea of standing up and fighting for themselves energized folk so recently driven out of their homes and enslaved. They credited Abisina with giving them this chance. As she worked with them, many embraced or thanked her. She shied away from the attention, but once again Neiall pulled her aside.

"They need you," he said. "Don't take that away from them."

"I don't want to get their hopes up," Abisina argued.

"They know what they're facing," he shot back. "If they're going to die, why deny them the comfort of knowing that they will die as Watersmeet? That's what you are to them, Abisina: Rueshlan and Watersmeet." He stormed away but had made his point, and Abisina tried to do what he asked. Though the attention embarrassed her, she met folks' eyes and listened to those who told her how much she looked like her father and how wonderful it was to have the rightful Keeper.

But she grew uneasy when one of the dwarves discovered a depression of land east of the Cleft. "It's the perfect spot to provide protection for the injured," the dwarf explained. Setting aside a place for healing suggested the chance of survival. *Someone might get sick or injured during trench digging,* Abisina thought, and seeing the dwarf's eager face, she gave in. Still, she was plagued by her worries that the folk believed she could save them.

Though Prane and Waite insisted that dwarves were always ready to dig, Abisina could see that the work at the wall, the grief at Watersmeet's loss, and the lack of food had taken its toll. The dwarves were panting and mopping their faces after an hour of trench work.

A crew was already out foraging, but Abisina visited each trench and pulled two or three of the most exhausted to add to the foraging teams. The work was less strenuous and offered the promise of food. By the time she met up with Erna again, she had twenty following her.

Erna enjoyed her task. She wandered among the trunks, trailing her fingers along the bark and humming. Abisina smiled as she watched the faun. *How could I have known that this tiny, timid faun would save me again and again?*

Erna flushed with excitement when Abisina asked what she'd found. "Now you understand, Abisina, it's still winter. If this thaw continues, we'll have fiddleheads in a few days. For now, I've found mountain ash; its fruit is nice at this time of year. Then there are wild leeks, hog peanuts, hairy lettuce, and so much rock tripe! Don't make that face, Abisina. Rock tripe is healthful!"

Abisina laughed. "Yes, rock tripe *is* healthful. If only it wasn't so bitter! But with the leeks and the mountain ash fruit, it will make a fine soup. It's a feast, Erna. Thank you!"

Erna smiled in relief. "You think it will help?"

"Immeasurably."

No one had brought a large cooking pot, though many gladly brought their small ones to the fire at the center of the camp. Abisina was going to oversee the preparations until the dwarf who had done most of the cooking at the wall bustled her away. "There are more important things for you to do, Keeper," he said—but his quick removal of the rock tripe from the steaming pot of mountain ash fruit made clear that it was Abisina's recipe that appalled him.

Abisina helped with the digging until darkness fell and the meal was prepared. Then she understood why the dwarf had been so eager to move her away from the kitchen. He handed her a bowl of warm mountain ash stew mixed with a hint of leek. Even before she took a bite, she felt better. Next to her, Prane ate something more suited to dwarves' tastes: a bowl of rubbery brown rock tripe, heavily flavored with leeks and a smattering of hog peanuts. "Like my grandmother made!" She sighed after her first bite.

Abisina's worries were never far away. *Their hope is false,* she thought, listening to the chatter around the fire after supper.

"Then they'll die with full bellies and for their folk," Neiall said when Abisina confessed her concerns. "And that's more than the fairies promised."

That night, like so many, Abisina's sleep was restless. She woke several times in a sweat, dreaming that something she couldn't see was chasing her into a Seldar grove. But the trees, rather than giving her comfort, left her cold and empty.

The spring thaw continued, and with the rapidly softening ground, the trench digging went better than Abisina had expected. Within days, the dwarves and their helpers started on the earthworks that would provide protection for the centaurs and fauns, and the archers climbed the trees to find the best angles for their shots.

At times, Abisina *wished* the battle would come. When she had stood on the wall thinking about her remaining days, her life had seemed so short. Now twenty days seemed interminable. Her mind teemed with thoughts she wanted to avoid: the other armies amassing south of the wall, Findlay and the folk off with the fairies, the coming battle. She sought out the hardest tasks she could to wear herself out and keep her worries at bay.

On the third day in camp, Abisina was working on a trench that had proven difficult to dig. Prane stood next to a half-submerged boulder, lecturing a group of Watersmeet dwarves—most of whom were twice her age—on proper boulder removal. The dwarves nodded approvingly, but when Prane said, "This is the technique we used to excavate Stonedun," she was met by blank looks. The Watersmeet dwarves had lived in the north for generations and had no sense for the history of the southern city of Stonedun.

Prane called for a break before they made the final effort to move the boulder. She chuckled as she joined Abisina at the edge of the trench. "Those dwarves have been living too long in the trees! They can carve through wood, but I have little cousins who dig better! They're quick learners, though, and eager to do a good job."

"I need your help, Prane," Abisina said abruptly. "Or I may."

"Anything."

"I need you to teach me how to open the gate in the wall. I may need to go south at some point. I'm not sure," she hedged. "It would help to know what we're facing. We're making all these preparations, but we don't know how big these armies are—if they have trolls or . . . something else."

"It's so dangerous!" Prane whispered. "I understand we want information, but *you* can't go."

Abisina regretted saying anything, but the idea had been growing. If it was possible that their other folk would come back to the wall, she had to do *more*. If she could go south, see their enemies up close, she might learn something that would help.

"I doubt I could teach you to open the gate, anyway," Prane said. "It's very, very complicated. I could do it myself, if I was standing there, seeing the levers, hearing the works turn, but teach you—it's impossible."

Abisina shrugged. "Like you said, it's too dangerous." They got to their feet to return to the boulder.

"Birds!" someone yelled from a treetop, and Abisina heard the eerie hiss.

"Take cover!" she called to a group resting in the sunshine of the glade.

"They won't see us here, Keeper!" Prane said to Abisina when they had jumped back into the half-finished trench.

Abisina knew her fear was plain on her face. She smiled at Prane's reassurance, but her mind was spinning. These birds had come from the *north*. They had to be the ones that the fairies were using to force the Watersmeet folk to the Fens. *The birds must have shaken off the fairies' control. The folk are armed and can fight back now.*

It had been only six days since the folk left the Motherland. If they headed back to the wall as Neiall predicted, they could be here in a week—before the other armies attacked.

*They'll be here for the battle and be slaughtered,* Abisina thought. The landscape around her transformed in her mind. They were no longer building a place for their last stand. If the folk came south, they had to *win*.

When Abisina found Neiall, he wanted to give up on the trenches altogether. "We can fall back to the plain between here and the Motherland," he said. "Meet the enemy on the battlefield instead of cringing in the woods. This plan of yours—it's a good one for an outnumbered force. But we won't be outnumbered! Watersmeet is on its way!"

"We've made real progress here," she countered. "If this is simply a stop on the enemy's march to the main battle, it's important to damage them as much as we can, especially if we end up fighting on the plain."

They went back and forth. Finally, Neiall agreed that it was wise to stay where food was plentiful and where they could deliver a big blow to the southern armies. He insisted that Abisina send a few scouts north to watch for the Watersmeet folk.

That night as she wandered among the trees out of sight of the central fire, Abisina again thought about going south. *The birds, the eels, the beast in the garden—they are part of the rift, but what is its final horror?*

"Abisina?"

She spun around. "Who's there?"

"It's Neiall. Come back to the fire. Someone's arrived."

"Who?"

"Just come."

Neiall led her not to the central fire but to a smaller

one where Alden, Waite, Erna, Prane, and Landry talked animatedly. In the middle of this group, tired and thin, stood Haret. Behind him, eyes darting around but with a shy smile on her face, was Frayda.

# CHAPTER XXV

"HUMAN." HARET GREETED HER GRUFFLY, BUT WHEN ABIsina threw her arms around him, he hugged her hard.

"Hoysta?" she whispered.

"Gone," he said. "Slipped away peacefully. I was there at the end." Abisina held Haret a little longer before turning to Frayda.

"Thank you for coming," Abisina said when she was sure her voice wouldn't shake.

"I brought this." Frayda touched her bow where it curved over her shoulder.

"How about something to eat?" Neiall asked. "You must be famished."

The tension broke. Everyone started talking at once, and bowls of rock tripe soup and mountain ash stew were rounded up. Frayda ate deliberately and seldom spoke, but Haret was anxious to hear the news.

Abisina wanted to talk to Haret alone. He would

understand why she wanted to go south, and he would help her. But she couldn't say anything here. Instead, she told him about her trip to the Motherland. He knew her well enough not to ask about Findlay or comment on Neriah, but when she said she had urged the folk to flee, he stared. "Leave Seldara?" he asked pointedly. In the garden, she had accused *him* of giving up on the vision of unity.

"Don't listen to her, Haret," Neiall jumped in. "Only today we saw the fairies' birds flying south. By now our folk are headed this way."

"What do we know of our enemy?" Haret asked. Alden avoided Haret's eyes, and Waite was suddenly engrossed in a cut on his finger.

Haret let his spoon drop into his third bowl of soup. "What are you holding back?" he demanded of the dwarf brothers. When they didn't answer him, Haret's frown deepened. "Don't you lie to me, Alden," he said. "I've just buried my grandmother. There's nothing you can tell me that could hurt me more."

"I know you can handle it," Alden said, stroking his beard. "But given your loss—"

"Enough!" Haret bellowed.

Alden's hand stilled. "The dwarves in the south are marching against us, Haret."

Prane nodded. "And they have a new leader. They say it's Ulbert—the hero who found the Obrium Lode."

"He's wearing Obrium," Waite added. "Head to foot. And he's coming this way, leading the dwarves of Stonedun."

Haret's lips tightened. "And you don't think I can handle it," he said.

The dwarves rushed to reassure him but then fell silent at a scowl from Haret. "You all know my weakness for Obrium," he said. "But I think I've learned something in the months since I left Watersmeet. When the time comes, I will resist."

The subject was dropped, but as Neiall described the plan for when the enemy arrived, Haret gripped his bowl as hard as he would grip his battle-axe. And he never finished his third bowl of soup.

Abisina had no chance to talk to Haret that night, and her dreams were worse than ever. This time she could see who chased her into the cold Seldar grove: Ulbert. The light of his armor was blinding, but she knew it was him. The trees looked pale compared to the gleam of the Obrium. She wanted to search for Haret, sure he had been with her, but the glaring armor dazzled her. She stumbled around the grove, crashing into trunks and calling for Haret. He never answered.

She left her bedroll at dawn and found Haret sitting by the cooking fire. They were alone.

"I'm going south, and I need your help," she blurted.

"What are you talking about?" Haret rasped, dragging her away from the fire so they would not be overheard.

She told him everything.

"And this plan of sending the folk east—where did you get it?" Haret asked.

"I got it from Vigar's papers."

He raised an eyebrow. "From *what*?"

She described her discovery in the library. Abisina saw the faded words before her. "She said something else, something I forgot. She said she would never flee again."

"And do you still doubt that you're Vigar's heir? That you have a special destiny?"

"What do you mean?"

"I thought even a human would see what it all points to." He crossed his arms, challenging her to disagree. "Well?" he prodded.

"You're saying . . . you're saying that Vigar vowed she would never flee again. And now I am also refusing to flee."

He nodded. "Just like Rueshlan. He *faced* the Worm."

"So I am behaving exactly as the heir of Rueshlan and Vigar would."

"No!" Haret said. "You're doing more than they did! You're trying to save *Seldara*."

"But—"

"Look at what Watersmeet has become. A Watersmeet that *accepts* the refugees. Look at Newlyn: their folk are marching to *you*."

"But, Haret! What if I still need the necklace?"

"The necklace has done its work already. Everyone knows it belongs to you. You are the Keeper. You learned no more from those papers than most of us already knew."

Abisina stared at him. "So I *can't* abandon this special destiny—even if I want to?"

Haret shrugged maddeningly.

"Then I'm going south."

"And I'm going with you."

"I should go alone. You need to stay here with Frayda."

It was a weak argument, and Haret dismissed it. "Frayda can take care of herself. She survived for two years alone in the forest. I'm going with you, human," Haret said again.

Abisina had one more argument, though she hated to use it. "Ulbert's there."

He sighed. "You're right, human. I've let you down before."

"No, Haret! That's not what I meant!"

"And I meant what I said last night. Right before she died, Grandmother talked to me about that time when I hurt . . . when I almost killed her." Haret's words were halting, but he did not break Abisina's gaze. "She said, 'It's time to let it go. For both of us.' That was all, but I understood."

Abisina understood, too. Hoysta had released Haret from his crushing guilt.

"I was like a boy again—before my father died, my mother. Before that terrible Obrium hunger destroyed my whole family. It was the last gift she gave me." He took a breath. "I can go south with you, human. Even if there are ten Ulberts."

Abisina and Haret approached Prane at the midday meal. Unless they could convince her to open the gate in the wall, they were going nowhere.

Prane's mouth dropped open. "Go south? Both of you?"

"I know you think it's too dangerous," Abisina said. "That's why Haret's coming with me. We'll stay no longer than we need to."

Prane raised objection after objection, even pointing to her arm, still bandaged from the überwolf bite. "I'm injured!" she insisted.

"Prane," Abisina said, "I've been watching you dig trenches for days!"

In the end, Prane couldn't stand up to the combined pleas of Abisina and Haret.

Neiall would be tougher, so Abisina told him only that she and Haret were going to the wall. "Most of the archers went back yesterday, and I need to work with them," she explained. But when she said that Prane was going as well, he flatly refused. "She's needed here."

"I need her expertise on the wall," Abisina said stubbornly. "She has this idea . . ."

"Take Waite or Alden," Neiall said. "They built it!"

Haret and Abisina had already discussed this. Alden could open the gate more easily than Prane, but they knew how cautious he could be. "He'll want a phalanx of centaurs to guard us!" Haret said. "It's got to be Prane."

"Prane is a master gate-builder," Haret told Neiall. "She's young; she knows the newest techniques. She thinks we can use the gate to bring the wall down on the advancing army after we've gotten away."

"Is that possible?"

"She's not sure," Haret said. "That's why we need her." He leaned closer to Neiall, whispering. "She didn't want to bring it up with Alden and Waite. They're old-fashioned. But she knew I admired her work in Newlyn."

As they walked away, having secured Neiall's agreement, Abisina had to ask, "Haret, is it true that we might be able to use the gate to bring down the wall?"

"What have I told you before, human? Dwarves do not joke about stone."

"Do they joke about gates?"

He broke into a grin. "Regularly."

They reached the wall after midnight, slipping past the sentries who were looking for wolves, not two dwarves and a human. In the morning, Prane would have to explain why she had come to the wall when dwarves were so in demand at the trenches, but it wouldn't matter. Abisina and Haret would be in the south.

Prane led them to the east side where the entrance to the gate was hidden. Amid a pile of discarded stone slabs, a shallow tunnel took them below the wall. Abisina, so much taller than the dwarves, had to crawl over the tunnel's rough and rutted ground. When they got to the end of the tunnel, Prane held a candle and studied the dizzying array of levers set into the wall: two hundred of different sizes and shapes. As Prane worked the levers, Abisina could see no pattern in her moves, but behind the wall, stone grated against stone as parts of the lock moved.

"Hurry, Prane," Abisina whispered.

"Hush!" Prane answered without pausing. "I have to hear the tumblers!" The dwarf's hands flew. Then she hit a lever that she clearly expected to move and snatched her hand away with a cry when it didn't. "The Earth!" she swore.

"What is it?" Abisina asked.

"Made a mistake," Prane mumbled. "Now hush!" Again she studied the levers until she said, "Ah!" and set to work. Haret looked on, shaking his head and smiling. A click echoed through the tunnel, and Prane's candle blew out. They were in the dark.

Abisina's nose twitched. Air blew at her, and it smelled of—decay. Not wet leaves and fallen branches—but fur and bodies and blood. The gate was open.

"You can't go over there!" Prane whispered. "I'm going to close it."

"No!" Abisina reached blindly toward the voice, found the cloth of Prane's tunic, and held her back. "We'll be careful, I promise."

"Then take me with you." Prane's voice was thick with tears.

"We'll need speed. I may have to carry Haret." Haret grunted in protest from the dark. "Carrying you would slow us, Prane. We'll be back after nightfall—not tomorrow, but the next day. Be ready to let us through."

Abisina pulled the dwarf into a hug and breathed in Prane's earthy scent, an antidote to the smell of death in the south, then crawled to where the passage ended. She got to her feet. "Ready, Haret?" she asked.

"As ever," he replied, and they walked through the open gate.

# Chapter XXVI

Prane's sobs followed Abisina and Haret until the gate clicked shut. A cold wind rushed down the Cleft. They slipped into the deep shadows along the Cleft's walls and set off.

They spoke little. Abisina kept an arrow on the naiad bow, and Haret had his hand on his axe. The land was silent. As dawn broke, they saw tracks of the usual forest animals—badger, skunk, squirrel—but nothing moved. No squirrel chittered. No bird called. They had both grown used to the quiet forests in the north, but there they had known the cause—überwolves or other predators had eaten most of the animals. Here, where the animal tracks were fresh, Abisina could not explain the brooding, oppressive silence.

By midafternoon, they walked through familiar land. Almost three years ago, the Watersmeet army had camped here, making a base at a dwarf ruin, a fragment of the Obrun City that the earthquake had thrust aboveground. Abisina's steps slowed. Where was the ruin? Had someone, or something, destroyed it?

"It's got to be here somewhere." Haret read her thoughts. His voice was rough from lack of use.

"There!" She pointed through the trees, catching a glimpse of stonework. In the tense days leading up to the battle, the ruin had been a place of refuge and friendship. Abisina could see Hoysta standing in a circle of dwarves in front of the crumbling stone wall, axe in her belt. She had traveled to join the battle against the Worm—and to find her grandson and Abisina.

Corlin had been here, too. He had led a ragged group of Vranian deserters away from the Worm's army—the same people he had eventually led back to build the village of Newlyn. Corlin had observed the Watersmeet folk and Rueshlan's leadership—and he saw what his people could become.

Abisina had first met Erna here. Like so many others, Erna and her mate, Darvus, had fled the Worm. When they found fauns, centaurs, and humans working together, Darvus had called it the "stuff of legends."

Watersmeet had been a beacon to these southerners. It still was.

"Let's go a little closer," Haret whispered, a trace of a smile on his lips. Breide had prepared meals for the camp. *Is he thinking of her?* Meelah had been Breide's assistant. Unwilling to be left behind, Meelah had put on a dwarf's hauberk and convinced Breide to take her on the march. Rueshlan had scolded both of them.

*Glynholly often sat there,* Abisina thought, looking at a stump forming a flat table near a corner of the ruin. A lane ran among the trees, where Abisina and Elodie had paced, considering how various weather conditions would change the flight of their arrows during the battle and laughing, as only Elodie could make her do.

*And Findlay.* Findlay and Abisina had been almost inseparable. She smiled. While they had not discovered their love for each other yet, anyone paying the slightest attention would have noticed.

Finally, of course, there was her father. Rueshlan—sometimes a man, sometimes a centaur—striding through the camp, checking plans with Glynholly, encouraging young soldiers as they readied for their first battle, tasting Breide's famous stews. Abisina had known she might lose her father, but she had no idea what else the Worm had set in motion.

*How strange to think longingly of the time before a battle!* They were precious memories now.

She touched Haret's arm. He wiped his eyes. "Where to?" he asked.

She knew they should go to the plain where the battle had been fought, gather as much information as they could, and get back to the gate, but there was one more place she had to go. "Follow me. It won't take long."

The plain was southwest, but she went southeast—to the site of her father's funeral pyre, home of the largest Seldar grove in . . . *Seldara.* She still allowed herself to use that name.

Abisina sensed that there would be no sentries or scouts

near the grove. Blinded by Ulbert's Obrium armor, what use would dwarves have for the soft glow of the Seldars? And their other enemies would also shun the Seldars' pure light.

As they neared the place, the fear that she carried was not about the enemy. Throughout the land, the Seldars were dying. Instead of coming upon a sea of radiant trunks and golden leaves, would she find only gnarled and blighted branches?

They reached the trees at sunset. They had walked several paces into the grove before she realized where she was. They stood in a forest of gray trunks stained with the sun's rays. Beneath their feet, dry leaves rustled; brittle limbs rattled in the low wind.

Abisina walked farther into the grove, willing there to be a thread of life in even one tree. Haret followed a few steps behind.

She reached the other side. She had seen nothing alive, had felt no answering warmth in the trees she touched.

*Hissssssssssssssssssssss!*

Haret pulled Abisina back into the trees. "It's safer in here," he whispered. Another hiss and then another rippled above them. They got to the center of the grove and sank into the leaves at the base of a tree.

"Let's stay here till dark," Haret said, "when those monsters can't fly. We'll work our way to the enemy camps, learn what we can. We told Prane we'd be back after nightfall tomorrow. We can wait here a bit and still make it."

Abisina nodded. Haret pulled some strips of dried meat from his satchel and handed one to her. She chewed and watched the light grow redder as she waited for the next hisses. They didn't come.

Haret snored softly, leaning against the tree, head thrown back, mouth open. Abisina sat up straighter. *I guess that means I'm on watch.*

Neither of them had slept more than three hours the night before, and the next thing she knew . . . *The moon has risen!* She scrambled to her feet. They had slept too long. But something in the angle of light was wrong. She looked for the moon, but the sky was black.

It was not the moon's light she had seen.

Behind her, a single Seldar glowed—its slender trunk straight, its branches supple. She had been leaning against it. Haret was curled in the leaves at its base. As Abisina watched, one golden leaf unfurled.

"Haret," she whispered, and he stirred.

"Mmm?" Then he saw the light and sat up. "What?"

"It's a Seldar, Haret. There's one still alive!"

His face relaxed. "Was it here the whole time?"

"I don't know. Maybe we couldn't see the tree's light until it got truly dark."

"Or it knows you're here," Haret said.

Abisina didn't argue as she usually would at any hint of her "special destiny." As she basked in the Seldar's light, her questions, her confusion, her despair melted away. She had often hoped, even expected, to hear the voice of her father in a Seldar grove, but this—

"It's enough," she murmured.

Haret stood next to her. "Got what you came for, human?"
She smiled.

"Then we'd better get going. We have to tell Neiall *something* once he learns that the gate can't bring down the wall."

Abisina followed Haret out of the grove. Nothing had changed. She had no hope that she would live past the battle. She carried all her worries for the folk from Watersmeet, the folk of Newlyn, and Erna's fauns headed this way.

But in some ways, everything had changed. She reached the edge of the Seldars. She could still see a small glow through the trunks. "It's enough," she said again.

It was a short walk from the grove to a rise overlooking the enemy camps.

"Forty fires, I'd guess," Haret said, surveying the lights dotting the plain. "Some of them large."

"Who's around them?"

Haret's night vision, like all dwarves', was sharp. "Centaurs and dwarves—in separate camps. No humans. That doesn't mean they're not at the fires to the west. Oh—and I don't like that!"

"What?"

"Trolls. Seven of them—no, eight. Enough for two rams—or one huge one."

Abisina headed back to the trees so they could work their way closer to the fires. Haret didn't follow. "What is it?" she asked.

"Ulbert—what if he *is* down there?"

"You're ready for him," Abisina said evenly. *But is he?* she wondered. *Can Haret face Ulbert?* She couldn't show him any doubt. "We talked about this, Haret. Remember Hoysta."

"Yes," he said without moving. "But, Abisina . . . it's possible that with Grandmother's forgiveness, I can face Ulbert?"

Abisina stepped closer. She knew he was serious when he used her name. She began to reassure him, then changed her mind. This was *Haret*. They told each other the truth. "I don't know, Haret, but yes, I think it's possible. As possible as my father sending me a sign through a Seldar tree."

For a moment, he stood rigid, and then his shoulders relaxed. "You're right, human. We can't know for sure. But there's one way to find out."

They headed back to the trees, assuming their usual nighttime stance: Haret walking in front, Abisina following with hands on his shoulders. They had perfected this style of travel on their first journey to Watersmeet.

As they neared the plain, Haret whispered, "Boulder to the right."

Abisina stopped. "Haret, get on my back." She transformed. "Once we're on the plain, we'll need speed." She stood next to the rock and waited.

All dwarves hated heights; none more than Haret. "No."

"This mission is only useful if we *return*, Haret, and I won't leave you."

"Human, we cannot have this argument now."

"Exactly. So get on my back."

Haret hesitated, but she knew she had him. He climbed

the rock and then climbed onto Abisina's back. "If we survive this, I will throttle you."

"Hang on," she said, though his hands were already clamped to her waist. "I'll go around to the right. We can get close to that fire there." She pointed to one set a little apart.

"Centaurs." Haret grunted. "I can see them moving around the fire."

"They're loud. We don't have to get too close. If we learn nothing, we can continue around the plain to the next fire."

She set off at a trot, thankful for the thawing earth that muffled her hooves.

Thirty centaurs gathered at the first fire. They were oddly crammed on one side, while the other side was wide-open. Abisina thought she recognized a few from her visit to the Cairn, although they were now even skinnier and dirtier. There was no raucous laughter or loud drinking songs. These centaurs stood with their heads down, staring into the flames. The hiss of the fire and the crackle of burning wood drowned out any words that passed between them. After straining to hear for a few minutes, Abisina moved on.

"Hardly an army to strike awe in its opponent," Haret muttered. "It's a wonder they've made it this far. And why were they all huddled together like that?"

Abisina was about to respond when a foul stench filled her nose. She gagged.

"Oh, the Earth!" Haret cried. "What is it?"

The answer lay ahead.

The cool moonlight illuminated an enormous pile of

bodies. It was as tall as Abisina and as wide as the base of a Sylvyad: a tangle of hooves and torsos, arms and legs. Broad backs of dwarves, hands still clutching axes, faces disfigured in pain or terror. Centaurs' tails mingled with beards and hair. Weapons glittered among the carnage—knives and swords, the graceful curve of a bow, the notched blade of a dagger. Moonlight shone off a shield, a leather breastplate. How had they died? It was impossible to tell. Some of the corpses were as skeletal as the centaurs at the fire. They might have died from hunger or disease or exhaustion or exposure. Others looked better fed. Had they died in some battle for power among the armies? Whatever the cause, the result was horrific. A muddle of death—no honor or peace to be found.

Abisina moved around the corpses as fast as she could, holding her breath. Haret's heart beat against her back. Neither spoke. *This is the smell of battle*, she realized. That smell was not yet in the north, but it was coming.

At the next fire, more emaciated centaurs huddled far from the pile of corpses. Abisina was on the verge of heading into the trees, sure they would learn nothing, when hoofbeats thudded across the plain, coming closer.

The centaurs heard them, too, and seemed to wake from a stupor. Their faces, etched with weariness and defeat, now hardened. Lips curled back from their jagged teeth. Hands went to swords. The centaurs moved apart, encircled the fire, and lifted their heads, ready to greet what was coming. The hoofbeats got closer, and the herd began to murmur a name:

"Icksyon, Icksyon, Icksyon."

But the Icksyon who stepped into the firelight was not the Icksyon Abisina had seen before.

Gone were the rolls of fat, the muddied flanks, the tangled hair and yellowed beard. This Icksyon was huge—easily as big as Rueshlan—and his shoulders were wide, his chest broad, and his abdomen muscled. The hair combed back from his head was thick and blond; his beard was full. The fleshy jowls had disappeared to expose a firm jaw. This was Icksyon as he had been in his prime: strong, hard, powerful. The only detail she recognized was the necklace of toes. She felt the terror of facing him for the first time in Giant's Cairn. She gathered herself to leap back into the forest.

"No, human," Haret growled. "We need to hear him."

Haret's steady presence kept her from running.

Icksyon breathed deeply before speaking, pulling the rank air into his lungs. Around the fire, his herd did the same.

Icksyon began: "What a night, my friends! The perfume on the wind—it feeds me better than meat! Better than mead!" He took another breath, and the ruddiness of his cheeks deepened. Around him, shoulders straightened, chests swelled.

"The humans are close. In two days' time, we'll march north, and you will satisfy your appetites! Once the north is ours, nothing will hold us back. Soon, the humans, dwarves, fauns, and fairies will suffer the pain you have suffered."

Icksyon's eyes raked over the gathered centaurs, but when his gaze came to rest, he looked right at Abisina. She was sure of it. His eyes stared into hers. Her knees felt weak, her legs shook. Each beat of her heart screamed: "Go! Go! Go!"

"Now, human!" Haret dug his heels into her flanks. She reared, pivoted, and leapt into the trees, weaving around trunks and branches, barely aware of the directions Haret shouted in her ear. "To the right! The *right* or you'll get tangled up in— Now, left! Do you see that rock?"

She jumped it and dodged right again to avoid a low-hanging branch. "Oh, the Earth!" Haret groaned.

Ahead, the trees thinned, and they flew across open ground. Abisina ran flat out. She didn't notice her waning strength, her heaving chest.

She slowed only when they approached more trees—first weaving into them, then transforming and collapsing onto the ground.

Haret rolled away from her and lay spread-eagle, as if to touch as much earth as he could. Then he rose and stood over Abisina. "We have to get back to the wall and then to the trenches—get our folk prepared."

Mechanically, Abisina stood. Haret walked north, and she followed. Her feet felt as if they belonged to someone else. She saw them moving—avoiding the remaining drifts of snow, stepping over rocks, coming to a stop when Haret stopped—but the only thing real to her were those eyes.

She finally knew what the rift had sent.

When she looked into Icksyon's eyes, she looked into the eyes of the Worm.

# Chapter XXVII

Neiall was with the sentries when they arrived at the wall in the afternoon.

"He must have figured out that we were up to something," Haret said. "What should I tell them, human?"

"Prane must open the gate. I want to talk to you and Neiall in the lever room." These were the first words she had spoken since fleeing from Icksyon.

Haret shouted up the instructions and then joined Abisina in the shade of the wall as the lock rumbled behind them.

"Prane told me what you did! It was too dangerous!" Neiall said when the gate swung open.

"Please shut the gate and wait outside, Prane. I need to talk to Neiall and Haret," Abisina said.

When Prane had disappeared through the tunnel, Abisina turned to the others. "The battle begins the day after tomorrow. We face the Worm."

"The Worm?" Haret asked, incredulous.

"Abisina—you cannot be serious!" Neiall said.

"We saw *Icksyon*, human." Haret spoke to her as if she were a child. "The moonlight was tricky. And you've always feared Icksyon. He may have seemed Worm-like, but it was Icksyon."

"We watched the Worm die," Neiall added. "All three of us!"

Abisina waited until they both stopped speaking. "You're right. We saw the Worm's body consumed by poison. We saw a centaur the herds *called* Icksyon, but it was not Icksyon. I can't even guess what happened to the real Icksyon. And yes, the moonlight *was* tricky, Haret, and I *was* terrified. But you are forgetting what we know about the Worm. All night and all day, I've reviewed the stories, remembered the conversations with my father, relived the moments in Vranille and in the battle when I came face-to-face with the Worm. There is no doubt.

"Think, Neiall," she said as he started to protest. "Vigar and the rest of Watersmeet saw the flood destroy the Worm. Yet when my father found Vigar, she warned him with her final breath that the Worm would be back."

"After Vigar killed the Worm, it vanished for three hundred years!" Neiall said. "It's been less than three since Rueshlan killed it!"

"Rueshlan told me once that the Worm feeds on hatred," Abisina said. "For a few months after the Worm's defeat, the conflict between the Vranians and the folk of the south ebbed, and the Seldar trees brought hope for unity. But quickly, the dwarves reclaimed Stonedun, Icksyon grew stronger, and Theckis built his rule in Vranham as if he were Vran himself. In the north, the fairies went their own way. Even Watersmeet began to divide. The Worm had plenty of hatred to feed on."

*"We didn't see the Worm!"* Haret insisted. "We saw Icksyon!"

"You know how the Worm first appeared to the Vranians," Abisina said. "He was a young, beautiful man. They thought he was Vran! The Worm is a shape-shifter. That young man they called Charach was one of its shapes. The white centaur on the plain—the one now called Icksyon—that is another of its shapes. Ulbert could be another. Whatever is leading the Vranian army will be yet another."

"It doesn't make sense!" Neiall's face was flushed, and his lips trembled. "The Worm cannot lead three armies at once! They come from different parts of the south."

"I don't understand all its powers, Neiall," Abisina said. "But Icksyon *is* the Worm. I don't want to argue anymore. I want to speak to the folk."

"You cannot tell them this!" Neiall said. "You'll scare them away! We need every soldier at the wall and at the trenches! We cannot afford to—"

"To tell them the truth? I will not trick them into facing the Worm. My father would never have done that. You asked me to be Keeper, Neiall. As Keeper, I will tell the folk the truth."

Haret stared at her, then slowly nodded.

Neiall stepped back, rubbing his face with his hand. "It's

really the Worm?" He sounded tired and frightened.

Abisina put her hand on his shoulder. "I'm sorry."

"You're right, Abisina," Neiall said. "You're the Keeper. I stood by your father when he faced the Worm. I'll stand by you, too."

All the archers and centaurs waited for Abisina as she emerged from the tunnel. The long secret discussion between their leaders had shaken them.

"What is it, Keeper?" Prane asked, running up to Abisina.

Abisina had to answer the same questions that Neiall and Haret had put to her, and more.

"How big is their army?"

"Do they have trolls?"

"Any birds?"

"Can we survive this?"

Thankfully, Abisina didn't have to answer the last question. Ravinne galloped up from the trenches, yelling, "They're coming! The rest of the folk! Our scouts met a messenger this morning. They've escaped the fairies, and there are four hundred ready to fight. They'll reach the Motherland in two days. The rest must follow more slowly."

A cheer went up, but Abisina could barely breathe.

Her first thought was of Findlay. He was coming back to her! For a blissful instant, this was all that mattered.

But it wasn't just Findlay. It was all of Watersmeet. They were not going east. They were going to fight—could they win?

Abisina went with Neiall, Prane, and Haret to the trenches that night. She faced the same questions and the same hope. The folk all believed that with the addition of four hundred soldiers, they had a real chance.

Abisina sent more archers and centaurs to the wall and then, at last, left to wrap herself in her cloak and sleep—a sleep, thank Vigar, without dreams.

She woke to a camp alive with digging, building, and final preparations. One group that had worked in the trenches through the night used their rest time to sharpen arrows, swords, and axes.

"We have to disguise the trenches better!" Prane argued to Waite as they bustled past. "We want all the enemy in the glade before they realize it's a trap!"

The excitement, the activity, even the weather seemed to mock Abisina. How could the sun shine, the snowdrops bloom, the tree buds swell when in a matter of days this could be a boneyard? But she knew she couldn't let anyone see her despair.

She found Haret to tell him that she was returning to the Cleft.

"Fine. Let me say good-bye to Alden and Waite."

"What do you mean?" Abisina asked. "Are you coming, too?"

"What did you expect, human?"

"I assumed you wanted to work on the trenches until the battle."

"We started this journey together, human. We should finish it together."

Back at the wall, Abisina and Haret called together the archers and the centaurs, talking them through the best ways to defeat their enemies.

"The longer we hold the armies, the better," Abisina explained. "We want to leave the wall at night, if we can. They'll assume we're stopping for dark, but we'll be on our way to the trenches. Each archer is paired with a centaur for the trip back. Once you get the signal, don't waste time. We'll need your skills at the trenches, too—humans in the trees, fauns and centaurs behind earthworks. That's where we'll make our *real* stand."

Waiting and idleness would bring fear, so Abisina had targets set up for practicing shots. She assigned folk to check weapons and make more arrows. She dispatched centaurs to the forest to find trees for building ladders. If the wall started to fall while they were on it, they would need more than one staircase to get down. She paced the wall, took turns at the targets, rubbed oil into the naiad bow, and urged others to sleep or eat—things she couldn't make herself do.

The waiting was worse once the sun went down. The camp buzzed with tension: a group of archers shot at targets as soon as the moon rose; fires usually doused after midnight continued to burn; arrows, already sharpened to a deadly edge, were sharpened again. Twice Abisina tried to sleep, only to bolt out of her tent and prowl through the camp. If she shut her eyes, she saw two armies marching to the wall: the Watersmeet folk from the north and the shape-shifter's from the south.

The trill of a faun's pipe from the top of the wall sent Abisina flying up the uneven steps, Haret on her heels.

"What is it?" Abisina panted. Three fauns, Farron among them, were peering into the shadows below the wall.

"I'm sorry, Keeper," Farron said. "We may have summoned you needlessly. The sentry thought she heard someone down there—calling for Watersmeet."

"And for Erna," the sentry added. "I'm sure someone called for Erna."

"We haven't heard it again, Keeper," Farron said, with a sidelong glance at the sentry.

"Erna's from the south," Abisina said. "She asked the fauns from her home to join us."

"Should we open the gate?" Farron asked.

Abisina stared at him as a realization came over her. "We have no one to open the gate! Prane and Alden are at the trenches. What if it's Darvus?"

"I can do it," Haret said. "Not easily, but I've seen Prane do it twice and heard it a third time. Should I get started?"

"Yes, Haret. It may not be them, but just in case. . . ."

Haret headed down the steps, muttering and moving his hands as he rehearsed the lever movements. Abisina stayed on the wall and called into the darkness below: "Darvus?"

After she yelled several more times, Darvus's voice floated up: "Abisina?"

"Yes, it's me!"

"I told you I knew her!" Darvus shouted to someone near him.

"How many of you are down there?" Abisina asked.

"Forty! Is Erna there?"

"Vigar's braid!" Abisina said under her breath. She had to get forty fauns back to the trenches. She needed the centaurs here, so the fauns would have to walk. Could Haret get the gate opened fast enough to give them time to reach the trenches? "She's near, Darvus," Abisina called down. "Stay where you are. We're working on the gate."

She turned to Farron. "I'm going to help Haret. You keep watch." She raced down the stairs and into the tunnel. Haret was pulling and pushing levers, but no sound came from inside the walls. "It's harder than I thought," he said. "I can tell by your face that I have to keep going."

"It's Darvus—and thirty-nine of his friends. Should I go get Prane?"

"There's no time for that, human! Leave me. I'll do it." He turned back to the levers and pulled one. Something in the wall clicked. He reached for another. "I said, leave me, human."

Abisina paced along the base of the wall, furious that she had nothing to do. And then it came to her. "Rope!" she said aloud. "Fauns don't hate heights. We could pull them over the wall!"

She ran to the small fire among the tents where a group of centaurs and fauns were gathered. Soon, all of them, and anyone else not on the wall, were combing the camp for bits of rope. Tents were taken down, their lines removed and their walls sliced into strips. By the time the moon set, they had already pulled four fauns over the edge of the wall. At dawn, when the gate ground open at last, only three fauns trotted through the lever room.

Abisina had tried to stop Haret, but he waved her off. "So I can do what, human? Pace around like you?"

Still, Haret was startled when the last faun went by. "Where are the rest?"

"We pulled them over," Abisina said.

"You pulled thirty-seven fauns over the wall?"

"Thirty-eight. Darvus forgot to count himself."

The night was over. The folk at the wall were now tired enough to sleep for a few hours, even Abisina. She woke at noon: the day of the battle. Next time she slept—if there was a next time—the fate of Seldara would be decided.

# CHAPTER XXVIII

THE CAMP HEARD THE MARCHING FEET LONG BEFORE THEY could see the advancing army. The steady *tramp, tramp, tramp* put folk on edge. The centaurs kicking a mangled pot back and forth stopped playing. The faun idly blowing on her pipes silenced them. The woman tying her bedroll left the laces loose, got her bow, and headed to the wall. By the time the enemy army appeared as a smudge of black crawling up the Cleft road, folk's hearts were beating to the *tramp, tramp, tramp*.

Abisina and Haret stood side by side atop the wall near one of the newly made ladders, two of twenty-five archers.

"Is there room for one more?" Frayda stepped from the nearest ladder.

"Frayda!" Abisina and Haret said together.

"You said you needed my bow, Keeper."

"Your bow is *most* welcome!" Abisina said. She wrapped her arms around Frayda.

"It's time I rejoined my folk," Frayda said. "I don't expect to survive this fight." She looked down the row of archers. "I guess none of us should. But it's the best way I have to honor him—fighting beside his daughter."

The first figures Abisina could distinguish from the mass pushing its way down the road were the trolls: eight of them, four marching on either side of an enormous tree trunk, the battering ram.

"Trolls aren't known for their sense of direction," she muttered. "Who's leading them?"

"There," Haret said, pointing. "A dwarf—no, several—walking under the ram. The trolls are shackled, and the dwarves hold their chains."

Though she feared the trolls, Abisina couldn't hate them. Trolls were violent, vicious, stupid, and slow, but these trolls were slaves; they fought and killed and swung that ram to avoid pain. They were no more likely to survive than she was.

Behind the trolls stretched the rest of the army—the rift army, as Abisina had started to call it. First were the minotaurs, the hags that controlled them nowhere in sight. Beyond the forest of minotaur horns came centaurs and men, some carrying spears, others bows. And at waists and across backs were long and deadly swords. Some of the men wore mail, a few of the centaurs had leather breastplates, and many of the dwarves had hauberks and helms. But Abisina also saw bare chests and heads. Her army lacked armor, too, and she expected that the folk from the north wouldn't have much.

You didn't grab your heavy mail shirt when you were running for your life.

Even with their differences, the soldiers were oddly uniform. As the lines approached, Abisina realized that the Stonedun dwarves all wore green tunics. The Vranian men were all blond. Even the southern centaurs, who wore no tunics, looked similar in their filthiness. She glanced down the row of human and faun archers on the wall. No two were alike. *Watersmeet!* she thought. Her love for her home strengthened her.

The one creature that would stand out was the shapeshifter, but Abisina saw no sign of it in any of its guises.

Archers along the wall raised their bows, but Abisina called, "Wait till they're in certain range!"

At some unseen signal, the *tramp, tramp, tramp* ceased.

"What are they doing?" Abisina asked.

"One of the dwarves is pointing to the weak spot on the wall," Haret said. "They've picked it out already. Vran take those Stonedun dwarves!"

The trolls, with their dwarf escorts, were back on the move, heading for the vulnerable point, the rest of the army following behind.

"Get ready!" Abisina called, and twenty-five bows rose with hers. "Aim at the dwarves below the ram!"

Before the trolls came within range, two groups of centaurs detached themselves from the rest of the army and ran forward with enormous shields.

"How can they fight with those?" Haret said. But they had

no intention of fighting. They surrounded the trolls and raised the shields, making already difficult shots even harder.

"The trolls will be right below us," Abisina said to Haret and Frayda. "Make your arrows count.

"Take aim!" Abisina ordered "Pick your target . . . and . . . arrows fly!"

The first volley arced in the air with the sound of a thousand insect wings. As Abisina readied a second and then a third arrow, a few spears tilted to the side, the hands that held them now limp. Gaps appeared in the ranks of centaurs and minotaurs; the dwarves, blocked by their taller companions, were safe for now. Then an answering volley of arrows flew at the wall, forcing the archers to shoot from behind the parapet. The line advanced.

Abisina spotted a gap between the centaurs' shields. Frayda had seen it, too. The shot was desperately tricky. The gap was narrow and intermittent, and because they shot from above, they needed to bend the arc. A centaur stumbled, and the opening gaped! The string of the naiad bow sang in Abisina's ear. Frayda released an arrow right after Abisina's, and one of the centaurs dropped her shield completely. With Haret's help, they brought down all the shield-centaurs on one side. The trolls were exposed!

There had been casualties on the wall, too. Three archers had fallen over the parapet, and two more lay on the wall, bleeding. "Get them down!" Abisina called. She aimed at a troll and hit its arm, but the arrow glanced off its hide. Frayda followed up and made the shot.

Seconds later, the wall shook beneath Abisina's feet. The trolls had swung the ram. "All to the trolls!" Abisina cried, and the archers slid into the places of those who had fallen. More archers were on the stairs.

Then, down the Cleft, a hiss.

The faun next to Abisina threw himself flat on the wall, and farther down the line a woman screamed. Abisina ran along the ranks, shouting words of encouragement and scanning the sky for the hulking birds. "Aim for the throat or the eyes!" she yelled, but her words were drowned by the next crash of the ram.

"One troll down!" Haret shouted as another hiss set Abisina's heart racing. *Where are the birds?*

Then one swooped in low from the north, ready to rake the wall with its talons.

"Birds at the back!" Abisina yelled as she aimed at the monster's eye. Her arrow caught the bird just before it reached the wall. With a scream, it banked to the left, catching a claw on the parapet and pulling part of it down. The bird banked again to avoid the Cleft wall, but its balance was off. Its wing scraped the black cliffs, and blood fell with each wing thrust before it circled and flew shakily south.

Abisina couldn't celebrate its defeat; Haret had taken out one troll, but the ram still crashed against the wall. Abisina loosed two arrows, one lodging in a troll's hand. The ram dipped and only grazed the wall. "Better than nothing!" she said.

Three trolls on one side of the ram bristled with arrows,

but the centaurs were regrouping, positioning shields on the exposed side. "Get them while you can!" Haret yelled, and the archers responded. Two centaurs fell, taking their shields with them, and one troll dropped the ram, swatting at arrows.

Dwarves were scurrying to rearrange the trolls. The beasts were angry and began to bellow and pull on their shackles. One dwarf got caught in the chain, and his leg twisted. Abisina couldn't hear his scream over the tolls' roars.

A second bird was bearing down. "This one's mine!" Frayda yelled, and crouched, arrow ready. She targeted the spot where its beak met its throat but missed. Instantly, she was on her feet, second arrow on the string. As the bird passed the wall, her arrow flew into the joint between the bird's wing and body. It kept flying, but its right wing dipped lower.

Abisina assessed their losses. On the ground, their centaurs were patching up archers. Four or five might be back. Three more lay still, and some had fallen over the wall to the other side.

Abisina glanced at the sun—red and low. *An hour till nightfall!* But an hour more of sunlight meant an hour more of birds. Two were bearing down on them, one behind the other. "Birds!" She pulled an arrow from her quiver.

She focused on the bird that bled from one wing. It swooped at the wall, talons extended. Abisina targeted the same joint on the other wing. The naiad bow responded as if it were part of her hand.

"Look out!" someone screamed, and she threw herself behind the parapet before she saw her arrow hit. Another volley flew overhead. When she regained her feet, the bird was fighting to stay aloft. It turned and flew south, losing height with each beat of its injured wings.

The second bird alit on the wall, tearing chunks off the parapet and striking out with its beak. Several stones fell onto the rift army below, but many archers plummeted after them. Haret ran at it with his axe as Abisina nocked an arrow. The bird's hooked beak slashed at Haret. He ducked and scrambled between its legs. Abisina sent another arrow at the bird's eyes. It screamed—a sound that made the centaurs on the ground clamp their hands over their ears. Abisina took shot after shot as the bird rose in the air with Haret clasped in its talons. Haret froze in fear. Then he shook himself, swung his axe to cut off the claw that held him, and fell back onto the wall as the bird screamed again.

Abisina rushed to Haret while Frayda leapt onto the parapet and shot into the bird's open beak. With a snap, the bird bit the shaft of the arrow, lashed its tail around, and smacked Frayda. Frayda grabbed at the air as she lost her balance. An injured faun reached out to catch her, and their hands touched, but the faun could not hold on. Frayda fell backward—panic, then peace on her face as she dropped out of sight.

Abisina raced to the edge of the parapet. Frayda's body had disappeared into the mass of minotaurs below. In the distance, the bird swung its head from side to side, opened its beak, and emitted a hideous choking sound before it crashed into the side of the Cleft and fell onto its own army.

Abisina sank back below the parapet. Haret crawled over to her and crouched down, holding his left arm gingerly.

"Are you okay?" she gasped.

He shrugged. "Not bad for facing a bird."

"Frayda fell."

Abisina put a shaking hand to her face. Haret's voice was pained, but he said, "This is not the time, human."

He was right. Pushing away the thought of Frayda, she got to her feet and surveyed the battle. The archers had brought down another troll, but minotaurs now had two smaller rams, smashing again and again into the weakest part of the wall. Hunks of stone fell with each blow. The bird had taken down a length of parapet and cratered the top of the wall with its beak. About fifteen archers shot volley after volley, targeting the rams.

Abisina glanced at the sun; one red spot, like a single coal, glowed above the horizon. As she watched, it grew smaller and smaller and then winked out.

"They will break through in several hours," Haret said. "Then it will take more time to make the hole large enough for the army. We did what we set out to do."

"We killed one bird, injured two," Abisina said. "But we don't know how many they have."

"The birds are their best weapon, and this is not the final battle. I'm sure they held some back," he said. "When the final battle does come, we'll see more birds than we saw today."

"How many have we lost?" Abisina asked.

"I lost track."

Two more archers joined the ranks on the wall, each carrying a few extra quivers. One of them ran up to Abisina. "This is all we have left, Keeper," he said.

"Tell them to make their quiver last until the light is gone," she said. "Then we leave for the trenches. By the time the army realizes we're gone, we'll be halfway there."

# Chapter XXIX

Abisina and Haret left the wall only after they had helped every archer onto the backs of the centaurs. Abisina had planned for some centaurs to carry two riders, but they had lost so many, three centaurs galloped to the trenches with no riders at all.

Abisina and Haret followed, and the rams faded to distant thuds. Her mind raced ahead to the next battle. How long could they hold the enemy at the mouth of the Cleft? How much damage could they inflict? Would it be enough to give Findlay and Elodie's army a chance?

And now she had to consider a retreat plan. Abisina had built her strategy around getting the folk at the wall to the trenches. Once there, her small force would weaken the Worm as much as they could without any thought for their own lives. But now, if the trenches were overrun, the survivors had to pull back to the plain around the Motherland to help Findlay and Elodie. At least two leagues of forest stood between the Cleft and the plain. How could she get a retreating army through safely? And whatever was left of her army would also have to cross the plain. Most of the drifts had melted during the thaw. They could cross in two hours, but they would be totally exposed. Birds, überwolves, the rift army. How many would actually make it to Findlay and Elodie in the end?

Abisina and Haret reached the mouth of the Cleft after midnight. The moon was high and just past full. Neiall met them. They helped the archers dismount; two of the injured had died on the journey. Neiall assigned the new arrivals positions in the trenches, behind the bulwarks, or in the trees.

"How soon can we expect the attack?" Neiall asked as the last faun trotted off to her place.

"We can't be sure how quickly their army will move through the Cleft," Abisina said. "I would expect some scouts—perhaps an advance force—a little before dawn."

Neiall lowered his voice. "Did you see the Worm?"

Abisina shook her head. "We took down a few birds, a few trolls. Some damage to the main army, but it will be a large and deadly force when it arrives."

"The numbers?" Neiall pressed.

"Four to one," Haret said.

Neiall looked across the glade where four hundred soldiers were hidden in the woods. An army of sixteen hundred headed toward them. How far would the element of surprise take them?

"You should sleep, Abisina," Neiall said.

"Have you been sleeping?"

Neiall shrugged. "It was worth a try."

"I could eat, though," she said. "Haret?"

"Always."

While Abisina sat eating some flat bread, Salat galloped up, Erna on her back. "Oh, Abisina!" Erna cried. "I am so glad to see you back safe! And thank you for sending Darvus on to me!" Abisina helped the faun down.

"About Darvus," Erna whispered. "He thinks I should stay in the healing area during the battle—it's safer, he says. I told him no. 'After what I've been through? I can handle being behind the earthworks where I've been assigned'—those were my exact words. Salat will be nearby. She'll watch out for me."

"What about Darvus?" Abisina asked.

"He'll be with me, of course. He's a very good archer. But he goes green at the sight of blood."

"Erna," Abisina said suddenly, "is your mother here?"

Erna gasped, horrified. "Of course not! Those in our village who were not up to the journey, like Mother, hid. Her mate's with her." Erna wrinkled her nose. "He's a good shot, or so Darvus tells me. He can protect her."

Salat listened to the conversation with an amused smile. "I think we should let the Keeper get back to her duties," she said to Erna, with a wink at Abisina. "I'll take you back to Darvus."

Abisina watched them go. *Vigar guard Erna during this battle!* she thought. *And Darvus. And Erna's mother—wherever she's hiding!*

After eating, Abisina walked among the trenches,

earthworks, and archer stands to speak to the soldiers. Most were focused and determined, but as the night dragged on, the tension grew. By dawn, she had soothed several folk who could barely speak for fear. She was talking gently to a particularly nervous young man—little more than a boy—when a centaur came galloping into the middle of the glade. Neiall ran forward, and, with a final squeeze of the young man's hand, Abisina joined them. Haret wasn't far behind.

"Three scouts," the centaur panted. "We killed two. Injured the third, a centaur, but she got away."

"How far away is the rest of the army?" Abisina asked.

"Sound echoes so much in the Cleft, it's hard to say. Two hours at most."

"The Earth!" Haret swore. "Our folk can't take much more of the waiting!"

"Extra rations, then," Abisina said. "Anything to distract them. Our plan relies on getting as many into the glade as possible before we attack. No one can act too soon. We cannot lose the element of surprise."

Two hours passed, and then three, and Abisina and Neiall struggled to keep the folk in their places.

When Abisina finally heard the dreaded *tramp, tramp, tramp,* she was in a trench with Haret. She had planned to be behind the earthworks where her bow would be the most use, but she didn't want to move now that the rift army was close.

"Together again, human," Haret said, gripping his axe a little tighter.

The thud of hooves and feet, the clanking of weapons,

and the jingle of mail became deafening, amplified by the Cleft's stone walls. Around Abisina, the faces of the dwarves settled into a stony determination. No one moved. *Please let them follow orders!* Abisina had been as clear as possible with the captains: no movement, no volley of arrows, no cries of "Watersmeet!" until the advancing line of soldiers stepped onto the rise at the end of the glade.

The first soldiers appeared. Again the minotaurs led. Abisina could almost taste their fear. Behind them came a contingent of centaurs carrying hags—bags of bones topped with thin dirty hair, clutching staffs to control the mino-taurs.

A few rows of dwarves followed. "Look at them," Haret whispered. "Their eyes."

Abisina saw the same wildness in these dwarves' eyes that she'd seen in Haret's when he'd felt the pull of Obrium.

"Ulbert is not far," Haret said.

After that came rows of men—blond, fair, and battle worn. Most stared straight ahead, but one Vranian's eyes were as wild as the dwarves'.

Abisina looked for Theckis, the leader of Vranham. *He'll be at the rear, where it's safer.* For Abisina's entire life in Vranille, Elder Theckis had shown himself a coward. He had allowed Abisina to live when her coloring, even as an infant, marked her for death. What seemed like mercy was actually fear: Sina had threatened to expose Theckis's support for a leader who spoke against Vran's teaching. And Theckis had made Abisina pay for his cowardice. He worked to ensure that of all the outcasts Abisina was the most hated. *No, Theckis will never pick up a sword to fight with his people. He will stay at the back of the army until the bloodshed has ended.*

The rows kept coming. Then shouts went up from the front of the column.

One of the archers must have shot into the rift army and exposed their position—too soon!

The enemy centaurs and men in the glade moved to defensive stances; the dwarves hefted their axes off their shoulders; archers crouched and scanned the trees.

Abisina leapt from the trench. "For Watersmeet!" she yelled. Watersmeet archers rained down arrows. In front of her, a centaur fell, tangling another as it tried to get away from the arrows. Along the tree line, soldiers collapsed; others scrambled for the cover of the trees, but the dwarves and humans waited in the trenches.

Abisina's plan had worked—but only for those soldiers who had entered the glade. The soldiers still coming from the Cleft had seen Watersmeet's positions. They marched forward with weapons drawn. Some cut to the sides, avoiding the open area and slipping into the trees. Several lines of enemy archers established themselves, and Watersmeet's archers began to fall to the forest floor with sickening thuds. Minotaurs met Watersmeet's centaurs in the glade. Swinging their horns from side to side, the minotaurs ripped flanks and sliced legs. The enemy soldiers who had gone into the trees approached the trenches from the rear, forcing those on the southern end of the glade to fight Icksyon's herd on one side and Vranians on the other.

Folk responded to this new threat, Abisina among them, leaving the earthworks and trenches to fight off the advancing Vranians, but the enemy had overrun many of the southern trenches before they could get there.

And then the birds came, swooping from tree to tree, plucking archers like fruit and slamming them to the ground. The birds that landed in the glade lashed out with beaks, talons, and tails, striking as many of their own soldiers as Abisina's.

Abisina focused on the birds—shooting sometimes as a centaur, sometimes as a human, whatever form gave her the best angle. She shot at a bird flying toward a tree laden with archers. Her first arrow missed. Her second hit it in the neck and stuck. The bird veered, crashed into a tall pine, and fell head over tail to the ground. Two birds in the glade took to the air, and Abisina, now human, readied another arrow, but a sudden, brilliant light blinded her. She shaded her eyes, and something smashed against her chest, knocking her back and cracking her ribs. Disoriented, she glimpsed the descending blade of an axe and rolled away, the axe burying in the soft ground where she had lain moments before. She scrambled to her feet as another axe was launched at her head. She ducked, tripped, and landed hard on top of a fallen dwarf. *Waite.* She hardly took in his vacant eyes before the whistle of another blow sent her ducking away. Her hand touched cold metal. Waite's axe.

She picked it up and swung out, striking something hard. Her arm ached with the blow, but she swung the axe again. Someone screamed. She threw herself behind a tree, desperate to get her bearings. A dwarf hurtled after her. Abisina saw the dwarf's mad eyes and green tunic as she lashed out again with Waite's axe, catching the dwarf across the face.

Two dwarves in green lay dead: one fallen against Waite's body, the other at Abisina's feet. More were coming, racing through the trees with the same wild eyes. A Watersmeet dwarf stood facing the glade, axe-hand slack at his side. Abisina screamed a warning—how could he not see the Stonedun dwarf headed right at him? He didn't flinch, didn't raise his axe as the other dwarf's blade cut across his middle.

Abisina understood. *Ulbert is in the glade.*

"Haret!" she cried, running. In front of her, three dwarves climbed from a trench, bodies slack, headed to the light. She paused long enough to shoot arrows into an überwolf drawn to the smell of battle and then broke into the glade.

Ulbert stood in the middle, among the crushed bodies, facing the rise. She squinted against the radiance of his armor, seeing only the roughest outline of him. Taller and broader than any dwarf Abisina had ever seen, Ulbert raised his Obrium axe and cut down four Watersmeet dwarves. More dwarves streamed from the trees, weaponless.

Haret was among them. She recognized his hauberk, his dented helm, the coarse dark hair at his neck. The battle cries, the running feet, the arrows whistling, the groans of pain faded—only her friend mattered, helpless in the face of his biggest weakness.

She transformed and galloped forward as Ulbert raised his axe again. She could see no weak spot in his armor, no seam or crease that would take an arrow. So she slammed into him, broken ribs grinding together.

Ulbert toppled back, losing his axe. The Watersmeet dwarves paused.

"Pull back!" she yelled at them. "Back to the plain!"

A few blinked at her.

"Why?" another asked.

Ulbert was getting to his feet, freeing his axe from the dirt.

Someone else picked up her cry: "Fall back to the plain!"

Abisina reared and brought her hooves down on Ulbert's chest as he started to rise. The blow reverberated up her legs. More pain, but it focused her.

"Haret!" she screamed.

Haret blinked, and his gaze cleared.

On the ground, Ulbert had his axe again. He swiped at Haret, nicking his hauberk, and then rolled away.

Abisina still had Waite's axe, and she brought it down on Ulbert's head. The axe shattered, but he was slower getting up. Abisina reared, striking him on the back; her hooves slid and she fell to the ground, human again, though she hadn't intended to transform.

On his feet now, Ulbert swung to face her and raised his visor.

The Worm's eyes bore into hers.

*I know you!*

The words echoed through Abisina's head, and she screamed.

The brilliance of the Obrium armor became the brilliance of white flanks. The gleaming axe extended into the cruel blade of a sword. A broad chest reflected the sunlight where the Obrium breastplate had been. Now, instead of armor around Ulbert's neck, a necklace of toes hung around Icksyon's. He threw back his head, and the helm fell away in ripples of blond hair.

Only the eyes stayed the same.

Icksyon reared, higher and higher, hooves flashing. He began to descend, about to crush Haret.

Abisina threw herself on top of Haret. "On my back!" she screeched, and his arm bent around her neck. She transformed, Haret clinging to her, as she regained her hooves and ran. A blow glanced off her shoulder, but she kept going. *Go back and fight!* she told herself. *End this!* But her hooves did not falter. Something deeper drove her away.

Haret's heavy boots kicked her in the belly as he tried to pull himself onto her back, and his grip on her throat cut off her air. They galloped for the rise. Bodies were strewn everywhere—centaurs, dwarves, humans, fauns, überwolves, minotaurs, hags. The bulk of three trolls rose like hills. Two birds lay in leathery heaps. A few centaurs were still locked in combat, and dwarves, who had come to their senses, searched for weapons. Haret's grip on her throat released; instead he squeezed her aching ribs.

As they reached the top of the rise, she turned back.

Icksyon stood where she had left him, gleaming white, a smile lighting up his handsome features as he gripped the brown toe on his necklace.

# CHAPTER XXX

OUT OF SIGHT OF THE GLADE, ABISINA PULLED UP SHORT. "Are you all right?"

"I'm sorry!" Haret choked.

"Stop," she commanded.

"I gave in! Again! I thought I—"

"And I ran as soon as Icksyon showed up. It doesn't matter now. We have to save our folk."

Shouts echoed around them: "Fall back!"

"Where's my axe?"

"Watch that dwarf!"

"Not that way! To the plain!"

There was a terrible scream.

"Weapons ready, Haret." Abisina reached for the naiad bow still across her back, though her quiver was light. "Have you got your bow?"

"Yes, but no arrows."

"We'll gather some—from those who fell."

They found three archers with slashes across their bodies and twisted limbs. The birds had pulled them from the trees and dropped them. Their quivers were full. "I'll use these to protect Watersmeet," Abisina whispered to the fallen as she gathered the arrows.

They hadn't gone far from the battle site when they came upon their first skirmish. Triumphant yells warned them to approach cautiously. A group of Vranian men had cornered some folk—Abisina couldn't see who—in a jumble of boulders. The Vranians were taking turns slipping from the safety of the trees to draw an arrow or two from their quarry, depleting their quivers before the final attack. For the Vranians, it had become a game.

The next Vranian—a man Abisina vaguely recognized from her years in Vranille—dashed out. The arrow from the boulders missed, but Abisina's didn't. As their comrade dropped, the Vranians turned. Haret's and Abisina's shots left most dead and a few racing into the trees.

In the boulders, a cluster of Watersmeet folk and a few southern fauns cowered. All were injured, two grievously. They had half a quiver of arrows among them and two damaged bows. Abisina wanted to help the injured, but she couldn't take the time.

"Gather the weapons from the fallen Vranians," she commanded the group. "Those who are too injured to fight will stay here. The rest of you, head north to the plain."

Similar scenes repeated throughout the forest. Watersmeet ran, the rift army pursued. Abisina and Haret pushed toward the plain, gathering more followers as they went. They collected weapons and passed them out to the unarmed. They sent the less injured to care for the seriously injured; anyone who could fight, they urged on.

So many injured, so many dead. They came upon faces they didn't recognize and faces of friends. They took weapons from the bodies of friends and enemies, then left the fallen to rot or be eaten by the überwolves slinking through the forest. Haret found the body of a good friend from his years in the south. Abisina came upon the centaur who had let her escape by the Cairn's stream. A few said they had seen Neiall or Prane or Ravinne or Landry, but they heard nothing of Alden or Erna or so many others. Abisina told Haret about Waite. He shook his head. "I cannot think of it now."

*Who will be left?* Abisina wondered, and she drove herself harder.

Half a league from the plain, they came upon the remains of their army. In a wooded hollow, a hundred or so beleaguered fighters sat or lay on the ground, some asleep with their quivers on their backs. Captains—most newly made when their own captains were killed—wandered among them, checking for injuries, counting arrows, giving a word of encouragement. Abisina and Haret hung back while the folk they had gathered stumbled forward to join their friends and neighbors.

*So few*, Abisina thought.

"Only six dwarves," Haret murmured.

"Do you see Prane or Alden?" she asked.

"Alden's over there."

"How about Erna?"

"Keeper!" The cry came from a knot of folk close to the lip of the dale. All heads turned to Abisina. She trotted down the slope and saw Neiall crouched at the side of a centaur with an arrow in his shoulder.

"Keeper, I am glad to see you!" Neiall called again, limping to her as a dwarf took over the centaur's care.

"Can you help me down, Neiall?" Haret said. "I've had enough of riding."

After Haret landed next to her, Abisina transformed. "Is this . . . all?" she asked.

"Some are still coming in, but I don't expect too many more." Neiall wiped his face with a bloody hand. "Ravinne is out scouting the enemy. We think they're on the plain. She has Farron with her. He'll come back with news while she goes on to find the rest of our folk."

"We're going to need them," Haret muttered.

"We've brought some weapons," Abisina said.

"Any food?"

"A little. No one had much."

Neiall glanced at the red sky. "We'll be left alone until morning."

"Gather the food and hand it out equally," Abisina said. "Do you have any healers?"

"No. And no medicines."

"Then I'll see to the injured."

"You need a healer yourself, human," Haret grunted.

"I'll be fine."

"Knew you'd say that." Haret sighed.

As Abisina checked wounds, wrapped broken limbs, and comforted those who had watched friends die, she heard stories of Icksyon and Ulbert appearing in the wood, bringing new strength to their followers. Abisina asked if they had seen a blond man, regal and charismatic. She feared the Worm might become Charach, the human form it used in Vranille. *Or what if it takes the shape of Vran?* The thought of facing the Worm in Vran's image scared her more than facing Icksyon. But no one had seen such a man. And no one had seen the Worm itself.

Salat and Erna were in the hollow. Salat had taken an arrow through her upper arm, but Erna was unharmed. As Abisina bound Salat's injury, Erna confessed: "When the first of Icksyon's centaurs approached, I threw my dagger." She hung her head and buried her hands in her hair. "I didn't wait to see where it landed. I ran and hid. I'm so ashamed. When I saw Salat during the retreat, I came out. I knew you might need me for foraging or something. She brought me here."

"You're right, Erna. I will need you. Your help foraging is far more important than anything you might have done during the battle. I'm glad that you hid!"

Erna lifted her head. "Really?"

"Of course! But," Abisina added, "what about Darvus?"

"He was much braver than I was. He shot a whole quiver before he hid. He's still hiding," Erna said. "I'm sure he'll be here soon."

Despite all the pain of the day, Abisina smiled. Erna's mix

of fear and faith was astounding and wonderful. And well-placed; Darvus arrived at the camp an hour later.

By nightfall, Abisina had done what she could for the wounded. She couldn't remember the last time she had her medicine pouch. Had they taken it from her in the Motherland? How many days had it been since she stood with Lohring and Neriah in the Mother's house?

Haret wrapped Abisina's ribs and cleaned a few wounds on her arms and then went to find Alden. This was the only time they would get to grieve Waite's loss.

Despite Neiall's protests, Abisina took one of the next watches. She needed to be alone with her thoughts. She settled into the crook of a tree and tried to focus on what lay before them. How could her weakened army face battle in the morning? *We have to! The rest of our folk are out there!*

She heard the squelch of footsteps in mud and sat up, readying an arrow. She spotted a figure picking his way through the trees—human, male.

"I've got my arrow on you," she said, and the figure's hands went up.

"Watersmeet?"

"Who wants to know?"

"Landry of Newlyn. I'm looking for Watersmeet."

"Well, you've found us!" Abisina declared, dropping her arrow. She recognized Landry's voice. "Lucky for you we're not rift folk."

"Faun tracks led this way. They don't have fauns. Is that you, Abisina?"

She jumped down to the ground.

"Thank Vran—oh! Sorry! Old habit," he said. "But I have great news!"

"We could use great news."

"Newlyn's coming!" Landry could no longer keep his voice down. "I met Eder in the wood!"

"Thaula's father?"

"Yes! He'd come on ahead of the army! Well, there's only about three hundred of them. But they're on their way! They were on the far side of the Cleft a few hours ago. And Corlin's with them!"

"He's alive?" Abisina clutched Landry's arm.

"I don't know how—we had no time for stories. But they're coming!"

Neiall and Haret still sat with Alden, talking quietly, but they stood up when they saw Abisina and Landry. "Over here," Abisina said, pulling them away from the sleeping forms littering the ground. The moon had risen enough that she noticed a gash on Landry's head, and as he talked, she cleaned it.

"The Newlyn army is mostly men," Landry said, "since— Ow!" He winced as Abisina touched his cut but kept talking. "The folk of Newlyn are not as ready to accept female soldiers. A few dwarves, too. They— Ow! Can you go easier, Abisina? They could be here in the morning. Corlin's leading them."

"The Earth!" Haret cried.

"How did you come upon Eder?" Abisina asked. She had

finished with Landry's head and was cleaning a wound on his arm.

"This." He pointed to his head. "I got knocked out and left for dead. Eder came through the Cleft and saw the remains of the battle. He found me as I was stirring. I didn't know what happened at the end of the battle. I'd heard the call for retreat right before I got knocked out. We agreed that he'd go back and tell Corlin what was going on, then come through the Cleft again. I said I'd meet him there after I found you."

"Watersmeet's coming from the north, Newlyn from the south! We'll have the rift army between us!" Neiall said.

"Do we know how many of the enemy are left?" Abisina asked. "Any sign of Farron?"

"I expected him by now," Neiall said.

A low whistle came from across the camp. "It's another sentry," Alden said. "Maybe that's Farron."

In a few minutes, Farron ran to them. He reported that the enemy was camped in the trees fringing the plain. The battle in the glade hadn't been for nothing. The enemy had sustained heavy losses—maybe as many as three hundred. Five leviathan-birds had landed near the camp, but one couldn't fold its wing, and Farron didn't think it could fly far.

"The dwarves are camped apart from the centaurs, and the men are farther off still," Farron said. "I saw a man kill a dwarf, and the whole camp threatened to explode. One man shouted over the rest. He channeled the hatred toward you, Keeper, and that brought them together for the moment."

"Who was this man?" Abisina asked sharply.

"He was young," Farron said. "He looked like all those Vranians—blond, fair. They called him something. . . . I don't remember what it was."

"Vran? Did they call him Vran?"

"No. I would remember that. It was something like— Wait! I've got it. Jorno!"

"Jorno!"

"Yes, he was a leader. An Elder, I think. Anyway, they listened to him."

"So that's what happened to Jorno," Haret muttered. "We never did find his body. . . ."

It was the last name Abisina expected—or wanted—to hear. What if she faced Jorno in battle? He had saved her life once, had loved her, he claimed. But he had turned on her when he learned she could shape-shift. He had killed Kyron, who had been like a father to her.

"They have about thirteen hundred," Neiall calculated. "From what I saw, most of their army is weak and lacking weapons."

"So are we," Abisina reminded him. "No one has an advantage there."

"There's infighting. That matters," he said. "We have a hundred here, plus the four hundred from Watersmeet and the three hundred from Newlyn. We are two-thirds their size, but we fight for our home. They fight only for hate. And we have you, Abisina."

She couldn't meet his eyes. *When I saw Icksyon, I ran.*

"I think Neiall is right. We need to draw them onto the

plain—get them between Newlyn and Watersmeet," Haret said.

"If we put our puny force on the plain, we'll draw the birds," Alden argued. "They could take care of most of us at one time."

"Unless we can draw the birds to the boundary trees," Abisina said.

Everyone stared at her.

"Explain," Neiall said.

"You know Erna can talk to the trees," Abisina said, lowering her voice. What she had in mind would scare Erna out of her horns. "Even the trees in the Motherland. It's how she got me out. If some of us crossed the plain tonight, making sure that the enemy sees us headed north to the Motherland, I think Alden's right, the birds would be sent after us at dawn. We could lead them to the boundary trees and, if we're lucky, lead them into the roots. The rift army will follow. That will put them between our two armies."

"There are some big 'ifs' there, human!" Haret cried.

"It's too dangerous," Alden agreed.

"Of course it's dangerous!" Neiall said. "It's *all* dangerous—but it might work."

"Some of us aren't up to a trek across the plain, Keeper," Alden noted.

"I'm thinking of a small group," Abisina said. "How many centaurs do we have? We need speed. We want them to see us go, but it can't be so close to dawn that the birds follow right away. How far is their camp, Farron?"

"About a league. Mostly downhill."

"We have twenty centaurs," Neiall put in.

"I need ten. And Erna."

"And me," Haret said.

She didn't argue.

"Landry, bring the Newlyn army as fast as you can," she said. "Once we've taken care of the birds, we'll find the rest of Watersmeet and tell them the plan."

"*If* you can find them—" Alden began, but Neiall had seized on Abisina's idea.

"You have to go now," he said. "We have little time if this is going to work. Yes—I know! Another 'if,' Alden! Once Newlyn's here, we'll join you. Landry—you, too. Get going!"

"He needs water and food!" Abisina said. Landry had already turned away, but he came back with a grateful look at Abisina. Neiall thrust his own water skin and two pieces of dried meat at him.

Abisina, Neiall, and Haret headed back to the camp to wake the centaurs and Erna. Alden stood scratching his beard, while Farron tried to convince him that this was the best chance they had.

The centaurs were eager to be part of the plan, but it took Abisina several precious minutes to convince Erna. She wasn't afraid of the trees. She refused to travel at night. Abisina had to promise that Erna could ride on her back with Haret behind her and that Salat, who was one of the chosen ten, would be close by. Abisina felt badly but she refused to allow Erna to wake Darvus and say good-bye, imagining the scene that would follow.

"He could come, too!" Erna said. "He won't slow us down!"

"Get on, Erna," Abisina said in a tone stern enough that Erna squeaked, but she scrambled onto Abisina's back.

Haret got up behind her. "Once this is over, I will *never* ride again," he grumbled.

# Chapter XXXI

Abisina led the centaurs first to the plain, then west toward the rift army's camp. The moon bathed the plain in silver light, a stark beauty. Now that the drifts had melted, Abisina could make out the Motherland's trees.

They slowed down when they smelled the smoke of the enemy camp, and Abisina, with Haret and Erna clinging to her, entered the trees again, deliberately stepping on twigs and rustling leaves. They needed the sentries to see them heading north. A screech owl called from their right, closer to the plain, and Abisina knew they'd been heard. She continued to make noise as she headed back to where the centaurs waited.

She paused before she stepped onto the plain. An oak tree stood next to her, leaves just emerging from buds. She had seen no oaks in this part of the forest, and it made her pause. An oak branch was sometimes used as a symbol of peace. She remembered her father carrying one when he attempted a parley with the Worm.

At the time, she had been angry, sure that their enemies' hate was too great to consider an offer of peace. It had been. But her father had pointed out that the parley was a seed. If Watersmeet were to win, the parley made clear that they were merciful. Rueshlan had hoped that it would convince the Vranians to join with Watersmeet and begin a true peace.

*My father understood something I didn't,* Abisina realized. *Newlyn, the refugees—these were the fruits of that seed.* She snapped off a branch of the oak and stuck it in her belt.

"Human, you can't think—"

"Hold tight," Abisina warned. She leapt onto the plain and set off at a trot, angling away from the camp. The centaurs, alert for her return, followed. Once out of sight, they would go at a gallop, but they needed to seem as if they were being careful.

Abisina saw the silhouettes of the five leviathan-birds against the fire. The moonlight silvered their backs; their heads were tucked under their wings. They looked peaceful. *They're not,* she reminded herself. *And tomorrow we need to destroy them.*

The centaurs with Abisina were tired, but like her, a surge of excitement carried them across the muddy plain. They arrived at the Motherland before the sun rose.

"Erna," Abisina asked, "where do you want us?"

"Take me to the fringe but not inside it," she said. "These trees are so unpredictable! I'd like to talk to them before you and the others come in."

Abisina did what Erna said, letting her down before the smooth ring of earth that marked where the roots lay underground, waiting for prey. Their plan relied on Erna making the trees understand. What if she couldn't? When they had been in the Motherland, Erna had said that not all the trees listened to her. Why hadn't Abisina thought of that before?

Abisina stood with the rest of the centaurs, watching Erna. As Erna began to tug on her hair, Abisina's worries increased. Erna motioned them to move back a little. Clearly this was not going well. And the sun was rising.

Dimples appeared on the halo of smooth ground, as if a battle raged below.

"Birds!" One of the centaurs pointed. "Four! No—there's a fifth, flying in slower!"

"Weapons ready!" Abisina cried. "Erna!"

They didn't stand a chance against five birds.

Bows were drawn by all of them, including Haret. He would bring out his axe if the fighting got close.

Erna screamed, and Abisina turned. A root had grasped Erna's wrist. The earth churned, but no roots broke the surface.

"No!" Abisina galloped to the faun, drawing her sword.

"Mine!" Haret shouted. He was far better with his axe. She brought him close to Erna. A few roots now rose from the earth, but others pulled them down. Erna screamed again as Haret leaned forward from Abisina's back and swung his axe, severing the root that held her.

The earth exploded with darting roots. Abisina grabbed Erna and reared away. A few tendrils touched her ankles but couldn't hang on.

*Hissss!*

The birds angled into the cluster of centaurs. Haret pulled Erna up behind him.

"Erna! What's going on?" Abisina yelled.

"Put me down!"

Abisina was busy shooting the birds. Two landed, and some centaurs abandoned their bows for their swords. Salat advanced on one of the birds, but another swooped in and caught her up. From the bird's talons, she hacked at its legs with her sword. It released her, but her back was torn to ribbons.

"Put me down, Abisina!" Erna shouted.

"But—"

Erna jumped. Another bird swooped in as the faun ran for the boundary. Abisina watched in horror, sure that the roots would snap Erna's neck. Instead they parted. Erna was in the middle of the halo of earth when a bird reached her, talons extended. Erna screamed and threw herself flat on the ground, but before the bird touched her, a thick root lashed itself around the bird's leg. The bird shrieked as more roots rose and whipped around its neck, its wings, its beak. *Crack!* The bird went limp, neck broken, and the roots pulled it underground.

"It's okay!" Erna cried. She stood in a cage the roots had formed to protect her. "You can come in now!"

"Don't you move, human!" Haret shouted, but they had to lure the other birds in. Giddy with fear, Abisina stepped among the writhing roots. Nothing touched her.

The four remaining birds had flown high. Now three of

them dived for the centaurs. The injured bird trailed behind.

"Scatter!" Abisina yelled. "Then into the boundary!"

All but Salat obeyed, though their tails twitched nervously as they followed their Keeper's command. "To me!" Abisina called to Salat; the centaur could barely stand.

One bird split off and then a second, chasing the centaurs along the edge of the boundary. Abisina didn't know if the centaurs could force themselves into the roots despite their trust in her, but as the birds flew close, two centaurs veered in. Around them, the roots rose.

A bird shrieked as roots lassoed its claws and tail. The air split with the birds' screeches. Haret covered his ears. The injured bird pulled out of its dive. Abisina worried that it would come for Salat, who had fallen outside the boundary, but it turned in the air and flew awkwardly away.

Abisina and Haret raced to Salat. The other centaurs, one carrying Erna, gathered around them. Salat had lost too much blood. Erna crept forward and laid her head on the centaur's chest.

Ravinne galloped up as Abisina closed Salat's eyes.

"Keeper! I didn't think I'd see you— Oh!" Ravinne put a hand to her mouth when she saw Salat.

"Have you come from the folk?" Abisina asked.

"Yes." Ravinne dragged her eyes away from her dead friend. "They're about an hour behind me."

*Findlay and Elodie.* "How are they?"

"Ready to face the rift army, Keeper. Ready to be Waters-meet again."

Abisina wanted to take off at once—Findlay was only an hour away!—but she couldn't leave the shaken and grieving centaurs.

Ravinne was embracing another centaur, and Abisina overheard her say, "I wish we could have a pyre. I hate to leave her here for überwolves."

"I'll get the roots to take care of it," Erna said. She had been kneeling at Salat's side. "We can move her body off the plain. It will be safe until we can have a pyre. . . ."

Abisina and the other centaurs helped lift Salat's body and carry her to where six roots rose from the ground. The roots wrapped around Salat more gently than Abisina could have imagined and passed her to the next group of waiting roots, until her body was conveyed to the Motherland and laid among the boundary trees.

Abisina again grew nervous and jittery as she stared in the direction from which Watersmeet would come. Finally Haret said, "Let's go, human. You'll wear yourself out more with the wait than if you just go meet him."

Abisina tried to stay at a brisk trot, but she kept breaking into a gallop. She gave up and let herself go. When they rounded a curve and she could see the Watersmeet army coming toward them, she pulled up short.

"What if he's not there? What if he still doesn't want to see me?"

"Stop it, human. If *he* could gallop, he'd be out in front of the rest. I guarantee he began to regret everything he said before he was out of the Motherland."

But Abisina walked slowly, scanning for blond hair. They were still far apart when she spotted him—and he was running. He had spotted her, too.

"Put me down, human," Haret insisted. "Go to him."

Abisina galloped, transforming just before they met.

"Abby—"

"Fin—don't say anything. Just kiss me."

They fell into each other's arms, both crying, both trying to say how sorry they were, how much they missed each other while also kissing each other as many times as they could. The cheer from the Watersmeet army drowned their words and brought them to their senses.

Elodie was the next to arrive, and she tackled Abisina, too. Soon, the folk had engulfed them. Abisina hugged everyone— friends, acquaintances, even Vranian refugees—while keeping Findlay's hand firmly in hers. They all called her Keeper.

Then Meelah was there, hugging her hard.

"Meelah! How are you here?" Abisina looked at Findlay.

"Oh, Findlay didn't want me to come," Meelah said. "But I pointed out that he promised he wouldn't leave me alone." She smiled, and Abisina could see a much younger Meelah following Rueshlan's army, wearing a dwarf's hauberk that was far too big for her. "My arm is almost healed, and I'm a good shot!" She touched her bow. "And I've faced the Worm—I can face anything."

Meelah's words sobered Abisina. "I need to talk to the leaders," she told Findlay. He nodded and raised his hand for silence.

"Human." Haret was at her side again.

"Breide?" she asked, realizing she hadn't seen her friend's fiery braids.

"I heard that she's with Lennan behind the army. She's fine—though not ready to fight."

Findlay called out names: "Elodie, Torlad, Anwyn, and Aldreck!"

"Aldreck is Alden's youngest," Haret said quietly. "Looks like his father but has his uncle's liveliness. Can't tell him about Waite yet."

Anwyn hurried up and embraced Abisina. "I'm so sorry, Keeper! We should have trusted you! Erith won't come near you," she said. "He's so humiliated. He's back there with Braim—the one who called the time *before* you came the Golden Age."

"All is forgiven. You—and Erith and Braim—did what you thought was best for Watersmeet. Callas?"

"Back with the army—recovering. We haven't found her mate."

Torlad, a palomino centaur, joined them, as did Aldreck—hair as red as Alden's.

Abisina explained that Newlyn's army, led by Corlin, was coming from the south.

At the mention of Corlin, Elodie gasped and burst into tears. Abisina smiled at her friend's joy, but the smile faded as she described the rift army.

"And the Worm is really with them?" Findlay asked.

"I haven't seen the Worm, but I watched as Ulbert

shape-shifted into a young, powerful version of Icksyon. I'm sure we'll see the Worm before long."

"We've beaten the Worm before," Findlay said. "We can do it again."

Findlay's optimism almost made Abisina smile again. *How can I be happy?* she wondered. The Worm was coming for them! *But it isn't here yet.* She drew in the feeling of her friends around her—Findlay's hand in hers, Elodie's joy that Corlin was alive—and wrapped it tight. She would need it later.

They resumed the march, Abisina walking between Findlay and Elodie. Haret marched next to Findlay, a hand on Aldreck's shoulder.

Another joyous reunion took place when Watersmeet reached the waiting centaurs. Abisina watched as families embraced.

Then Findlay turned to her.

"Abby." He touched her face. She could see him choosing his words carefully. "I know what you'll do," he said. "What you have to do. I want to stop you, but I can't." A hint of a smile—but he became serious once more. "I've known since . . . maybe since the moment I first saw you in Watersmeet. You wore the necklace." He touched her neck as if it still hung there. "I saw it then—your destiny, though I didn't call it that." He lifted his hand to her cheek again, and she leaned against it. "I know you'll fight with all you have. So will I. We're fighting for Watersmeet and Seldara. But—"

"Fin—"

"Let me finish, Abby. Please. Please try to survive. I can't imagine going on without you. I would, because that's what I want *you* to do if I don't survive. But please—try. Do what you have to do, but be careful."

Abisina reached into her pocket, withdrew the green waist-cord, and slipped it into Findlay's hand. He seemed to know it by touch—and now he did smile as he brought it to his lips and kissed it. "I'm bound to you, Abisina," he said.

"And I am bound to you, Findlay."

He pulled her to him, and she buried her head in his neck.

# Chapter XXXII

After consulting with the other leaders, Abisina placed the spear-carriers at the front of the army's main column; behind them were centaurs with swords. Humans, fauns, and dwarves brought up the rear. The archers were divided and placed on each flank where they could shoot the approaching force from both sides. Erna stayed in the roots where she could direct an attack against any enemy who came too near—and where she'd be safe.

Abisina stood in the center of the front line, watching the rift army get closer. The enemy was organized into separate bands of men and dwarves, their divisions heightened by the uniformly blond hair of the men and the dwarves' green tunics. Only the centaurs mixed with other folk; they still carried hags, and the minotaurs stood shoulder to shoulder with them. Abisina felt a flicker of hope. Their separation weakened them. Each group would have soldiers with different specialties; they lost the strength of these specialties by dividing them. It seemed odd that the Worm had arranged its soldiers so poorly.

There were a few trolls in the middle of the front line; this time men controlled them. Abisina could see no überwolves, though she knew they were near. *If they've finished with the feast we left them at the mouth of the Cleft.* The wounded leviathan-bird was nowhere in sight.

"Human." Haret had fought his way forward. "You need to talk to your army."

Abisina remembered Rueshlan rallying his soldiers before the battle with the Worm, filling them with courage and determination.

"You can do it, human."

"How is it that you know what worries me before I do?" she said. She took a deep breath and trotted out in front of the army.

"Watersmeet!" Her voice wobbled, but the folk answered her, sure and confident.

"Hi-yah!"

"Vigar!"

"Hi-yah!"

"Rueshlan!"

"Hi-yah!"

She caught sight of a refugee near the front with a spear. "Friends of the south!"

"Hi-yah!"

"Seldara!" she concluded.

"Hi-yah!" The final shout was deafening, and she used the energy of it to strengthen her words.

"We are in a strange position. Before his battle with the Worm, my father said that we had to use our swords to convince our enemy that we were merciful. Our task is the same. Even now we would join with them—if *all* folk—north and south, centaur and human, faun and dwarf—were free."

Cheers drowned her next words, but she held up her hands and they subsided. "For years Watersmeet has lived one way, the fairies and the folk of the south another. My father knew that these divisions could not last. The opening of the Cleft simply made what he saw clearer. When one folk is free, how can they let another be enslaved?"

Cheers erupted again. Then Abisina withdrew the oak branch from her belt, and the shouts hushed. "Yes, I will attempt a parley."

A few cried, "No!" and others joined them. Abisina stood still, holding the branch above her head until all were quiet.

"We stand on a battlefield as we did three short years ago. Again, our enemies' hate longs to destroy us. For a time, we, too, were fractured. Now, behind the enemy, folk are coming from Newlyn. Even a few of the dwarves of Stonedun will fight with us. Look at *them*!" She pointed the branch at the rift army. "Divided by kind! That will never be Watersmeet! That will never be Seldara!"

Soldiers raised their weapons in the air and shook them, calling out "Watersmeet!" and "Seldara!"

Abisina shouted over the din. "You have asked me to be your Keeper! You have said that I am Vigar's heir, Rueshlan's heir. But"—she paused and looked over the variety of faces focused on her, hanging on her words—"we are *all* the heirs of Vigar and Rueshlan!"

The roar that met these words shook the ground. Then the faces changed—from solidarity to anger. Abisina reared and turned. The Worm's army ran at them, weapons drawn. She raised the oak branch, knowing it was futile, and a spear flew from the line of galloping centaurs and knocked it from her hand.

The battle had begun.

Abisina shot an arrow into a troll's eye before racing to the side. Shooting more arrows as she ran, she scanned for Icksyon among the herd of centaurs headed at her, but she didn't see him.

She joined the ranks of archers, and as she targeted a Vranian, then a minotaur, she kept scanning for Icksyon, Ulbert, the Worm, Vran. The shape-shifter could be anything, but she had no doubt she would recognize it. Its eyes would find her.

The archers had done their work—only one troll still swung its huge fists, taking out a centaur and then a human before an arrow from the right flank struck it in the throat. The rift's advance guard of centaurs had broken through Watersmeet's line of spears to face a barrage of swords— Findlay's was among them, but Abisina couldn't see him. She did see Torlad, the palomino centaur. His bright hair blazed a path through a group of green-clad dwarves as he worked his blade. Ravinne and a few others attacked a column of Vranians. Abisina could see nothing of Haret or Elodie.

She shot down a dwarf who was ready to take the head off a faun, and she killed a centaur bearing down on a weaponless dwarf who was running for a fallen axe. But the thought of the shape-shifter was always before her. When the sun flashed off a sword, she looked for Ulbert. A white centaur galloped toward the archers, and she braced to meet Icksyon.

They weren't there.

A phalanx of Vranians came at the archers near Abisina. The front men carried shields to protect their faces and torsos; the ones behind put their shields above them to deflect the incoming arrows. They came close before Abisina took her own shot at them, focusing on breaks between shields. Some of the other archers shot at their exposed legs. A few stumbled, but most of them—about fifteen—came on. Ravinne saw the danger, set her spear, and charged the phalanx. She hit a Vranian, and her spear sank into his side, knocking him into the man next to him. The back of the phalanx fell in disarray; the front kept coming.

They were right in front of Abisina when they dropped their shields and raised their swords. Abisina shot and killed two men, while a third came on with sword drawn.

She reared and brought her hooves down on his arm. The man yelled in pain as his sword clattered to the ground. Abisina was drawing her own sword when he looked up, and she saw his face.

"Jorno!" She held back her stroke.

He met her eyes. "Kill me," he said. "I was ready to kill you."

"You told me to run when the mob was after me," Abisina said, lowering her sword. "You saved my life."

"That was before I knew what you were. I regret it now. I regret knowing you. Loving you." Abisina could hardly hear him above the din of the battle. "Seeing you like *this* . . ." He looked at her legs, her hooves.

"Keeper!" someone shouted.

Abisina looked away for no more than an instant. When she looked back, Jorno had retrieved his sword and was coming at her again.

She knocked his first blow aside, but she was off balance. He pressed his advantage. Backing up, she managed to duck his first stroke. Then she transformed, and he stepped back, surprised, before coming at her again with renewed fury.

"Demon!" he spat as he brought his sword down toward her head.

*Clang!*

A second sword met Jorno's, and before Abisina could see who had saved her, Jorno was down, blood pouring from his chest, his eyes dimming. "Demon," he said again, and closed his eyes.

"Abby!" Findlay stood next to her. Jorno lay dead.

"Keeper!" The call came again, and Abisina saw the speaker—a dwarf, pointing across the field.

Ulbert stood among the Stonedun dwarves, his armor gleaming in the sun, battle-axe swinging. Already, some of the Watersmeet dwarves had dropped their axes and were running toward him, though two near Abisina gripped their weapons tighter and kept fighting.

"Fin—"

"Go!" he said.

She transformed and galloped toward Ulbert. She knew her sword and bow would be useless. *I brought him down in the glade and will do it again. Somehow.*

She dodged wounded dwarves, jumped a sword leveled at her, zigzagged between clashing centaurs. "Fight!" she yelled at the unarmed dwarves moving toward the Obrium. "Remember Watersmeet! Remember Rueshlan!" A few faces cleared. Others were too far gone.

*Haret?* she wondered, and fought harder to get to Ulbert.

She snatched a spear from the back of a fallen Vranian and held it in front of her. Suddenly, the enemy was falling back on either side as if opening her path.

She put on a burst of speed, hoping to use the spear to knock over Ulbert. Before she reached him, she saw Haret barreling at the shape-shifter. Haret, too, was going for brute force.

They reached Ulbert at the same moment—Haret crashing into his chest, Abisina into his neck. Her spear splintered. Pain exploded in her head and shoulders. Ulbert fell back, Abisina and Haret on top of him. Shards of metal pierced Haret's face, the remains of his axe. "Visor," Haret croaked, reaching his bleeding hands for Ulbert's helm.

Abisina drew her sword.

As Haret touched the Obrium visor, his face went blank. Instead of lifting it, he caressed it, then moaned.

"No!" Abisina cried. She stood on shaky human legs—when had she transformed? "Haret, my dearest friend, stay with me."

Haret's hands trembled.

"Keep fighting!" Abisina lifted her sword. "Think of Hoysta!"

Haret's fingers tightened on the helm, but Ulbert was rising, and Haret slipped off. Ulbert raised his axe as Haret threw his arms around Ulbert's legs, bracing his feet against the ground as he sought to topple him.

But Haret no longer held the legs of a dwarf—he held the legs of a centaur.

"Icksyon!" Abisina cried.

Haret fell to the ground as Icksyon reared and grabbed Abisina, pinning her arms to her sides and lifting her as if she weighed no more than a fairy. He leapt over Haret and set off at a gallop, dodging anyone who got in his way.

Abisina had dropped her sword. Icksyon tossed the arrows from her quiver. He left her the naiad bow, but it was useless.

Abisina fought the panic that threatened to engulf her. *I am not that frightened girl anymore!*

But a small voice whispered her fear: *This is not Icksyon! It is something worse!*

Icksyon galloped away from the battle. When he stopped, Abisina could hear no cries, no clash of swords. He set Abisina before him, a hand on her throat, squeezing.

His eyes were as black as the rift. Her knees buckled, but he held her up.

"I knew you would come," he said. His breath blew over her, smelling like the carcasses on the plain. "Your kind is always heroic. I fought your father a hundred times—in so many guises. Our battles raged over generations, in land after land. *He* was a worthy opponent. But you and Vigar! She was a mere human. You, only slightly more." He pulled her closer, putting his face inches from hers. "You want to save those fighting back there. But there's nothing you can do, daughter of Rueshlan."

Abisina strained to hear the battle. How far had he taken her? He held her so tightly, she couldn't turn her head. Her world had contracted to those eyes—and this struggle to keep breathing.

"You can kill me." She forced the words from her burning throat. "Like you killed Rueshlan and Vigar. But you won't win!"

"I have already won." He smiled, exposing perfect, strong teeth. "Even if somehow you destroyed me, it is too late. These armies—the centaurs, the Vranians, the dwarves—will destroy the land. More than they love their homes, they hate each other. I've made sure of that." His grip loosened a little, and Abisina managed a breath.

"You drove Vigar and Vran out of their home and across the mountains," she said.

His smile widened, and then his face began to change. This new face had high cheekbones; a smaller, delicate mouth; and soft blond curls. His body became a man's—still muscled and strong, but no longer huge and bulging.

Only the eyes remained the same.

"Are you Vran?" she gasped.

"Very like him. Vran got old before he had done all that I wanted him to do. And just as I did with Icksyon, I took Vran's place. Now you know the true history of your ancestor."

"I am also related to Vigar!" Abisina said.

"Vran and Vigar—brother and sister." He shook his head in mock amazement. "Think of the hate Vran bred in this land. But Vigar's folk—even now, they hold a shred of her ideals. If you were there to lead them . . . but I will not take that chance. I will destroy you, and your death will make your folk mad for revenge. Revenge leads to hate—as Vran and his petty desire for the necklace showed so well. When the Green Man gave it to his sister, I had what I needed. Vran took revenge on anyone who looked like her."

The black eyes stared into Abisina's. Vran's face began to stretch, his nose drawing into his flesh, his mouth widening to reveal teeth growing to points as his hair sank into his skull and the eyes multiplied around his head. Abisina screamed.

The White Worm.

She could see its tail lashing in the air, spraying poison. The Worm supported itself with one short, muscled arm; the other arm held her, claws digging into her neck. Abisina pulled at the claws, kicked the Worm's fleshy trunk, dug her fingernails into its arm as she struggled to breathe.

The Worm had finished playing.

As it squeezed her harder, the darkness closed in. All she

could see was the Worm's eyes. She shut her own, refusing to die with the Worm as her last sight.

An image came to her: Rueshlan. He was smiling, then throwing his head back and laughing. Slowly, she saw more of him, as if she were moving away. He was a man, dressed in the simple tunic he often wore in Watersmeet. Light danced on his face—the soft orange light of a fire. And now Abisina saw where he was. He sat in his favorite chair at home. In his chamber. She had just been there. Her last time in Watersmeet. When she had left Vigar's papers.

Her eyes snapped open. Abisina used her last breath to say three simple words:

"Vran *loved* Vigar."

The Worm's grip loosened a fraction.

"Vran loved Vigar," she said again. "I saw it written in his hand."

The Worm's face started to contract, its teeth to shrink, its nose to emerge. "He hated her!" Vran's mouth screamed. Then the face expanded, the mouth widened from Vran's to the Worm's.

Abisina had caught another breath. "Then why do I have Vigar's and Imara's eyes?"

The Worm's features, suspended for a moment, collapsed into Vran's. The lashing tail disappeared, and the hand at her throat had no claws.

Vran stood before Abisina again, but the beautiful face was harsh, twisted.

"You said Vran took revenge on anyone who looked like

her. But he saved Imara—and all the generations that followed her. She had green eyes—like mine. Imara was Vigar's cousin—not Vran's. Vigar was his half sister. Vran loved Vigar. And Vigar never stopped loving Vran."

Abisina lifted her hands and touched the shape-shifter's face. His grip loosened more, and she breathed; but she kept her hands on his face, smoothed his brow, his scowling lips.

She held the image of Vran's letter, Vigar's papers in her mind as she became a potter, his face her clay.

*Your loving brother, Vran.*

Under her touch, his lips grew fuller. The cheekbones became wider, the curve of the cheek softer.

*Because he took my cousin, I have to believe . . .*

Vran's nose straightened, and then the golden curls and fair skin darkened. At last, the eyes changed.

They turned green.

Abisina stared at the face of Vigar.

The hand at her throat tightened.

Abisina kept touching the shape-shifter. The green eyes remained as the face reformed: her mother, Sina—another of Imara's descendants. *And someone who carried no hate*, Abisina thought. The coloring shifted, and she saw her father. Another shift and she saw Hoysta, then Kyron. The hands squeezed still harder, and the darkness closed around her, but she fought it and kept thinking of those who had taught her love. Haret's, then Findlay's face. The hands became claws; blood trickled down her neck. Elodie, Corlin, Meelah, and Erna. Her lungs threatened to collapse. She saw Thaula and Breide. Face after face—from Watersmeet, from Newlyn, from Vranille. The shifts happened so quickly now, the faces blurred. *Am I dying?*

And then the procession paused on a single face: black skin, brown eyes, thick hair.

Neriah. *My sister.*

Her anger surged. *My sister who betrayed me.*

Neriah's face began to lighten, her teeth to grow; her eyes turned blacker.

*And saved me,* Abisina thought.

The face froze: she could see pieces of Neriah, of the Worm, of Vran. The eyes were green.

*Neriah feels our father in the Seldars. . . .*

The last words the Fairy Mother said to her returned: "Neriah is having second thoughts about the necklace."

*Neriah is my half sister. We're like Vran and Vigar. She's hurt me, but I can love her anyway. And she can love me.*

An explosion of light threw Abisina to the ground.

She needed to stand! To find the shape-shifter and destroy it! But she couldn't see; she could only breathe—long, gasping lungfuls of air.

Slowly, her vision cleared, and she forced herself to her feet.

She stood on the plain in a blackened patch of earth.

She was alone.

To the east, a cloud of dust rose on the horizon. The battle continued.

*These armies will destroy the land. . . . More than they love their homes, they hate each other!*

The shape-shifter's threat.

Over the sound of her hooves, Abisina could hear screams, jeers, clashing swords, metal striking metal.

Newlyn had arrived. Together with Watersmeet they had formed a huge circle in the middle of the plain. They all faced inward, watching, rapt.

A smaller cluster of folk stood to one side of the circle, facing each other. She spotted Findlay, Elodie, Erna, and Haret—*Thank Vigar!* The blond man next to Elodie held her hand. *Corlin.* Her friends threw glances toward the larger circle and seemed to be arguing about something.

Abisina shouldered her way through the folk of Watersmeet and Newlyn. They were cheering and laughing—but the laughter was harsh, and the cheers were mocking.

In the center of the ring, the rift army fought on. Men against dwarves against centaurs against minotaurs. It was a massacre.

Abisina broke into the circle. She had no sword or spear. She had no necklace. The words of the shape-shifter drove her forward:

*Vigar's folk—even now, they hold a shred of her ideals. If you were there to lead them . . .*

Abisina didn't glance at the combatants. She didn't keep

watch for stray arrows or spears. She raised the naiad bow above her head and began to gallop around the ring. She passed neighbors, friends, women from Newlyn whom she had taught to shoot, a man Findlay had taught to forage, folk who had never met her but knew Rueshlan, folk who had only heard the stories of the centaur-man and his daughter.

As she passed, she met the eyes of every centaur, faun, human, and dwarf.

A wave of silence followed her. First, only those on the outer ring hushed. But the quiet was deep enough that a centaur from Icksyon's herd about to take the head of a Vranian held back his sword. A dwarf from Stonedun paused before lowering his axe on a Vranian Elder, still wearing his sash. A hag released a dwarf and dropped her staff. A minotaur stopped its horns before they connected with a centaur's chest.

Findlay's group joined the circle with the others.

Across the battlefield, the silence spread, until the folk of Newlyn, Stonedun, Vranham, the Cairn, and Watersmeet could hear nothing but the thuds of a single centaur's hooves.

# CHAPTER XXXIII

THE KEEPER REFUSED TO LEAVE THE PYRE, THOUGH SHE fell asleep on her feet more than once. Findlay and Haret stayed by her side; Elodie and Corlin were seldom absent. Erna divided her time between Abisina and Darvus, who had been wounded in the battle.

Abisina watched the bodies of so many she knew and loved committed to flame: Prane, Alden, Landry, Anwyn. Salat's body had been retrieved from the boundary trees, Waite's from the glade, and Frayda's from the wall. It had taken a long time to find Neiall's body, but the Keeper had insisted that the fire not be lit until he, too, was laid with those for whom he had died.

The Keeper had the bodies of Icksyon's herd, the dwarves of Stonedun, and the Vranians laid on the same pyre. If some disagreed with her decision, they kept it to themselves. They referred to "a united Seldara" in her presence, but Abisina was not naive. She saw a few Watersmeet dwarves scowl at the befuddled dwarves of Stonedun who had not yet shaken off their Obrium stupor, and she saw the Watersmeet centaurs eye the matted hair and tails of the Cairn's herd. The southerners were more obvious in their hostility. Some had left as soon as they had been given a few pieces of bread, and Torlad had been injured when a Cairn centaur attacked him with her hooves.

As Abisina stood watching the flames and smoke and ash rise to the sky, she thought of the other pyres that had marked her life. So many of them were connected to the Worm!

Had anything really changed?

*Yes!* she thought. *There are reasons to hope.*

Her mother and others had been victims of the tyranny of Vranian Elders. That tyranny was broken. Most of the Elders of Vranham had died in this battle. Theckis's body burned with the rest.

She had seen Corlin talking earnestly to one of the Vranian Elders, offering Newlyn as a home for the widows, orphans, and older men who had been left in Vranham when the call for battle came. Even the Elders responsible for holding him in a cell would be welcomed. The south was *not* as divided as it had been after Rueshlan died.

*And the north?* No one standing at Rueshlan's pyre would have predicted the collapse of Watersmeet. *But Watersmeet has learned to work with the refugees—to see the refugees as folk like them.*

The rift had been blown apart. There were still über-wolves, the eels, minotaurs, hags, and trolls, but no new terrors were coming from the mountain. There would be a staggering amount of work ahead and, Abisina had to admit, more loss of life; but they no longer faced an unknown and limitless fear.

Building a friendship between north and south would take years, but she believed it was possible. Watersmeet had helped the centaurs of the south with their most pressing fear: the leviathan-birds. And Haret said that several Stonedun dwarves had discovered family connections with Watersmeet dwarves.

They needed one another. The shape-shifter had been right—the land was all but destroyed. It would take many hands to rebuild, to forage, to plant. Communities would have to come together.

"Abby?"

Abisina looked up, surprised to see how low the pyre had burned. The heat still shimmered off it, but there were no flames and no smoke. It was a bed of red coals.

Findlay took her hand and pointed off to the west.

A dark line moved toward them. Abisina went cold. *An army!* Findlay's grin made her look again.

It was Watersmeet.

She picked out Breide first, dragging her injured leg behind her but with dancing red braids and a wide smile. She saw Gilden, his long beard ragged and dirty, ambling along with a cane for support. She picked out Lennan, healer's pouch at his side, helping Callas, still weak and pale, but alive. Finally, she saw Glynholly.

The faun walked on the edge of the crowd, shoulders hunched, head down.

Abisina transformed and galloped toward Glynholly. At the sound of her hooves, Glynholly glanced up, then she crumpled, as if trying to make herself as small as possible.

Abisina slowed.

Her gallop had begun a general rush between the folk of Watersmeet, separated for so long and through such hardship. Though some watched Abisina and Glynholly, most were too caught up in their own reunions to wonder about their past and current Keeper.

"I thought you were him," Glynholly whispered to Abisina. "Come to get revenge on me for what I did to Watersmeet."

It took Abisina a moment to realize that Glynholly was talking about Rueshlan. "No, Glynholly! Rueshlan loved you!"

"I destroyed all that he worked for," Glynholly sobbed.

"Look around you." Across the plain, father embraced son, cousin greeted cousin, mate clung to mate, and a mother shouted with joy at finding her children. "Watersmeet survives."

"It will survive despite me. I—I can't go back, Abisina. I'm not sure where I'll go. . . . But there is one final service I can do for my home."

Glynholly reached into her satchel and drew out the Keeper's necklace. Was it the real one? The chain, the pendant were black. But as Glynholly lifted the necklace to Abisina, a spark of light kindled at the tip of the pendant and grew, slowly at first but gathering speed, the light consuming the blackness until the necklace burned with white brilliance.

"Where did you get it?" Abisina breathed as she took it in her hand.

"Neriah. Once the birds left, the fairies had little choice; they could've fought us, but they would've had to leave their children unprotected. They let us go. That night I woke up, and Neriah was there. The necklace was as dark on her as it had been on me." Glynholly smiled with no joy. "I suppose that should comfort me. She was no more fit to walk in Rueshlan's shoes than I was."

"Did she say anything?" Abisina asked.

"She said, 'You know what to do with this.' She didn't have to. I had always known what to do with it. That moment with Neriah was the closest I've ever felt to a fairy, even after all those months with Reava. Neriah and I understood each other. We *needed* the necklace. You never really did."

"I do need it, Glynholly." Abisina still stared at the twisting Obrium. "My mother and my father wore this necklace. It keeps them with me. The Green Man gave the necklace to Vigar." She held up the necklace, tracing the strands with her finger. ". . . smaller threads of water, weaving . . ." she murmured.

"Oh!" Abisina cried. Hearing the words she had read in Vigar's papers, holding the necklace— "It's *not* Watersmeet! All this time, I've been sure that's what it was. My father even told me that it was an image of the three Watersmeet rivers coming together. But if Vigar was standing on the

Mountains Eternal, she would see not just Watersmeet. She would see the entire valley! All the rivers 'weaving' into one! It's not Watersmeet, Glynholly!" she said again. "It's Seldara!"

Abisina grasped the startled faun's hand to keep herself from falling over. "The Green Man gave this to Vigar because she saw one united land. And now, for perhaps the first time, we have a real chance of making Vigar's vision, the Green Man's vision, a reality."

# EPILOGUE

ABISINA LEANED BACK AGAINST FINDLAY'S CHEST, LOOKING at the array of stars, smelling the perfume of fruit, and letting the peace of the garden settle over her. Nothing disturbed the peace now. When they had come through the tunnels, Abisina had seen no trace of whatever rift monster had lurked there.

Findlay rested his head against her hair, and Abisina sighed. "You were right. I'm glad we came," she said.

"Mmm."

Clearing the überwolves out of Watersmeet had been difficult. Findlay's sword arm was heavily bandaged from a recent skirmish; and now, even months after the folk had returned to Watersmeet, überwolves still infested its northern reaches.

For the eels, Abisina had enlisted the help of the naiads again. Though the naiads could not fight the eels themselves, they could describe the grottos and caverns in the Sylvyad roots. The folk opened the eels' central dens to the light, and the eels fled. When a few of the Sylvyads fell, more light reached the eels, driving them to the north—where the folk left them, for now, with the überwolves.

Abisina shifted so that she could see the glow of the lone Seldar that grew in the garden. She had gone to it as soon as she and Findlay arrived that afternoon. Like the Sylvyads, not all the Seldars had survived. But in both of the groves near Watersmeet, a cluster of Seldars had stayed strong. In the past weeks, Abisina had been overjoyed to see several saplings break ground. These trees, more than any other sign, gave her hope that Seldara would survive.

The death of so many trees in the Motherland's boundary had been a benefit. Erna had explained that the boundary trees were not naturally vicious. They had grown so close together, they had to fight for light, air, water, and the earth that sustained them. Erna, Darvus, and the other folk who had fallen in love with the Motherland's inner forests could cross the boundary with no fear now that all the trees could find the sustenance they needed—though they did seem to keep their taste for überwolves. Those in the Motherland were busy strengthening the delicate floors of the fairies' abandoned houses and building stairs instead of ladders so that they could live in them. Abisina and Findlay planned to visit soon.

"I wish we would hear from Elodie and Corlin," Abisina said.

"I knew that you couldn't stop worrying, even in the garden, Abby." Findlay ran his fingers through her hair and kissed her lightly. "If they had sent a message the moment they reached Newlyn, there are still plenty of reasons it wouldn't have reached us yet. Next spring we'll go down there ourselves. All of Seldara will want to see its Keeper."

Abisina looked down at the necklace. It lay on the dark

blue of her tunic like a drop of sunlight on a lake. She still wasn't used to the title—Keeper of Seldara. She had hardly gotten used to the idea of being Keeper of Watersmeet. And there were plenty up and down the land who rejected the very idea of a Keeper, not to mention a unified Seldara.

"Stop, Abby," Findlay said. He wrapped his arms around her. "I can feel your worries. Haret will keep Watersmeet safe while you're away, and Breide will look after Haret. For tonight, you are not the Keeper of Watersmeet or Seldara or the Motherland or the Cairn. The only thing you're keeping right now is my heart. And I'm keeping yours."

Abisina leaned into Findlay's embrace and gave herself up to the peace of the garden.

*Not just the garden,* she thought. *This is the peace of love and friends and knowing that, eventually, this whole land will be my home.*